Aberash

A Mysterious Land Downunder

Helene Smith

With Illustrations by

Amy Trevaskis

For
Warren, Joey, Kenny & Maureen

and

the Noongar People
of the South West[1]

---

[1] Please see notes at rear regarding Noongar words used within this book.

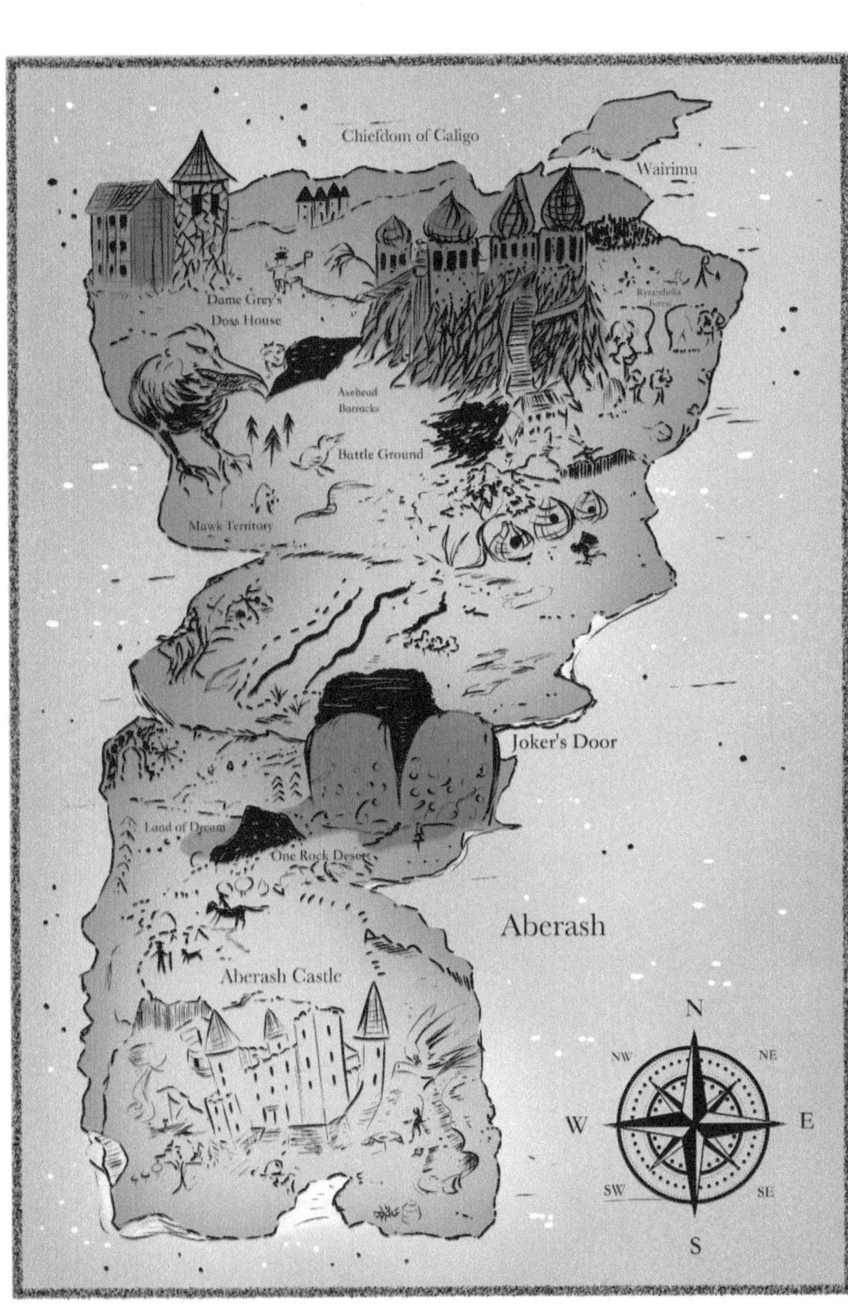

Chiefdom of Caligo
Wairimu
Dame Grey's
Doss House
Ryzanbella
Forest
Axehead
Barracks
Battle Ground
Mawk Territory
Joker's Door
Land of Dream
One Rock Desert
Aberash
Aberash Castle
N
NW
NE
W
E
SW
SE
S

1 The Parents
Brightday City

Mr and Mrs Mason leapt from Bus 303 into the chill of a blinding fog. Shivering, they stood on the kerb with one thought in mind – their children.

'We can do this,' Petronella said with a tremulous smile.

'For Lori and Cade, we must. Our very own twins. Bless them, but we must not weaken.' With a sad half smile, Robert stroked his wife's cheek. 'Will you be okay at the end, Sweetheart?'

'If…I don't look back…I shall.' Blinking away a tear, Petronella checked her shoulder bag one last time, though she knew the contents by heart. For each twin, a lightweight water-proof backpack fitted with neither too much, nor too little. 'You have the lucky coin for Cade?'

'It's right here.' Robert patted a pocket somewhere near his heart.

'And I have the good luck charm for Lori.' Petronella kissed the pale gemstone that hung on a cord round her neck and then bent to tighten the laces of her sturdy boots. When it was done, she reached for Robert's hand and with giant strides they ran. The echoing boom…boom…boom of their footsteps would come to the twins like the distant beat of a drum. Their father's sight was sharp and their mother had a talent for reading oncoming traffic. They dodged dogs, joggers, cyclists and skaters.

'Excuse me…our children…you see…we must get to them by four.' Petronella raced on, her carefully straightened hair, woolly and wild. Her eyes wide. Lori…Cade…we won't let you down. Her darling twins were too young to be doing this thing on their own. But there was no other way. The clock in the bell tower chimed 3.45. Fifteen precious minutes was all they had.

Meanwhile, in the Undercroft of Brightday High, Minnie, the canteen lady peered into the murky fog. 'Lori and Cade Mason? Are you okay?'

'We're fine,' Lori called, though she wanted to shout to the world, that no, we are not fine. How can we possibly be fine? Miserably, her gaze flicked to the empty seats all around.

'Where have Mum and Dad got to?' Cade huddled into his jacket beside her. 'We should be looking for Ms Alayah.'

'Of course, we should. But where would we look? In some kind of otherworld?'

'That's exactly where we should look.' With his clear-river eyes, his dark brows and that fringe of black hair, Cade looked a little other worldish, himself. Lori's own reflection in the shiny metal wall of Minnie's kiosk wobbled. Sea-green eyes (her mum called them aquamarine), birdwing brows, reddish brown hair. A gangly teen with freckles on her nose. Too skinny, too pale, too quiet. A girl who had lost the will to do the one thing she loved to do.

The enormous Undercroft was a special meeting place for the students of Brightday High. Minnie recalled that on this same day last year, they sat at her tables stuffing themselves with muffins and her lemony lemonade. They laughed themselves silly and sang the latest songs in lovely snatches with Lori Mason leading. But today there were no customers but two and a dismal silence.

When the last bell rang, the other kids had bolted. Like runaway horses on Cup Day – falling over each other to be first on the bus. A few lucky kids were picked up by parents in four-wheel-drives loaded with surf boards and fishing tackle. Nothing like that for the Mason twins. It might have been better for the poor loves to have joined Ms Rake's bootcamp. Minnie's wistful gaze shifted to the far end of the Undercroft where the surface of the wall shimmered and shifted. Like the closed curtains of a grand stage. Weird.

2 Desertion
The Undercroft

Petronella and Robert skidded to a stop. No time for questions – just a lot of telling. 'We're going to a business conference,' Robert said, flatly. 'And you lucky kids are going for a spell in the country.'

A spell in the country? Lori and Cade exchanged a look. They were city kids all the way through. Their sky was lit by neon lights. Their sounds the pounding of feet, the stop and go of red and green, the glare and clatter of well-stocked supermarkets. The rush and roar of traffic on land and the far-off hoot of ships at sea. They didn't know anything about the country.

Robert waved towards the west, where on a clear day you might see across the waters, a haze of green with a rosy glow of sky behind. The name *Aberash* had been whispered among story tellers. They spoke of a strange other world. A forbidden zone in no-go waters. A place where the fisher-folk of Brightday Seafood Cooperative refused to go.

'You'll be fine,' said Petronella with a stiff bright smile. 'You're going to Samuel. He's your first cousin – thrice removed.'

'Thrice removed? That's hardly a cousin at all,' Lori protested. 'Besides, Uncle Albert reckons Samuel is a quitter.'

Cade raised an eyebrow. 'He runs a Lightfoot goat dairy, so he can't be too much of a quitter.'

Lori leapt from her seat. 'I bet they're fierce and smelly as old cheese.' She wrinkled her nose. 'I vote we stay home by ourselves.'

'And who are the parents here?' Robert glared. 'Like it or not, you're going for a spell in the country.' Each time the twins opened their mouths to protest, he held up his hand in the stop-please sign. There'd be no argument and certainly no pleading for *everyone to go home and forget the whole stupid idea.*

'We know you and Mum need to go to your conference,' Lori reasoned. 'It doesn't worry us a bit. In fact, we'd like to be home by ourselves.'

'Stock the fridge with food and we'll be sweet.' Cade smiled uncertainly.

Absently, Lori caught a swathe of her reddish-brown hair, twisting it around her forefinger, while nodding vehemently. 'Yeah! We need time to…chill…no…we need time to…to think.'

'Better not to think.' Robert fixed each twin with a stern frown. 'All you gotta do right now, is to wait for your taxi…it's long and it's green…right?'

The twins turned to their mother, but sadly, she shook her head. There was nothing more to say. The dense fog closed in while their dad went on about the taxi. 'It's extra-long…and it's extra green. You'll know it as soon as you see it.'

'Ok Dad. We get it.' Cade's words were drowned by a deep rumble. Like the ocean in a storm, the fog swirled, coiled and rose before breaking with a slap on the concrete. It was followed by a long-drawn sigh. When it cleared, whichever way you looked at it, the Mason twins were alone.

3 Reflection
The Undercroft

Why were they in such a hurry?' Cade tossed his new lucky coin. It had come with an urgent whisper from his dad: *Read the coin and read it well.* In fact, Cade hated reading anything, even a coin. He tossed it again while a puzzled Lori studied the pale gemstone her mother had placed in the palm of her hand. It wasn't even pretty.

'Mum knows I don't do jewellery.' With a resigned shrug, she looped it round her neck.

Cade grimaced. 'As for Mum's water-proof backpacks, there's nothing in mine but my tatty old blanket, a chamois that might do for a towel, undies, water bottle and a packet of sugarless chewies. For teeth cleaning if we can't get to a bathroom.'

Lori rolled her eyes, but peeping into her own backpack, she was secretly pleased to find her friendly old blankie. A set of headlights probed the fog and a black and white taxi crunched over the driveway with a flickering red sign on top. Cade jumped up to squint at another vehicle just behind it.

'Not ours,' he called. A long line of hopeful drivers followed. Not one was extra-long or green.

'Maybe it was something made up by Dad. Maybe they've simply run out on us.' There was a sick feeling in the pit of Cade's stomach.

'Like forever?' Lori pictured Cade and herself after the school gates shut. Hurried on by night guards. Huddled in doorways among the homeless. 'At least we'd have our blankies…but why are we talking this way? Like we don't even trust our own mum and dad?'

'We don't trust ourselves.' Cade sighed. 'Not since you-know-who messed with our heads.'

Lori frowned, 'Can't you talk about him…about what happened? Are you too scared or what?'

'He was a wizard…he jinxed our school…and eyed us…of course I'm bloody scared. 'When I think of him I'm so scared, I want to throw up.'

'Me too.' Lori shivered and sighed. 'We were the ones he was after…and it was Ms Alayah who saved us.'

'We owe her, big time.' Tears welled in Cade's eyes and he blinked them away. Images of the wizard crowded his head…along with the tag he left behind. Cade focussed on his lucky coin. Smooth between his thumb and forefinger. Warm to touch. He tossed it…higher than he meant to. Caught and held it in his open palm. Stared at the strange marks on its surface. As if to find an answer to a riddle that teased like an itch. The more you rubbed and scratched, the worse it got. He turned the coin over and the letters wobbled and grinned.

Oh Dad, how far is one little coin going to take me? And why do I need to read it? Cade was good at spotting things, and he rarely forgot anything he saw or heard, but the minute he tried to read, the letters wriggled and squirmed, changing themselves about. The word, FLAT, became FATL and sometimes T-A-L-F with a silent L like HALF. The letters poked tongues as he stammered out their sound. Or they shot out an extra leg to make him stumble over words, clapping little hands over mouths to stifle cruel laughter. *Watch this boy slide the slippery dip*, they mocked. *He's a disgrace to Brightday High.*

If only I'd passed my reading test and if only Lori hadn't messed up that split leap in her dance class. Maybe things would be different, but you couldn't go back. Nor could you change something that was in your face every day.

OPEN!
MILK
NO
SHAKES
CASH
ONLY
COCONUTS!
Toasted
Ham
No cheese
4$
Cheese
No Toast
$5
FOR
THE
CHIPS
Sunshinell

4 The Snatching
Brightday School

It leapt from the pages of newspapers all over town. It blared at you from TV news and radio talkback. Every word pounded in Cade's head.

Brightday High Mystery: Popular school teacher, Ms Alayah – snatched in broad daylight....

Another sighting of the mystery flying machine – assailant vanishes in a pall of smoke....

A friend of Ms Alayah claims – days before the snatching Alayah told me the school was jinxed by a wizard.

Social media blazed with claims and counter-claims: Next you'll be saying the world is flat. As if there is any such thing as a wizard...

I reckon Ms Alayah set up the snatching herself and then did a bunk (5,000 likes).

Well I don't reckon she did...when I took my kids to school, I swear this thing jumped me...it felt kind of other-worldish and weird (6, 000 likes).

Cade sighed. 'I should have tried to stop him...instead of standing at the window like a witless fool.'

'Stop it...it was my fault too.' Lori's pale face tightened, and she closed her eyes. 'Ms Alayah stood up for us both...' The clock in the bell tower ticked on. Cade glanced at his sister. Her hands were shaking.

'Did you eat today?' he asked, accusingly, and received a shrug for an answer. 'Minnie's kiosk is still open, so I'll get us some chocolate.' It was all he could think to do for a sister who gave up on eating whenever she was worried.

'Whatever.' The world was a sour taste in Lori's mouth…and this awful fog like a big wet blanket hanging over them. Was it some kind of insidious warning of bad things to come? *Insidious…insidious…*a hideous word, but it said everything.

Cade's money pocket was empty except for the coin, but he'd give it a go. Without the other kids milling around, he studied Minnie more closely. Her bones were old and frail as a tiny bird's but her blue eyes were bright and clear.

'A lucky coin and a promise will buy you two of my specials.' Her shining gaze locked with his and he couldn't look away.

'Um…I have a lucky coin,' he stammered, 'but a…a promise?'

'For every bit of chocolate, you eat, you give a bit away, but you always save a bit for the bag. Do you promise?'

'Okay…yes, I promise.' The words jumped out of his mouth.

'Then you'll not go hungry out west across the waters.'

Across the waters where the sun goes down? To Aberash? A place where even brave fishers refuse to go?

Lori accepted the chocolate from Cade and went along with the promise he had made to Minnie because she didn't want to look like a quitter. The worst thing you could be in her family was a quitter and Lori didn't want to be one. She tuned in to the distant roar of traffic from the freeway. The rumble of a train passing. And then, in the spooky silence of the Undercroft, a voice.

Cade grabbed her arm. 'What is it?' he whispered.

'It's Minnie crooning…listen.' The words coiled around them.

A mortal boy, a mortal girl
Eyed by a wizard, must fall to his spell
Or pass the test,
Yet, with a coin and a key may prove the best,
The prisoners of a wizard's bind to free.

What can it mean? Cade quite forgot to listen for a taxi. He didn't hear the ebb and flow of traffic. All he could think about was Brightday High, his very own school, jinxed by a wizard.

5 Jinxed
Looking Back

Weeks before the snatching, Cade felt it. A shadow, where no shadow should be. A whisper without a mouth. An ugly invisible toad. When Mr Brown – the big boss of schools inspected Brightday High, a dark blobby 'thing' leapt on to his shoulder. A wizard for sure. Cade knew right away. It spoke through Mr Brown's mouth with terrible warnings. In just an hour, Principal Trihardy and the teachers were frightened out of their wits. You could feel a ripple of fear in the walls. The teachers stopped smiling. They yelled at the kids for no reason at all and Mr Trihardy showed the first sign of his twitchiness problem.

The worst day began with a call over the PA system: 'Cade Mason, please report to Mr Trihardy with your reading test results.' Trent and his gang sniggered.

Looking up from his desk, Mr Trihardy turned a worried face to Cade. He lined up his pens. Red to the left and blue to the right. He fiddled with his tie (the blue one with red spots). He twitched and he swallowed. He lined up his pens again and blurted, 'From now on, only good readers are wanted in our school…even good isn't good enough. You need to be excellent from day one.' A long-drawn pause. 'It's not about you, Cade, it's about our reputation. The reputation of Brightday High. It's our place on the ladder we must guard.'

While Mr Trihardy turned to his computer to tap out some kind of report on the matter, Cade stood at the open window, taking deep breaths of air to calm himself. From the assembly area outside, came the rise and fall of voices, the stop and go of recorded music. It was Ms Alayah with her dance class.

'We'll try that split-leap again,' she called. It was Lori who messed up. That was the reason Ms Alayah called her back when the others ran off to their regular classes. Lori tried another split-leap. It was a bit wobbly, but good enough. In the background the buzz of a city at work went on. From a distance, teams of construction workers looked like hurrying ants in orange hats and vests. Powerful machines drove giant cranes between great towers of steel.

What happened next was like a full stop in the middle of a sentence. The workers, the machines and drivers froze. In the assembly area outside the office window, Lori and Ms Alayah were still. Like statues leaning towards each other with a sheet of paper suspended above their hands.

Cade yelled at his sister. 'It's some kind of spell…you need to….' What Lori needed to do was left unsaid because now she and Ms Alayah were laughing as they snatched at the paper sail floating away on the wind. At the same time the thrumming of an aircraft filled the air. A shadow appeared over the assembly area outside. Fat bellied and fuzzy at the edges.

'It's an aircraft and it has landed,' Cade shouted. 'A triple decker…a tipsy, tin can of a thing…Mr Trihardy?'

'Let me sleep,' Mr Trihardy groaned as he cradled his aching head in his arms on the desktop. Meanwhile outside, a wizard leapt from the aircraft and the rules of when and where, were like a pack of cards strewn across a room. Dressed in something dark and flowing, with splashes of purple and a tinge of green, the wizard moved with the stealth and speed of a shadow.

One moment here, one moment there. Now this moment. He stood at the open window capturing Cade's gaze. It was impossible to look away from those dark orbs. They drew you in and held you fast.

Ms Alayah called urgently, 'Don't let him *eye* you!'

Gasping, Cade tried to warn Lori. It was like a bad dream. When your tongue feels too big for your mouth. When your words dry up and your legs turn to mush. The best Cade could manage was a raggedy croak. Then nothing. He was drowning in the wizard's words.

Your story I will take, your story I will make

Not for you to mend, not for you to end.

Come, be my slave in Caligo.

Each word burned into Cade's skull. Like hot needles laced with poison. He wanted to be sick. He wanted to scream. But all he could do was chew on his fist while the wizard turned on Lori. Now she too, was held by the wizard's eyes and stung by his words.

The searing gaze flashed from Cade to Lori. 'You'll both be my slaves,' he screamed.

'Not while I am here.' Ms Alayah's voice rang out. 'Are you afraid of these children? Is that it? You want to crush their truth and steal their magic? You want to weave your own wicked plot and choose your own ending, is that it, Mister Wizard Man?'

While she held the wizard's gaze, Ms Alayah frantically signalled to Lori. She waved towards the open office window where Cade waited with arms outstretched. With one impulse in her legs and heart, Lori ran to link fingers with her brother. Using a rescue grip learned at scouts and her toes as leverage against the stone wall, she scrambled inside. There, to witness Ms Alayah dragged away by the wizard.

A knot of dark clouds gathered over the school. An ear-splitting blast of thunder shook the walls and a picture crashed to the floor. Lightning arced down from the sky. A daemon dancer, holding hands with the wind. On a rampage, it smashed a one-hundred-year-old red gum. Its low friendly branches reduced to smoking rubble. So too, a tree-house and a garden made by the kids of Brightday High.

'I should have helped, Ms Alayah, not run away,' Lori whimpered. The twins huddled together while the storm raged. Rain slapped against windows. Curtains were drawn, shutters pulled down. Drains flooded. Water oozed into classrooms. It was Minnie, the canteen lady who spoke through the PA system. 'Today is a dark day for Brightday High.'

During the worst of the storm, Mr Trihardy wakened from a deep sleep, a little surprised to see the Mason twins shivering and terrified in the gloom of a power outage. Storm or not, Mr Trihardy went on, his voice high pitched and desperate.

'Only schools at the top get the prize.'

'Ms Alayah 's gone,' Cade sobbed. 'She's been snatched…and it's all my fault…'

'Snatched by a wizard,' Lori added, and it's all my fault…'

'A wizard?' Mr Trihardy snapped 'You saw somebody?'

'I saw his eyes,' Cade said. 'They were terrible…and his words *burned* into my skull.'

'A case of too much sun.' Blinking furiously, Mr Trihardy held up a protesting hand. 'I blame Ms Alayah for your wild imaginings.'

'Did you sleep through all of it?' Cade asked, incredulously. 'Didn't you see that wizard?'

'Enough!' Mr Trihardy barked. 'All this make-believe stuff has turned your head. I won't have it.' But the principal had to have it. A few students who witnessed the snatching through a window, ran into his office without so much as an "excuse me" or a knock.

'A vampire came after Ms Alayah and he snatched her away.'

'No, it was a wizard.'

'It was a dragon breathing flames.'

'It was an ordinary person in high heeled boots and a greenish leather coat thing,' said sensible head boy, Dean. 'He may be a hypnotist…it was like he wanted Lori and Cade to follow him. Ms Alayah blocked him and the hypnotist lost his cool. Then the storm came and it was too dark to see.'

Nobody knew what really happened but Ms Alayah had disappeared and they wanted her back. The class teachers who rushed in to see what the fuss was about, agreed. All except Ms Rake who turned away with her mean little smile. The police cordoned off the crime scene with yellow tape. They took measurements and marked the ground with chalk. They combed every bit of it for fingerprints and DNA but found nothing.

In desperation Mr Trihardy called Pronto@Investigators. It was a famous undercover service. For reasons involving national security, nobody but Mr Trihardy and the deputy got to see the Pronto team. With rumours flying, the kids were ushered out of their classrooms into the Undercroft.

'With the Pronto team,' Dean said, 'it's like – all hush-hush, don't tell anything to anyone. Even your own spouse.'

'Your own kids?' somebody piped up.

'Especially your own kids!' Nobody argued. If Dean said something, everyone believed him. The Pronto team found a graffiti tag burnt into the bitumen surface of the assembly area. It was a picture of the deadliest scorpion in the world with small pincers but a vicious sting coiled and ready to strike. With a chill in the air and a thick white fog pressing down on the city, the students of Brightday High shivered.

6 Soldiering On
The Undercroft

While waiting for some weird taxi that was supposedly long and especially green, Cade couldn't stop reliving those painful days after the snatching.

At assembly, the kids droned out the national anthem and Mr Mac's band fell apart.

'Ms Alayah is my aunty,' Eddie sighed unhappily. 'My family need her back.'

'We all need her back,' said Dean, 'and we need to find her quick.'

'You mean quickly, with an el and a wy,' Mr Trihardy barked. 'Didn't anybody teach you about adverbs?' He went on about it being up to the authorities to find Ms Alayah and then sounded off at all kids in general. 'Tuck in your shirts…and do up your shoe laces.' If he saw a jumper tied around a waist by the sleeves, he turned blue with rage. By day two, his legs and his arms twitched violently. Even so, he spent hours testing all classes in mathematics, spelling, and reading. The testing flopped and the kids mucked around while the teachers squinted into their iPads clicking pass or fail with no in between. Cade failed his reading test. Lori failed in mathematics. Worst of all, while Mr Mac was on stress leave, the visiting music teacher told Lori: 'Your voice is too strong for such a quiet girl…a big fail, for you, Miss.' She was banned from the choir and even singing the national anthem, with a tap on her head.

'Now I can't sing, even when I'm alone,' she confided to Cade. 'It's like I'm half broken.'

'Bootcamp,' Mr Trihardy cried. 'You lot must put your names down for Ms Rake's bootcamp in the holidays and your parents will pay.' Even sensible Dean was bawled out. A rumour flew around the school about Mr Trihardy. It came from Ms Rake and she got it from Mrs Trihardy. He was having nightmares about the school sliding down the big slippery dip to the bottom rung of some ladder (whatever it meant, the kids thought it must be awful for a grown man to cry in his sleep). It followed that Mrs Trihardy who helped out in the library, was so upset, she messed up the Dewey system and was no longer her smiling self.

Cade came to himself. He was still in the Undercroft. Still waiting for an extra-long green taxi. Earlier that day, Dean had called through the open window of their bus. 'You two ought to come with us. The bootcamp won't be that bad.' He and the others were even able to laugh about it but of course their parents lingered for last minute hugs, air kisses and a few extra dollars tucked into their baggage. No such thing for the Mason twins.

The empty space left by sensible Dean, Eddie and the gang on this last day at school for the year was kind of lonesome. Cade turned to Lori who stroked her gemstone while murmuring soft words. 'You're quite smooth and warm on my cold fingers.'

To his surprise, Cade's own fingers ached for the touch of his lucky coin. Something to toss and hold. So why had he wasted it on two chocolates neither he nor Lori wanted? But what was this? A thinly sliced *ting…ting…ting.* Spinning around at his feet, the coin, sparked with flashes of light in the gloom.

'So…you've come back to me…how strange is that?' He caught and held it for Lori to see but she was hunched into herself.

'I wonder if anyone's ever starved to death waiting for an extra-long green taxi,' she murmured. Cade ran his fingertips over the surface of his coin. It was almost possible to read the tiny letters by touch. To be fair, he should return it to Minnie but her light was out and the shutters of her kiosk were firmly closed.

Beside him Lori shivered. 'We'll be okay, Sis.' Cade turned towards her. 'If we do need to eat, we always have our choc…'

A soft horn-beep and Cade gulped at the sight of an extra-extra-long taxi nosing to a stop. A car-shaped wonder, it appeared to be cut from a single stone. A glittering jewel of a thing, reflecting back every shade of green.

7 Cousin Samuel
The Taxi

'Are there a couple of Mason kids here?' The driver, a boy of about eighteen, leapt out of the taxi. 'I'm Samuel, your first cousin…thrice removed, I'm told.' Not much taller than either of them, he straightened his crumpled jacket and finger combed shoulder length hair. It was reddish-brown and his skin was that kind of fair that blushes easily and often. *Just like mine*, Lori thought.

'I hope you're okay riding up front with me.' There was a hint of laughter in his goldie-brown eyes. 'The back cabin's already taken.'

'Sorry kids,' a man's sleepy voice called through the half open window. 'First in, best dressed, don't ya know?'

'Hi there.' A woman at his side yawned. 'Ruby and Roger here – to be sure you have a fun trip to the Otherside.'

Lori peered through the window to speak to the couple. 'Fun? The other side? Of what? We're meant to be going to our cousin's goat…I mean *Lightfoot farm* in the country.'

'Whatever.' The woman yawned and the pair went on juggling ear muffs, eye masks and neck pillows. They sank into a nest of blankets until there was nothing to see of them but a pair of bunny-eared beanies.

While Samuel took a driver's break, the twins slipped into body hugging front seats – familiar and comfy. But the dashboard of the taxi was something else again.

'It's like a holy place,' Lori said in a hushed whisper.

'That's what smart cars are all about.' Cade gaped. 'This sure is a dazzler…but…it's…so…' So, what? The kind of vehicle he dreamed about after a crap day at school? 'It's like trying to hold onto a rainbow up close or the light from a stained-glass window.'

'Or a keyboard with notes shaped like raindrops.' Lori wanted to reach out and stroke them. Glittering jewels in earth colours - red, orange, yellow. Mixed with water and sky – Green, blue, indigo, violet. Seven colours in seven shades. Colours like music. Colours like a rainbow reflected in water, wobbling and wavering. But how did it all come together? Cade had nothing to say, though Lori knew his mind would be leaping around like a grasshopper, trapped in a box.

'Aha…I get it.' He exhaled sharply. 'It's so simple you wouldn't believe it. Each key triggers an action.'

Lori moved the forefinger of her right hand towards bright yellow. 'Like the keys of a piano…like you strike a chord to make a sound.' She twisted her wrist to catch the beam in her palm – a small quivering splash like sunlight on her skin. Moving her head closer, she picked up a sound, soft as a heartbeat. 'The engine might be dozing, but it's still awake, I reckon.'

'Yep. Bright yellow keeps it ticking over when the taxi's stationary. But take a look at that.' Cade pointed to an image above the dash. A sculpture of an eagle. Deep brown, with russet plumage and wings spread wide. It's proud head and fierce beak pointed downwards to an old-fashioned bronze compass with a rotating bezel attached.

'Eagles always know the way home,' Lori reflected. 'No matter how high or how far they travel.' She'd never seen one in the flesh…only online and a stuffed one at the Natural Science Museum.

'The compass thing is kinda quirky.' Cade was into smart-cars, even if the rest of his family were not. He checked out any new models show cased in the city mall. A young sales guy had allowed him to sit in the latest wonder-car with a pop-up door. Cade kept up with the newest car-planes too, and had watched the amazing TFX on YouTube. But this was something different again. A bit too off-centre, weird and wobbly for his liking.

'Hey, Sis, check out that brownish key with the half note above.'

'You mean burnt sienna.' Lori leaned closer. 'There's a different picture symbol on each part…you can choose a steering wheel or a joystick to drive it.'

'Sure…the idea's not new, but there's something else. I'm wondering about power…is it electric or what?' Cade ummed and aahd. 'From the shine of the car's surface, I'm guessing solar…or…or wind…'

'Or something…' Lori's half smile didn't quite match a flicker of fear in her eyes. There was some other force…something whacky…something spooky about this car and they both knew it.

Nervously, Cade tried to read the fancy black script beneath blood red. After silently mouthing the letters, he took a deep breath and swallowed. 'Jeepers, it says Barrier Breaker.'

'What kind of barrier? Oh brother.' Lori's finger tips pressed against her temples. 'What have we got ourselves into?' They stared at each other, half scared, half thrilled. Wanting to stay, yet wanting to run as fast and as far as their legs might carry them. Was this some kind of dark magic?

Before they were ready for him, Samuel appeared. 'Everything okay?' Their cousin froze – half in, half out of the taxi. His knowing eyes shot from one twin to the other. 'No second thoughts, then?'

Cade tried to make sense of it. *This car…is hardly what you'd expect a farmer of Lightfoots to come up with.* He risked a quick look at his sister's face trying to read the expression in her eyes. When she was scared the pupils, like now, were tiny dots and the blue-green irises smoky and distant.

'Well?' Their cousin waited calmly enough, though Lori sensed his colour rising. Her own face flared. Oh yes, he was a cousin all right…with a blushing problem that equalled her own. He should be trustworthy, but was he?

'At least you're giving us a choice,' Cade whispered.

After an awkward moment of stillness, the twins blurted, as one, 'No second thoughts.'

'Then prepare yourselves for take-off.' With a decisive click, Samuel secured an opaque panel that separated the front and back cabins, then slid his seat into the central position. He spread his hands. Clever looking hands, though more like the hands of a pianist than a driver with his thumb on blood red. A bright jewel in the handy middle C position. A faint purring, a crushed peppery smell, and something unfolded from the top of the taxi.

They braced themselves for whatever lay ahead. Blood Red cast a fiery glow across their faces. A faint rumble gathered momentum, like the long roll of a giant king wave. Veering deeply into the enormous Undercroft, the taxi skittered between two rows of seating with a hair's width to spare. Without pause, it hurtled towards and then through the shimmering back wall of the Undercroft. That mysterious 'out of bounds' place where the students of Brightday High were strictly forbidden to go.

A sensation of passing through something feathery and soft and then they were off. With knuckles clenched, the twins held on to each other. Were they turning outside in or inside out? Or were they being jettisoned into somebody's fantastical story? There was no time to quibble about the wrongs and the rights of it, or to compare it to anyone else's entry into another realm. They were nosediving into their very own mysterious Otherside.

8 The Journey
Into the Blue by Taxi

'We're gonna hit it,' Cade yelled. A rock face of sheer granite loomed.

'Then shut your eyes,' Samuel snapped. Up…up…up and up, they soared, gritting their teeth, eyes wide. With a sudden burst of power, the car shot over the rock face to the other side – a millisecond of silence – and the engine thrummed steadily on.

'Should be okay now, kids.' With one hand on the joy stick, Samuel took a good long swig at his water bottle and then wriggled down in his seat with eyes focussed ahead.

'We seem to be floating on a cushion of air,' Cade said.

'But…but…the sea, is there, just below us,' Lori spluttered. 'I can even smell it…salt…sea spray…what's going on?'

'We're gliding above it,' Samuel told her, calmly.

Peering through the wind screen, Lori willed herself to look ahead. 'Couldn't we…kind of…like…nose-dive into the water?'

'Without a life-jacket…or a whistle?' Cade attempted a weak grin, while feeling pretty queasy at the thought.

'We're pulled by a magnetic stream that doesn't rely on what you can see.' Samuel pointed to a key on the dash, leaf green with flecks of dappled light.

'So, we're doing what turtles and birds do.' Lori sat back, more at ease with the slower pace. It became a steady stream, on and on, until it was smooth as butter on your tongue.

'We're heading for a land…out west across the waters.' Samuel's words came with a reddish glow from the controls. Soft and warm on Lori's eyelids.

Uneasily, Cade stirred. 'The fishers will ride out the biggest storm but they won't go there.'

'Ms Alayah calls it Aberash…. Lori's words fell away. 'It means something about light.' She was almost asleep but went on. 'It's a place where you live by the old stories.'

'With magic and wizards?' Cade asked.

'And those who wash up on its shores…all mixed together kinda thing.' Lori's voice faded. 'But we need…we need….'

'Yeah? What do we need?' Cade wanted to shake her but she was asleep and already off in her dream world. He could tell by the little frown between her eyes. Once when she was little, Lori was so ill even Mum and Dad thought she might die. But afterwards she said, she was okay 'cos a giant bird had saved her. Of course, when she spoke of it, the kids at school laughed and teased her about it.

Oh, my dreambird, where are you now? Lori's thoughts were with the big bird. When I couldn't breathe, you gave me air. When I was cold, you warmed me…and now, I've lost the will to sing and it's like I'm not whole any more. I need to be whole, you see. Whole and strong, clever and brave. Brave enough to go find Ms Alayah.

Cade touched Lori's shoulder, stifling a moment of panic. His sister was talking gibberish. Though her eyes were shut, the lids quivered. Was she sick with a virus, or what?

'Lori is sleeping but are you okay?' Samuel glanced at him.

'I'm fine,' Cade shrugged but there was a great lump in his throat.

'If you're tight as a drum when you're fine, how are you when things get tough?' Samuel's lips twitched in a wobbly half smile.

'When Lori talks in her sleep, it spooks me and then, there's Ms Alayah. I can't stop thinking about her…wondering if she's hurt or even alive.'

'Lori will be okay, believe me. Breathe easy and wait, the answers will come.' His cousin drove on in silence, his face flecked with round splashes of colour from the dash. Warm and bright as Cade's lucky coin.

Read the coin and read it well. His dad's words echoed in his head. Cade hadn't bothered to read it and even spent it, without any thought to consequences. Yet the coin came back to him. It was a gift. A great gift. *So why didn't I say thanks Dad, instead of being such an ungrateful twerp?* He drew the coin from his pocket and placed it on the palm of his hand. This time, the words inscribed on its surface leapt at him – a tiny glowing trail in gold. *A Returning coin issued by the Supreme Council of Wizards in the year of the Horse.*

The busy hum of the engine shifted to a purr. Now active, the light from misty blue blurred the outline of Samuel's features. The taxi slowed. There was little sound but the rustle and rub of the cabin's cloth padding and faint vibrations of parts. The taxi was more puzzling and prettier than any car-plane Cade had ever seen. But something had changed.

'Are we being pulled by a magnetic force? A centre of gravity?' He put away his coin. Cade liked to know where he was in space. Always had. To know the sun rises in the east and sets in the west. He liked to distinguish planets from stars and to find south by looking at the Southern Cross and its pointers. He liked to hear his Noongar friend Eddie naming star clusters and the mysterious spaces in between.

Samuel broke into his thoughts, offering him a sweetmeat from a jar in the tuckerbox beside him. 'Made from a wild berry and quite chewy.' With a mouth full himself and slurping a bit, he went on to tell Cade, 'You can take a turn at driving if you like.'

A rush of blood flooded Cade's face. 'But…it's…not legal…is it?' He gulped and coughed to retrieve a delicious morsel of the candied fruit going down too soon. 'I'm…um…only just through second year high. A long way from getting a licence.'

'You'll be fine.' A touch to the controls and Samuel's seat glided to the right-hand side while Cade's slid soundlessly to the central position.

'If you say so…but what about Lori?' Cade was used to sharing.

'Your sister is busy with dream work.'

'Really?' Cade shrugged and then turned to the dash. Familiar in a peculiar way. A bit like his special art piece at school. Ms Alayah had praised him for what she called, *A fine work of imagination.*

Samuel stirred beside him. 'I figured you'd prefer the steering wheel option, rather than the joystick.'

The wheel, when it glided from its slot, was smooth and warm under his palms. A touch to red ochre under Samuel's direction and the engine turned over, full throated and powerful.

'Now shift to Resume.'

'That'd be this one?' Cade's hand, hovered over misty blue.

'You got it!' Samuel grinned. 'You've been watching and you remember.' The taxi lifted but the throbbing engine faltered, so Cade increased the revs with a touch to red ochre. 'Now…chill on misty blue, but steer towards that dark spot ahead of us.'

'It looks like…is it a real live eagle?'

'We call him Pathfinder. He's truer than any compass you know.' Samuel leaned back, loose limbed and cool. Driving on, Cade slowly came to know and to anticipate each move. He kept a sharp eye on the dash and Samuel. A nod or a hand movement, a single word or a smile of assent, to guide him. The different sounds and colour tones involved in driving the taxi wound together in a kind of dance with a russet plumed eagle leading. But it was only when Samuel took over the driving again, that Cade allowed himself to sit back in his seat, grinning.

Beside him, Lori stirred. Her dream had taken her to bushland that was scarred and blackened by fire but a season of rain must have passed. The seeds among the ashes were sprouting green. Her heart lifted at the sight of a lone tree between fallen logs. Tall as three grown men, the trunk was marked by the sting of fire, but the tree top bloomed with bright orange blossom. It was alive with the busy drone of insects and the excited trill of feasting birds. Her Dreambird wasn't here, but the tree with its blossom gave her hope. It felt like a good omen. *Is it possible that you are near?*

Lori woke up with a start and then she was on the edge of her seat. They had come from darkness into bright daylight. There were no highways or roads on the wide sweep of land beneath them. No townships or fences. Everything was curved as if it had never been marked by anything but rain, wind, and waves.

'This is Aberash, my homeland,' Samuel said.

Dreamily, Lori watched silvery waves of shifting light made by the wind as it ruffled trees and wide fields of grass. There were mountains on the far horizon – lofty giants with spidery networks of rivers and streams at their feet. It seemed right that a real live eagle led the way.

'Hey…you've gotta love this,' she whispered. The taxi flew low to a point where she saw clearly, a stand of bright trees. Wet by a recent shower, each leaf of each tree sparkled and shimmied like a mini ballet dancer.

'Our place is on the southern tip of Aberash.' Samuel's smiling face darkened. 'In the north there's a place that isn't so kind.' In a few words, he told of a state called Caligo ruled by a powerful wizard, jealous and mean spirited, who was intent on taking away the light. Taking away freedom and happiness. At this, Cade drew in his breath, then in a guarded tight voice, asked the question that was really an answer:

'His tag is a scorpion with small pincers and a large red tipped sting?'

'His name is Wairimu,' Samuel replied.

'Wairimu, so that's what it is,' Cade said, softly. 'We had no idea we were coming closer to where Ms Alayah might be.'

'While she is a prisoner,' Lori murmured, 'Miss Alayah won't get to see those leaves dancing.'

'If she hadn't protected us, she wouldn't be a prisoner,' Cade said, 'but why did Wairimu come after us in the first place?'

'Because you're the boy and the girl in his story.' Samuel's eyes focussed on the way ahead.

'But a story is just a story,' Cade argued.

'For mortals, yes, but for we, who live in Aberash, our stories are everything.'

Minnie's chant played in Cade's head, something about a boy with a coin and a girl with a key. What key? Something about the prisoners of a wizard's bind to free…. Was it possible?

'If we want to see Ms Alayah again,' he said, 'we need to go to Caligo and bring her back.' At this, Lori made a fist of her hand and reached. He did the same. One fist over the other. It signalled a promise that could not be broken.

9 The Country
Aberash

The dream bird is falling. Her wings are broken. Lori woke up with her heart racing. 'Oh…I fell asleep again…are we there?'

'A bad dream? Aww…I'm sorry…and yes, we are there.' Somebody touched her cheek. It was Ruby, the backseat passenger. The beanie had gone. Her shining dark hair lay round her shoulders and she wore an emerald green dress – all soft and shimmery. She patted down the skirt and stepped back from the taxi. They all looked down at her boots. Red and bright as the blush now spreading from her face to her neck. Lori met Cade's gaze and she thought he would agree. *Those boots are sure made for walking and so clunky and tough, you wouldn't want to mess with them.*

As if to smooth over an awkward moment, Roger announced, rather grandly, 'You are now under the protection of Samuel, Chief Wizard of Aberash.'

Ruby then spoke, too quickly, handing out advice on the best way to take a bird bath when water might be scarce and the finer points of teeth cleaning. Beside her, Roger stood uneasily in a slim-fit olive brown suit. With a worried frown, he clasped a slightly battered Akubra to his chest, his eyes blinking and glazed.

'Do we know you?' Cade asked. Images of the pair wobbled and quivered like reflections in water. Embarrassed and giddy, the twins edged away to huddle close to Samuel who whispered in a fond way, 'They do mean well.' He handed Ruby the keys to his jewelled taxi, saying carelessly, 'It's yours for as long as you need it for the inter-zone travel. We walk on our own two legs from here.'

With a disappointed shrug, Cade shouldered his backpack but lingered for a last glimpse of a wondrous set of wheels, the first and possibly the last of that calibre he'd ever get to drive. As it rose upwards, its wings flashed double swirls of light before streaking away and dissolving into the blue.

'They are so weird, but kind of nice.' Lori breathed in air so fresh and clean it almost burned. As they walked along the shore, her ears tuned to the whoosh and sigh of waves. In and out in the same old way towards the solemn yellow stones on the sandy shore. So, this was Aberash.

The beach was not so very different from Brightday, but the land as they turned to it, was something else again, shifting and shimmering with green and yellow light, then solidifying into something you might touch and smell. Springy and soft underfoot, the path smelled of moss and the damp decay of fallen leaves.

On either side of the path, the scrub hummed with the sound of small wings, soft slivers of birdsong from nesting wrens and spring birds in the shrubbery. With a quick darting flight two olive green parrots swept by from the trees above. Then, with high calls, parrots, with wings bright as poster paint flashed green, blue, yellow and purple. Lori's gaze met Samuel's, and for a moment, he seemed sad. *He's my cousin, should I say something?* She looked to Cade for a lead, but he was rushing ahead, excitedly calling, 'Wow…look at that for a tree!'

The odd moment passed and Samuel smiled. 'There are wild fig trees in the forest, but this is one you might know. Some call it The Tree of Life.'

'It's like a mountain!' Cade yelped.

Lori had seen figs in the supermarket…too expensive for the Mason family. But she hadn't seen a fig tree up close, ever. Or any fruit tree this big. It was so…so what? So wide…so darkly green and alive. Stepping right up to it, she put her ear to its gnarled trunk half expecting to hear a heartbeat.

Samuel's lips twitched and there was a smile in his eyes. 'There is also great *koorak* if you know what to look for.' He grinned. 'I mean, bush tucker.'

A rustle and stir of coarse green fig leaves. Whispers and giggles. The faint juddering of a branch. A voice said, 'Hah it's Samuel…he's back!' A boy looked down at them with surprised dark eyes. More faces appeared among the foliage, a mix of races, but somehow alike, each one with a headful of shaggy hair. Bare footed and dressed in coarsely woven sack-cloth dyed in the soft greens, browns and mushroom tones of the forest.

'These are the cousins?' somebody asked. With limbs stretched, the tree kids straddled the branches or they sat 'no hands' with calloused feet dangling. A flash of colour…a small person wearing a crooked green turban and a grubby face scrambled along a branch. He was followed by two dark-eyed girls wearing head scarves. There were more voices. Kids everywhere picking figs.

'I'm going for a big un.'

'Good size for the market.'

'Want to swap?'

'Mine is for drying.'

As the twins moved on, the voices faded.

'Is this a regular orchard?' Lori waved towards another tree – big as a mountain. It dripped with plums – yellow and bright as the moon. Its branches so heavy their tips folded back into the ground to make a cave-like skirt around the central trunk. This was not like the neatly laid out orchards she saw from the train near Brightday City, all raked and clean with clear cut edges.

Lori breathed air laden with the heady scent of fallen fruit. Alive with the stir and flutter of small birds feasting and the voices of busy fruit pickers. They called Samuel back to answer their questions. 'What's with your everyday mortals? Did they wash up on the shore, like we did?'

Lori was puzzled. 'Who are these kids? Where do they live? With their parents?'

Cade shrugged. Squinted against the light.

'What?'

'I don't know who they are, but I reckon I know where they live. Look into those trees over there. What do you see?'

'A tree house…more than one, a dozen or more.' Lori stared. Tree houses…each one with a wraparound veranda joined to its neighbour with rope walkways and ladders. 'Just look at that.' She had always wanted to live in a tree house. 'The kids here are not playing cubbies…they live in those trees.'

'*Kaya…kaya*,' somebody called from the treetops and a chorus of replies criss-crossed the strange green highway. *Kaya…kaya…*

'It's the homing hour.' Samuel had caught up with them, panting a little. He forced a smile, but his eyes were seriously worried. 'The half-light is almost on us…time for all of us to be indoors.'

Cade's own smile vanished and Lori shivered. The tree shadows had deepened. An icy wind ripped through the canopy around them. There was a change of mood and with it, a stab of sorrow. Lori thought of Ms Alayah and the vow she had made with Cade. *The quicker we find you the better Ms Alayah* she thought. *Without you, everything soon goes sour on us and out of kilter.*

The first sign of the village came with a secretive gush and gurgle of a swiftly flowing stream. Beyond its banks, houses – some in neat rows with thatched roofs and stone walls. Others were like upside down pottery cups with veins of dark wood, or tent like structures made of drift wood with woven walls of brush. Zig-zagging around and between the houses were vegetable and flower gardens, small dairies, bakeries and the workshops of artisans. The air bristled with mixed up smells of a thriving village. Yet strangely, the market place and lanes were empty. Every door was closed.

They hurried over a stone bridge to a bright green field. Following Samuel's lead, Lori and Cade kicked off their hikers, stuffed them into the backpacks and ran. The cool moist blades of grass were rough, but welcome on the underside of their feet and between their toes. The fresh smell of grass ran with them, along with a slither of fear. But somehow when they reached the top of the rise, they were laughing…and then they were gaping.

'Samuel…you live in a castle,' Lori gasped. 'I thought…I thought you'd live in a farmhouse with a veranda.'

'Not in Aberash,' Samuel grinned. 'You can blame our building wizards from olden times. When they arrived here they brought ideas and customs from their birth countries, along with their seeds, vines, and fruit saplings.'

'So, they made a castle,' Cade murmured. 'Like the castles they knew.'

'But its framework is made with the beautiful hardwoods of this land.' Samuel grinned. 'And there are gum trees in the garden.'

Aberash was small as castles go, with little turrets and hide-away niches. It wasn't grand but it had a nice warm feel to it. There was a lot to see at short notice.

'Well…do you like it?' Samuel grinned.

'I think so.' Lori blushed. 'I mean…what I mean is that it's…rather…fantastical.'

'Only rather?'

'You have to admit, it's a bit off centre,' Lori said. 'But it is a proper castle…with a rooftop garden and everything, even a tower with ravens sitting on top.' The windows winked a welcome, like eyes wide open and then came a blink and the shutters went down.

Samuel laughed. 'I call it a mish-mash of yesterday's dinner and a grand feast of a castle in one. But that's what I like about it.'

An arched wooden door swung open and the Castle Keepers appeared. Though Samuel greeted them cordially, a haughty nod from the towering pair was all they got. It was almost evening now and their shadows were long. Members of an ancient race, Mr Caius and Ms Cora looked down long proud noses. A ray of light from the setting sun lit up their bronzy skin and glossy black hair that hung long and loose in smooth capes round their shoulders almost to their knees. Each one looked at the world through silver-white eyes and gazes that moved from one object to another. Now and then, they held each twin in their sights. *As if they know more about us, than we know ourselves*, Cade thought.

With another nod to the twins, Mr Caius turned to Ms Cora and between them they unfolded a gorgeous cloak. Velvet and dark as night, yet somehow alive, it flickered with veins of blue, green, purple and gold.

'It's like the sky that time we saw the Aurora Australis.' Lori held her breath as the cloak wrapped Samuel in its folds. Until this moment their cousin seemed like an ordinary boy with a ruddy complexion. A little unusual, but unremarkable. Clothed in the cloak he looked taller, broader, the light in his eyes, though friendly, older and wiser. He looked quite suddenly, like a most distinguished young wizard.

'My friends,' Samuel's voice deepened and though soft, carried all over. 'As I put on this garment that we in Aberash call the Mage, I promise on this day, as I do every other day, to use the magic it gives me wisely and never for my own self-aggrandisement.'

Neither Lori nor Cade knew the word 'self-aggrandisement' but they were impressed. They watched open-mouthed as Samuel raised his arms while Mr Caius and Ms Cora sang in a low faintly off-key chant:

Glossy and dark as a raven's wing
threaded with the colour of our dreams
Without the Mage we are lost
to the whims of Wairimu
Ah, ah, a-ah…

A flock of little ravens took up the chant, ending with a drawn out, 'Aah.' It was followed by a more tuneful orchestra of birds from the swampland.

'We call the swampland by the Noongar name, *moyootj*,' Samuel said. They saw at its centre, a massive tree with an arching trunk and reaching limbs that seemed to go on forever. 'For that one too, we use the Noongar, *mangatj*.' Samuel went on, 'It is the biggest of its kind, a place of refuge for our magical songbird.'

'A magical songbird?' Lori held her breath.

'Renana…is our Night Protector,' Samuel said, softly.

Renana? Are you my Dreambird? Lori's heart swelled with hope.

10 The River Boys
The Grounds of Aberash Castle

With Samuel beside them, Lori and Cade stood on a little jetty over a creek that wound around the castle. The Lightfoots were coming home from the plateau beyond Rocky Barrier, driven by their keepers. It was a strange moment for Cade. The eyes of each keeper locked with his as they passed. *Noongar* brothers Aren, the eldest, and Nyan with little brother Archie riding on his shoulders. *They'll help us find Ms Alayah,* he thought. *I don't know how or why I feel it.* He leaned towards his sister, wanting to tell her about it, but her eyes were on the Lightfoots.

Lori breathed in the animals' scent. Sweet as newly cut grass. She couldn't keep her eyes off the soft furry creatures. The delicate curl of fluted horns. Pretty pink udders swollen with milk. Once in the home paddock, they played like children let out of school. Lifting dainty feet, they chased each other wildly, yet landing so lightly, they might have been floating. The keepers joined in a game like tag and it looked like a giggling Archie was the prize. The little guy was tossed from one brother to the other and finally placed on the back of a gentle nanny Lightfoot. There to nestle into its coat that was soft and light as a cottonwool cloud.

Now and then as they passed, Aren and Nyan pulled on the hoods of their jackets and instantly became one with the soft greys, cream and beige of the Lightfoots and the dun coloured ground.

'Like chameleons!' Cade looked at Samuel with a question in his eyes.

'The magic is in the hoods of their jackets, but the River brothers are putting on a show for you….'

It made Lori's head spin, for she sensed the movement of the boys at one with the Lightfoots, swirling around the field like wind in dry grass. It stopped when the lead animal stood still, panting, its large black fringed eyes flashing. The boys threw back the hoods of their jackets with big grins. The twins clapped and the boys bowed, laughing as they herded the Lightfoots on to the dairy.

So, this is our 'spell in the country' Lori thought. Boys who vanish by blending – a look-a-like goat herd with footprints no heavier than a breeze. Then there is the *moyootj*, a wetland full of shadows and light with a great *mangatj* tree at its centre – Renana's tree.

Renana, are you my Dreambird? Oh, I do hope so, cos I know you'll make me feel whole again…and brave. Brave enough to go find Ms Alayah….

The sombre half-light closed in. Lori shivered, but was comforted by Aren's voice as he rounded up the tail-ender Lightfoots for the night. 'Come along there, *kwoba, kwoba*…good…good.'

11 A Spell
Aberash Castle

As they stepped through the grand wooden doors of the castle, fear of the half-light fell away. The twins breathed warm silky air and the clay tiles under their bare feet were soft and welcoming. In a sitting room off the main hall they warmed themselves in front of a glowing turf fire. A snack had been laid out for them – scrumptious cherry muffins and a bowl of fruit. Lori's eyes lit up as she bit into a juicy pink fig while Cade drooled over a fat yellow plum. Afterwards they sat cross-legged on a woven mat while Samuel stood at a little distance. The Mage lay in rippling folds around his shoulders.

'It feels so warm up close to the Mage,' Lori whispered.

'Like soft gold.' *Was there such a thing?* Cade didn't know, but the words seemed right as they were both lulled into something like sleep. With shallow breaths, they sat – still as the yellow stones they had seen on the white shores of Aberash. Quiet as their own shadows. Lori heard only the odd word when Samuel chanted, but she sensed his wisdom and love for Aberash. A place for rare and precious things. Like flowers and seeds, like birds and words, lost children adrift in broken boats and the family of children who belonged to the River Tricky that flowed from the Mountains of Dream.

The candlelight dimmed, flickered, then leapt. Samuel turned to them with a smile and a warning. 'You've been eyed by a wizard who wants you in his net.' He offered a hand to each of them in turn with the silky brush of the Mage against their arms. Was this a protection spell? The twins were no longer silent but spilling out their hopes and their fears.

'When you're eyed by a wizard, do you meet the eye-er face to face and eye him back?' Even before Cade formed a question, Lori knew there were no ready answers…only more questions. Will the Mage protect us? How can we find Ms Alayah and bring her back? Is she suffering? Is she alive? Is it really okay to just wait for the answers to come?

12 A Feast
Aberash Castle

In the guest wing of the castle, Cade stepped onto the landing. He was dressed and ready for dinner but woozy from napping and disturbed by a dream. Looking down at the spiralling stairs, he sensed a presence. Maybe a ghost dancing with shadows in the splashes of moonlight from the long narrow windows.

Do you mind that I'm here? An ordinary kid, who, if he were really honest, would rather be at home right now. Safe with Mum and Dad. Maybe chopping up vegies for a Friday night stir-fry, arguing with Lori about adding kale to the mix.

Fear of Wairimu and the dreaded Castle of Caligo sent a chill through his body. He closed his eyes, trying to block out scary thoughts when a cold hand touched his arm.

'What? Ah…it's only you.'

'Who else would it be? Of course, it's me.' Lori was dressed in a hand-woven outfit like the one that had been laid out for him, easy-fit pants and tops in an earthy beige. She grinned. 'Did I scare you?'

'Not much…'

'Really?'

'You're so dorky…*and* you're dressed like a Lightfoot keeper.'

'You too, brother, but the River brothers have blending hoods.' Her eyes danced. 'Without those, you're nothing.'

He pulled a face.

'Tell me if I'm right,' she went on, 'You had a bad dream, and you feel like crap.'

Cade wanted to whack her for reading him so well, but he nodded. 'It was more than a dream.'

'Tell me about it, please…pretty please.'

'OK, but listen without butting in.' He lowered his voice. 'I am in this underground place…it's dark and my legs feel weak and wobbly.'

'You were trying to run away…'

'Yes and no…because I needed to keep looking…for…'

'Ms Alayah…of course you did.'

'I hear a cry and I think she's coming…'

'Oh brother, this is one of your premonitions. It means we're gonna find her.' Lori clutched at him but he shrugged her off.

'You jump in before I finish…that's why I don't wanta tell you stuff.'

Lori made a silly face and then turned to watch the shadows on the wall. Scary…but more than likely, tree shadows from the garden. 'You were saying?'

'It was only a dream.' Cade shook his head. 'I'm in this underground place…like I said…and when I hear somebody. I'm like, *it's gotta be Ms Alayah*. But it's not and I just kinda freeze.'

'Then who?'

'A boy. He's about our age and he's holding a lantern, like the hurricane lanterns you see in that little history museum around the corner at home.'

'And?'

'The boy shakes his head and looks at me. He's like, *can you undo my chains?* And I'm like, *you're shackled?* Cade closed his eyes, as if he couldn't get the image out of his head.

'So, he didn't speak at all…that's bad.'

'There wasn't any need…but I felt useless.'

For a moment they were silent, each one thinking of the boy…and Ms Alayah. From somewhere below stairs a dinner bell rang. A door opened, bringing in light, a clatter of crockery and cheerful voices, along with the aroma of delicious hot food.

'This feels kind of weird,' Lori said, 'Like we just go on as if nothing bad is happening. Like it doesn't matter that Ms Alayah is locked up and that boy is in chains.'

They took the stairs with none of the usual playful push and shove, or argument. Before entering the dining hall, their eyes met and they made the hand signal. One fist on another.

'I don't know how,' Cade said, 'but we're gonna find Ms Alayah and free her…and that boy.'

Lit by candle light, the castle hummed with the voices of guests from the village. Now and then a burst of laughter. A shouted greeting. Some folk wore simple pantsuits. Others were decked out in colourful gowns edged with beading and stitchery. There were elders who wore wizardly hats or traditional robes, like the village wise man who was said to cure headaches and heartache.

A smiling Chief Wizard Samuel led them to the table. He looked grand in the Mage. Even though his hat was quite modest and ordinary, Lori thought its jaunty angle perfect for their cousin. There seemed to be as many girl wizards as there were boys.

'Here in Aberash, it's what you do that matters,' Samuel said. A haughty-looking girl in a huge purple hat, laughed. In a swirl of silk and shining sequins, her gaze flicked towards the twins.

'But mortals must have their definitions and categories,' she said. 'Apologies to present company.'

'Of course,' somebody echoed. 'Hello present company.' It was Nyan, keeper of Lightfoots on the opposite side of the long table with Aren and little brother, Archie.

Nyan's grin was open and friendly as he reached into his curly crest of brown hair for a pair of knitting needles. With quick, sure hands, he cast on stitches, stopping now and then to unravel more wool or to count each loop of yarn. As more villagers took their places around the table there was just the rhythmical click-click of his needles and a burr of voices.

'Most folk come to Aberash by sea.' Nyan's dark eyes moved from his work to the twins and back again. 'They come in broken boats and driftwood, whereas we belong to the *bilya* – the Tricky. Our sister, and we brothers – tied ourselves to a raft in the year of the flood and that's how we landed in this part of Aberash.'

Aren took up the story. 'We remember very little about out past life but Samuel took us in. Like he takes in all the lost ones.'

'See these walls,' said Nyan. 'They look like any old walls – but they're made of wizard elastic. Watch and you'll see. The more people come, the more these walls stretch.'

'Err…they certainly look strong,' Lori stammered. 'The walls, I mean.'

'Oh yes…really strong,' Cade added.

'And very bendy,' said Lori. You could tell she felt stupid, Cade thought. The mere mortals seemed to have run out of things to say to these smart boys who could summon up magic whenever they felt like it, as well as sharing an exciting story about their beginnings.

In the uncomfortable silence that followed, Lori felt a huge emptiness. *Maybe I'm hungry…Yes I am hungry.* 'Cade…I'm starving,' she mouthed quietly to Cade. 'Are you?'

'Ravenous! Do you think it's a side effect from Samuel's spell?' Anxiously Cade looked towards the Castle Keepers. Mr Caius and Ms Cora padded from the kitchen to the dining hall with jugs of fruit juice and spring water. The drinks were followed by tiny hors d'oeuvres – dainty savoury tarts, soft cheeses mixed with a variety of fruits – grapes, wild berries and plums. But very soon their glasses were empty and the hors d'oeuvres all eaten.

After a rousing sea shanty from an old sailor, the village storyteller began a long-winded tale about a man and his unhappy two-headed dog, something about two heads being more trouble than one.

'Get to the point Wizard Teller,' said the purple-clad wizard in a trumpet like bray. 'You can do better!'

'Not while I'm so hungry,' Wizard Teller retorted. It all became quite heated until Samuel soothed ruffled spirits with his good humour and the promise of a nature concert on the rooftop garden for those who wished to stay on after dinner.

'Nature concert?' Lori whispered. 'What can that be?'

'I guess we'll find out…if we ever get to eat.' Cade looked about. People grumbled between themselves until some guests nearer the door, cheered.

'The fisher has come,' Wizard Teller called.

Samuel signalled for silence. 'Our esteemed Mia!'

More cheers as Mia came into the light. Her sun browned face framed in dark braids burnished with light. It matched the gleam in her eyes. Without the touch of even a finger, she balanced a huge basket of fish on the crown of her head.

Tall and proud, with strong brown hands by her sides, she cased the room slowly. As if she sensed – and then found – strangers. In one so dark, her clear-water eyes made her strangely beautiful, but her words, although unspoken, made Lori cringe.

They're city-raised, for sure – a boy and a girl who couldn't milk a Lightfoot if they were dying of thirst, nor could they catch a fish if you handed it to them on a plate – all gutted and scaled and ready for the pan!

'Meet my sister,' Nyan said, dryly, bending to resume his knitting at a furious pace. Everyone was silent as Mia carried the day's catch to Samuel. Lowering her body, she lifted the load from her head to the table, giving it a mischievous tilt. It was Ms Cora who saved a hefty pair of *yolka* from landing in the twins' laps. Calmly, she caught a fish in each hand and without a word, hurried to the kitchen.

'Take no notice of my sister,' Aren said. 'She can't abide strangers. It's in her nature, but she'll be your best friend when you need her.'

'I doubt that,' Lori muttered and she looked at Cade with a question in her eyes. As if she knew that in spite of the girl's rudeness, he liked her. He liked her a lot. Aren caught Lori's eye. He followed up by glaring at his sister. A faint blush tinged Mia's cheek and then she turned quickly to smile at the hungry crowd.

'Bravo, Mia, thank you for saving the day!' The people cheered.

When the noise subsided, Mia spoke with a break in her voice. 'We are so blessed in Aberash. But the wild fisher birds are the ones you must thank. I am only their guide.'

Mouth-watering aromas from the kitchen were soon followed by dish after dish carried to the table by the Castle Keepers and many willing guests: sizzling fish fillets, crispy and golden with chips, seaweed wraps, baked sweet potato, caramelised carrot, stuffed aubergines, a selection of greens with sweet cherry tomatoes. For dessert there were heavenly jellied fruits, berries and an extra creamy ice-cream from the dairy.

After the meal, they played party games (all that is, except Mia).

'A pinch and a punch for a soothsayer's hunch,' Aren cried. 'No returns but pass it on.' There was much pinching and punching amidst laughter along with umming and ahhing as each person tried to think of a soothsayer's hunch.

With a quickening heartbeat, Cade stood up to raise a trembling hand and to blurt in rapid fire, 'In a hundred years from now, who will sit at this very table wondering about who will sit at this very table in *another* hundred years?'

'So long as it's not Wairimu,' Wizard Teller's words carried all over, and Cade knew by their silence, the villagers didn't like the conversation. Abruptly, they broke into false smiles and bright chatter about a planned summer festival and other events. Everything else in their lives but Wairimu. The game was over and Cade's face was on fire. He daren't look at Lori or anyone but when he felt the touch of a hand on his, he forced himself to lift his head. It was Mia on the opposite side of the table.

'I shouldn't have said that,' he said.

'You asked a question, that's all. It was a good question.' Her eyes, were the colour of the sky you see in clear water.

Cade's gaze dropped to his own fidgeting fingers. 'How do you get to know…the rules in a place ruled by magic? That's where we are, aren't we?'

'Yes and no. As for the other — unless you are sure, you wait and you find out — that's what we do in Aberash.' They sat for a time without speaking until Mia went on, rather stiffly. 'Samuel gives us a home and a place here but never holds us captive. He knows my true home is with my fisher birds on the water. Every one of them is a loner like me.'

'Fisher birds?'

'I call them by the Noongar name, *Yoondoordo.*' She drew herself away, distant now, with a moist slick on her eyelids. Nyan glanced at his sister, uneasily. He tugged at the ball of wool in his hand and went on knitting in spite of her thunderous frown. The silence was awkward until the little brother who sat on Aren's lap, called out, 'Story…' he said. 'Tell Archie.' His searching eyes as he looked at each twin in turn, were calm pools of light.

'Our little night owl…our *Yartj* wants you to tell us your story.' Nyan too, looked from one to the other. 'How come? How come, you are here?'

'We were sent to Cousin Samuel by our mum and dad…we didn't know,' Lori said, with flaring cheeks, 'that we'd land in a place where there's magic and stuff.'

'You're among friends here,' Aren said, and so between them, the twins opened up about their lives and the troubles of Brightday High.

Afterwards Aren invited them to join him in lighting fresh candles from the stumps of the old. It was then that Lori saw close around her – a circle of faces, beautiful in the radiant light.

'I feel like, there's a warm cloak around us,' she whispered to Cade. *What Aren says is true,* she thought. *The walls of the castle stretch for a crowd and then retract.* Now that most of the villagers had gone home, the dining hall seemed smaller and the spiralling staircase less grand. The clay steps that led to the roof garden were quite worn but somehow inviting and the hand rail sturdy. She tried to imagine those who had come and gone over the years. How many feet had touched those stairs? How many hands had touched the railing? *If only we could know them.* Thoughtfully, she watched the Castle Keepers slowly mount those same stairs, and within a moment could not look away.

'Did you see that?' Cade whispered.

'If you saw what I saw, then yes.'

'Mr Caius and Ms Cora – the Castle Keepers transformed into ravens.'

Lori nodded. 'They have joined smaller ravens at the top of the tower.'

Cade's eyes darkened. 'It makes sense…they'd spot the first sign of trouble from up there.' His thoughts flew to Ms Alayah with Wairimu standing over her. Suddenly fearful, he checked to be sure Lori was near. They were ordinary kids – mortals and they had crossed a line.

13 Wairimu & Mandel
The sky above Caligo

In the guise of a handsome youth, Wairimu sat at the controls of the Hellican, a stolen three-tiered aircraft, from another time. At a touch, his tag shot out from its underbelly to drift in the wind – the outline of a deadly scorpion and the letter W for Wairimu.

He frowned at his dreamy eyed wife, Mandel, and her pink 'n grey parrot, Djak. She was gazing past the smudged letters to a patch of blue. What was she thinking? This was her one and only outing for the year.

'It's a privilege, not a right,' Wairimu muttered. Mandel's pleasure in seeing the sky, puzzled and angered him. Her job was to make the tea. That morning he'd used strong magic to transform his eyes a magnetic greenish gold. They were his 'tiger' eyes, so admired by his own dear mother, Bazilia. Remembering her praise, he threw Mandel a withering look. It left a coin sized burn on the most tender part of her neck. He smirked when she grimaced from a wound that would sting for days. When he saw her dabbing it with a smear of coconut butter he laughed.

Preening himself in front of a small mirror that dangled from his neck, Wairimu flicked out his tongue. *Brilliant,* he thought. A transformation spell he did that morning had turned his tongue a ghastly green with a blood red tip glistening with venom. An illusion of course, but a trick nobody else could do.

He smiled faintly, remembering a fellow wizard who had tried. *The pathetic nincompoop.* With blazing tiger eyes, he stared Mandel down and she soon dropped her gaze. Mimicking the dialect of the castle ghouls he kept in his private chambers, he went on.

'So, you know all about the spoilin' I've been doin' lately?' Disdainfully, he boasted about the trouble he had inflicted on the mortals of Brightday High. Mr Brown, the Big Boss of Schools was a push over. A whisper into his ear about not trusting Principal Trihardy and the over-anxious man did the rest. The whole dang lot of 'em went into a panic. Like Mother says – you knock one domino over and hey presto, the rest fall down!

The Chief Wizard of Caligo adjusted the controls of the Hellican and then continued to boast about his successes, while silently brooding about the unfairness of his losses. One of those losses stood out, like a bad taste in his mouth. After stalking the Mason twins for days, why hadn't he been able to grab the brats? As for Ms Alayah…that woman…part wizard for sure…had gotten all she deserved for blocking him. 'Despicable upstart,' he muttered, 'spreading happiness around like it's a Covid virus.'

Who could blame him for upping the dark side? Funny thing was, Ms Alayah might have broken away from him if she hadn't been so worried about the brats. As if she knew exactly why he nailed them. Of all the teachers in the school, only she knew how smart they were. *Well Ms Perfect, all the better for me when I make them my basement slaves. Happy days in the Dungeon of Caligo– loser lady.*

On the bright side, each twin had looked him square in the eye. There was only one person who could stop him now, and that was the young upstart, Samuel – Chief Wizard of Aberash. By himself, he was nothing. But he had the Mage with its formidable magic and Renana, the Night Protector. A weird bird for sure. Created by magic, alone – living on little but moonshine.

Unexpectedly, the power behind Wairimu's tiger eyes faded, and he flinched in pain. 'Pigs mud and damnation. Just thinking about Renana mucks up my transformation every time.' He cursed while his eyes spun in their sockets. Not a pretty sight, so of course the fool of a parrot screeched in fright and Mandel shrank from him.

'Ah my eyes, my eyes…Mandel, you fool, can't you see I need eyedrops?' He snatched what his wife timidly offered. Some cheap home-made rubbish he was sure. Just a bit of soda and salt in boiled water if he wasn't mistaken. He flushed his eyes out, blinked and cursed Renana for upsetting him. He double-cursed Mandel and that fool parrot for staring at him.

Mandel knew when not to speak but still it wasn't enough for him. *If only I could stop her thinking her own thoughts.* He had tried often enough and got close, but her mind always drifted away…like now. From the dreamy look in her eyes, he could tell she was thinking about Sunny Isle, with its crystal-clear pool of water. To this day, Mandel knew nothing about the curse he put on that pool and her people. *Ah well…let her dream.*

Mandel sighed. How well she remembered. The sparkling pool where her family gathered. 'My heart country,' she whispered. With a flood of feeling, she recalled her last day of freedom in those distant days.

For the last time in her life, at just fifteen, Mandel ran bare footed and free. Over the hot yellow sand into the cool green sea. She squealed with laughter at the rush of cold water on her warm brown skin. Young and strong, Mandel dragged her canoe into shallow waters while Djak, her pink 'n grey feathered friend, watched from the bow of the little craft. They were soon in deep water, where she dived for crayfish, swimming with ease between two bright shelves of coral. A knot of sea snakes drifted by, parting, like yellow streamers to let her through. Within moments she rose to the surface – blinking droplets of water from her eyes, breathing hard…grinning at the bird. She had retrieved a fish trap with crayfish inside.

'Food for the family.' Djak flapped his wings. Unlike the thick tongued birds of his kind, Djak spoke in a clear deep voice. He might once have been a man, transformed into his present state by a jealous wizard. But for now, he was content – a gifted pink 'n grey, carried to Mandel by the wind in a storm. Wherever she went he followed, helping her to spot fish in the tidal pools or to scrape oyster shells from rocks. And so, Djak was with her when, for the last time she shared her catch with her people. He was with her when, for the last time she was able to see and know her own smiling face. It was a perfect mirror image reflected in her people's *manang* – their only freshwater pool.

Wairimu, the Chief Wizard of Caligo also remembered. On that day, long ago, while trying to lure Mandel into his net, Wairimu used dark magic to disguise himself. He was the shadow behind every tree and every rock where he watched and waited for his moment. He was Scorpion – devil.

The first time he saw Mandel while fishing near Sunny Isle, something strange happened to him. Each time she smiled at her reflection in the people's *manang*, he wanted to do that. Every time she laughed, he wanted to laugh. When she stroked a pearly shell, he wanted that same shell. When sea snakes parted for her, he wanted the sea snakes to part for him. In so many ways, he wanted to be like her.

When he was alone, he tried to see himself in the people's pool, and it clouded over. He tried to laugh and his laugh sounded tinny and strange. He tried to make the snakes part for him but they hissed and spat their poison. He tried to love the things he found but when he tried, it made him feel foolish.

For a split-second, Wairimu imagined Mandel might teach him these things but he was both proud and vain. And so, he was angry and brooded. The more he brooded, the meaner and greener he became. When next he looked in the people's pool, he saw his own reflection and it stared back at him – a green jealous creature with rage in its eyes.

'Give me your laugh,' he screamed. 'Give me your happiness.'

'I…can't give it to you…just like that.' Mandel stared at him with fear and something else that made his wicked heart sing. It was her pity. A few muttered words of cunning magic and in a flash, he became a charming youth with shiny caramel skin like her own. Without delay, he pulled something from the deepest pocket of his cape – a rare orchid that lived and bloomed under the ground. It was named Rhizanthella by a plant wizard from a far country.

How well the Chief Wizard of Caligo remembered – the doe eyed island girl breathing in the orchid's strange chocolate smell, stroking the ruby red florets embedded in its sepals. She smiled up at him with wonder in her eyes, believing the orchid to be a token of his love.

'Does this mean two hearts joined as one?' she asked.

'Oh yes,' he lied, and a false wedding took place on that very day with feasting and music. It was loud enough to block out the weeping and wailing of Mandel's aged Nanna.

'Devil! Devil! An evil spirit is here,' she cried, as if she knew the mock-up ceremony marked the end of Mandel's happiness and the end of her people's way of life.

Wairimu left his bride waiting on the shore, while he slipped back to do his mischief. Wasting no time, he transformed the people's *manang*, their only source of fresh water, into a crystal stone. He slipped the crystal into the pouch that dangled from his neck along with his own little mirror and he muttered a mean curse. 'Mandel won't see her face through her own eyes again, and she won't see the one door to my castle that leads to the sky.'

There were stories among wizards of how the people of Sunny Isle were forced to leave their homeland. With no fresh water to drink and no way of knowing their own faces, many died heartbroken or were forced to live among tribes that didn't respect their customs and beliefs.

In the meantime, Wairimu escorted Mandel down dark passages to Deep, the ice-cold lowest level of Caligo Castle. It was home to the ghost of a dreaded pirate where he lived with the relics of his past.

'Meet my ancient ancestor, Zagan,' said Wairimu.

Zagan stared her down with ice cold eyes, sending a shock of shivers down her spine.

'Are you a ghost?' Too afraid to say more, she swallowed down her anger and her sorrow. Between Zagan and Wairimu, they forced her to weave a rope with sticky invisible threads. When she finished, Wairimu hooked it round her ankle. 'You can go to the kitchen now and bake my bread,' said he, 'but, before you go, give me back that orchid.' How he hated things to bloom…even underground.

'Captain Ironbar!' He shouted for the chief of the Axehead giants who guarded the chiefdom. 'Throw the Rhizanthella on to the castle rubbish tip and cover it with stinking black mud from the Axeheads' pigsty.'

If ever he wanted to leave Mandel while he went off to do his spoiling, Wairimu tied his end of the invisible rope to a pole in the kitchen. Within the castle, it was kept on a hand reel. The pink 'n grey, Djak, was also tied with a rope clipped to a little collar round his neck.

'I'm your master now, smart bird,' said Wairimu. It wasn't until he was in his basement where he did his darkest magic that he was brave enough to look into the Sunny Isle crystal. It showed a mirror image of himself. One look was enough.

'Cursed crystal,' he raged. 'That's not what I want to see.' With an unspeakable curse, he dropped it into his tankard of wine. There it stayed. Always hidden by the ghastly black dregs. Wairimu came back to the present with a start.

Again, Mandel turned her face to the calm blue sky. It reminded her of the Sunny Isle pool, her people's *manang*, and how she would see her own face in its clear surface. *Ah my sisters, do your children do as we did? How I long to be with you all.* Knowing nothing about Wairimu 's theft and his curse on her people, Mandel soothed herself with this thought and by stroking the one thing from her past he allowed her to keep. It was a gift from her Nanna…a message stick she couldn't even read.

'You don't need to read,' Wairimu often said. 'I tell you all you need to know. As for that old stick, better not to mess with it.' In truth she wondered if he was afraid of the message stick. Fondling its smooth handle, she murmured, 'I am so pleased I still have you, but I do wish I could read you.'

14 Mandel's Secret
The Sky above Caligo

How the years have passed,' Mandel sighed as the Hellican skimmed closer to the ground. She touched her message stick for luck, but the invisible rope that bound her to Wairimu dug deep. She rubbed her ankle. The rope was so strong, she had forgotten how to stand without it. One day in the chilly basement of Caligo Castle, she slipped free, only to stagger and fall. Wairimu laughed to see her lying on the ground. 'You are hopeless Mandel,' he chortled.

The trouble is, thought Mandel. I can't help believing what he says about me. But I do hope Ms Alayah doesn't weaken. Fearfully she recalled her secret. Mandel's only link with the outside was a two-way cupboard in the castle kitchen. It allowed traders to deliver food and goods to the castle. Earlier that day, Fisher Wizard Jim from Freo Shore had agreed to send a message to Samuel, Chief Wizard of Aberash. Jim would go through the young fisher, Mia, who was said to be as secretive and suspicious of strangers as her fisher birds, but trustworthy. She would pass on a message to Samuel.

'Please tell her Ms Alayah, is still alive but locked up in the dungeon at Caligo Castle.' Mandel had wrapped the money owed in a cloth on which she had drawn a map of the prison. It placed the dungeon on the western side of the castle with pictures of the viewing room above – the cells below and deeper still, a deadly maze of passages.

'What have I dared to do?' Now in the presence of Wairimu, Mandel's heart shrank inside her chest. Anxiously, she watched while he steered the aircraft towards Rhizanthella Forest. For years, Wairimu had attempted to break an invisible barrier that blocked him. As always, he charged towards it. But it was like trying to stop rain or the sun from rising. Whatever Wairimu did, he could not pass through the border to that forest.

'Dratted weirdo drop-outs,' he snarled. 'The creatures in there must have radar eyes.' He pulled at his carefully styled hair in a fury. 'My powers fall in a heap every time I try to cross the e'fin border.'

When Wairimu threw the Rhizanthella orchid to the pigs, a magical forest had grown up around it and a tribe of Lost People made it their home. From that day, even with strong magic, nobody could go there without their permission.

When it happened, Wairimu had been forced to have a bridge built on the western side of Caligo Castle to the rest of his holdings. The very thought of it, made him simmer with fury. With an ugly scowl spoiling his youthful mask, he recalled the day he paid a tribe of self-serving Axehead giants to build and guard the bridge. To this day the selfish dolts demanded coinage, fresh bread and even a measure of black wine for their labours.

'Greedy grumblers.' With a fierce burst of temper, he turned the Hellican too sharply and Mandel gripped her safety strap in fright.

'What is it?' she gasped.

'Don't ask,' Wairimu retorted savagely. 'And when we go home, don't even think of feedin' the wretched prisoner.'

How does he guess what I'm thinking? Miserably, Mandel heard the rub and rattle of the Hellican's parts and the reckless wind smacking its underbelly. Now and then, the noxious smell of old mud rose from the ground. She glimpsed beneath them, the Land of Bad Dreams. A place of which, few people would speak, except in a whisper.

With steely glints in his revived tiger eyes, Wairimu steered the Hellican to a section of his land that was ruled over by his ally, Dame Grey. A fluttering grey flag marked her latest business venture. A retirement lodge (no charity cases, thank you very much). With her false smiles, the Dame was able to fool old wizards who'd lost their magical powers and their wits. But Wairimu knew her true nature – at home without face paint – driving her ghastly devil birds, the mawks into submission. As for the Lodge, it was little better than a doss house. That being so, her domain was still part of his kingdom and a good measure of her profits went to him. It was a stepping stone into the Swamps of Murruk where only the fittest young workers survived to labour for him. They did so without complaint.

Mandel expected Wairimu to try a curse on Rhizanthella Forest, but he was quieter than usual. *It means he's planning something big*, she worried.

15 A Concert
Aberash Castle

On the rooftop garden, Nyan spread knitted rugs over the turf floor and invited them to sit. Lori sat like the others, legs crossed, back straight, a warm rug close. She breathed deeply, taking in the sweet fragrance of moonflowers and the night, but where was the stage and who were the performers?

'Look down there.' Cade pointed to the *moyootj* below. Partly in shadow – a swamp land. Sheeny and bright. As if glazed with a brush dipped in silver. The big *mangatj* tree stood in the centre like a black velvet cut-out pinned to the sky. The swamp's soft murmurings came up to meet them, the melodious moorp…moorp…moorp of frogs and the sky brilliant with stars.

Beside her, Mia, so haughty and distant at dinner, was soft eyed.

'We call them *koorni*,' she said. 'But have you ever heard the music of wings?' Within moments, there was a sound. Soft, yet powerful and strong as a drumbeat.

'I haven't…not like this.' Lori met Mia's gaze, knowing she felt it too, a thrill that no words could explain. The sky was full of water birds on their way to the rookery. Necks outstretched. Wings spread. Each one a perfect double curve, rising and wheeling in great loops across the sky.

Mia spoke with love of the wild creatures that belonged to the *moyootj*. 'They help me remember who I am and where I belong.'

When the water birds had gone, a moment of silence and then one tiny bird flew towards Lori. With brown speckled wings fluttering, it landed on the back of her hand. Clinging to her with tiny feet, its small body throbbed with warm energy and purpose. Its white face stared into her's before raising its head.

'Plunk, plunk, plunk.' The song was like the strings of a violin being plucked, and a signal for a whole flock of the same species. They were everywhere, singing their little hearts out. Large flocks of chats, known also as moon birds. Like the tree-top dwelling kids, they too, had found a home in Aberash.

*Bravo…bravo…*the audience clapped and cheered as more creatures performed. In a soft undertone, Aren and Nyan spoke the names of each species in the Noongar tongue – *kaawar, werloo, nyoolam, dirl-dirl, dwarnart…*each name seemed to echo the birdsong. Along with the birds and in between, waves of sound from the *koorni,* filled the night. There were tappers, bleaters, moaners, rattlers, clickers and now and then an explosive 'plunk' from old man bull frog. All were interspersed and ended with the musical, *moort…moort…moort.*

Afterwards, the silence was a song in itself, weaving a net of enchantment. And then as if waking from a dream, the small audience were on their feet. An explosion of birdsong from a single songster filled the night. A thrilling whip like call rose to the sky. Swooped and dived, rose again and spread in a continuous melody. Like bubbling water in a swiftly flowing stream.

'Renana,' Samuel said, softly. 'Our songbird and Night Protector.'

My dreambird. With her heart soaring, Lori scanned the horizon above the swamp, until she spotted the giant bird. With wide wings spread, it landed on a branch of the *mangatj* tree.

'I see her…oh I see Renana,' Lori whispered. Bronzy gold with a muted green, like forest moss. The bird lifted her fine head and spread her wings wide. As if to draw light from the moon.

'Hello,' Lori whispered. Renana nodded, a greeting that felt like a feathery hug. She beckoned to Cade, hoping he would see the bird with his own eyes but he brushed her away.

'I'm looking at the craters of the moon.' He adjusted a telescope that Aren had lent him. Lori saw in a flash, that her brother was afraid of Renana. Her call was too strange and strong for him. Was it something he feared in himself? Cade liked to keep a handle on where he was in time and space and she loved him for it…but sometimes…like now…he puzzled her.

'You don't see the Night Protector,' Nyan said with the sting of jealousy.

So why can I see her? Some instinct warned Lori not to speak of it.

'You must be dreaming.' Aren shrugged. 'People with the gift and her enemies, are the only ones who see her.'

I'm not dreaming, Lori reasoned, and Renana knows I'm not her enemy.

'Like all the best songsters,' Nyan argued, 'Renana is sure to be quite a small bird with a specialised voice box that can make more than one sound at a time.'

'You've got it all wrong,' Aren said. 'Old Sailor from the village reckons Renana is not a bird, but half woman and half cat. What do you think Mia?'

'Go back to your star gazing and leave Renana be,' Mia snapped. 'Shouldn't you boys be in bed at this hour?'

'We don't really know what Renana looks like,' Aren retorted. 'She uses magic to protect us, but we'll never know what she looks like.' Without saying a word, Lori turned her eyes back to the shining bird.

While she watched and waited, Samuel spoke quietly to Mia. 'You say you have a message from Mandel, wife of Wairimu?'

'Ms Alayah is alive. But she's a prisoner in the Dungeon of Caligo Castle. Even if she is as smart and cool as Lori and Cade say, she'll be one unhappy lady and in need of some help.'

When the River brothers and Cade excused themselves, Lori stayed on as if in a dream, with her eyes on the big tree.

'She'll need Renana,' Mia said. 'It looks as if this girl and her brother really are the ones. But they're mortals…and they know so little.'

'While I have this Mage, I shall keep my cousins safe.' Aware of a creeping chill in the air, Samuel held the garment close.

Unaware of their concern, Lori went on talking to her dreambird.

'*Renana*…that's a lovely name,' she whispered. 'Thank you for the birdcall and that gorgeous melody too. Thank you for everything…for being in my dream…and for being here for me…even though I'm just an ordinary girl.' Lori stayed for longer than she knew, until the big bird lifted its great wings skywards. *I am the Night Protector* it reminded her.

'Of course, you have work to do,' Lori whispered. She waved to Samuel at the far end of the garden and turned to Mia.

'I forgot to say goodnight to the others. I forgot everything.'

'You did,' Mia said softly, 'Goodnight, mortal girl.' At the same time, a dark cloud covered the moon. The fisher girl shivered. *Wairimu is near,* she thought. *I feel it in my bones.*

16 The Night Raiders
The Sky over Aberash

With one hand on the wheel of the Hellican, Wairimu turned to his crony, Dame Grey. They were on a spying mission to check out the granaries and other riches in Aberash.

Wairimu glared at the dame. 'You said Renana would be resting. Attending a concert, you said.'

'I told you to get out in the half-light before Renana wakes.' Her eyes narrowed. 'But you, Sir, refused to budge. Her song put you in a trance.'

'You should have prepared for that,' Wairimu's colour rose along with his temper. 'Why didn't you get your mawk spy to warn us?'

Dame Grey's jaw tightened. 'You've been fooled by Renana. Not for the first time. Wairimu, you messed up.'

'You, Madam, will eat those words. I don't mess up.' Without his disguise, the Scorpion's surly face hardened. Steely eyed, he turned away from the dame to that luminous creature who hovered near. Renana – Night Protector of Aberash. Flying slightly in front and above them, the giant bird cast a purple shadow that fell across their faces. A powerful symbol impossible to ignore.

The pair from the north flew on, with the faint hum of the engine and Wairimu 's curses. When they came to the outer reaches of the land, Renana swooped in and they saw at close quarters – the bird's great wing span, its giant muscular haunches and fierce eyes. But it was her cool assurance that offended Wairimu most.

'Renana,' he roared through a speaker, 'Call yourself Night Protector of Aberash? Pretender! Without magic you're nothing…without Samuel and his Mage, you die.' With a malicious snarl, he pulled a lever to release a blast of filthy bilge from the Hellican. 'Take that, pretender!'

The acrid slime splashed across Renana's gleaming coat. Pop-eyed and gleeful, the pair from the north looked on. But their lude grins turned to annoyance when the bilge simply fell away. Renana's gorgeous plumes glowed even more brightly. She looped twice around the Hellican and each time, Wairimu and Dame Grey were forced to see at close quarters, the jewel-like gleam of her huge hooked claws.

'So, you'll do nothing while she tears us to shreds?' Dame Grey turned on her ally. Wairimu bristled, but held his tongue as he spun the wheel sharply towards his own border. The big bird had fallen behind only because that was her choice and it filled him with rage. Why had the people of Aberash given Samuel the Mage when the old Chief died? A boy – so young and inexperienced. The Mage was nothing without Samuel to release its magic and Samuel was nothing but a stammering boy without the Mage. Then there was Renana…so weak and yet, so strong. Why?

The allies drove on, their differences forgotten as they glimpsed the fair land below.

'All that is now Samuel's…should and shall be mine,' Wairimu vowed.

'May it be so,' said Dame Grey, with a sly smile and a long slow nod.

17 Ms Alayah
Caligo Dungeon

In the viewing room, above the holding cell, Mandel served afternoon tea and retreated to her corner. Fearfully she waited while Wairimu swooped on the cake. He broke off a large chunk, scooping off extra cream topping with his finger.

'So!' he turned to his more fastidious mother, Bazilia. 'Here we have Ms Alayah. Stupid woman is making some kind of joy list.'

A flicker of spite crossed Bazilia's face. Her nostrils flared, distorting even further, her flat nasal voice. 'Just look at her – the hussy – I'll soon put a stop to her joy list.'

'Ah yes.' Wairimu licked a big sloop of cream from his fingers and slurped the last of his tea. 'This is a job for you, Mother. Scare her plenty and take Judd with you. See if you can't toughen him up a bit.'

'Call him *Slave* Judd if you don't mind.' Bazilia's pale eyes flared with annoyance.

'*Slave* Judd…if you insist.' Wairimu brushed at the crumbs on his chin. 'But I really don't know why you snatched him from the mortal zone. After all this time, he hasn't changed a jot.'

'I'll break him yet.' Bazilia sipped the last of her tea, placed the dainty china cup on its saucer and wiped her mouth with a snowy cloth. Lifting her head expectantly, she clapped her hands three times, smirking when Judd ran from the servants' quarters. Panting a little, he stood to attention. A big fair boy with beads of sweat on his upper lip, a mop of fair curly hair, a tip-tilted nose and dreamy blue eyes. She had trained him to bow when he said her name and he did so without flinching.

'Mistress Bazilia.'

Ah yes, thought Wairimu, *Mother is the best scare person I know*. With a slave to boss about and a prisoner to scare, it was the closest she ever came to smiling. Of course, she trained as a scare person in the mortal zone of Burnwood City. *Those were the days*, he thought. A sorcerer, a witch or a bad wizard in disguise could use a knucklewhack any time he or she liked without anyone saying a word against it.

When Bazilia first went to Burnwood City school, nobody guessed the new teacher was a sorceress – one who could transform children into animals. Nobody that is, except a few discerning boys and girls who had a nose for such things. One of those boys was Judd.

Wairimu recalled his boyhood when he was left in the care of servants while Bazilia passed over into the Mortal Zone. At the time, his ancestor – the dreaded pirate, Zagan, had slipped back into another time zone where ghosts and villains created havoc on the high seas, raiding countries from all over…dealing in slavery, thieving and thuggery. It was Wairimu's own dear mother who kept in touch, sending her little messages via helpful cross-zoners.

Bazilia too, remembered. From the very beginning Judd looked at her with eyes that told her, *I know that you are a sorceress from some dark place*. Then he gazed at a patch of blue sky through the classroom window, as if he were faraway. Using her knucklewhack to beat him, Bazilia muttered evil magic, expecting him to transform into a mouse in a trice…but nothing happened. Judd went on being Judd, whatever she did. She tried a worm transformation – a ferret – even a rat. But Judd went on being Judd.

'If I can't break you here, then you will come to Caligo with me.' Bazilia fixed him with an icy stare. 'You'll be my slave…see if that won't break your spirit, stubborn boy.'

With the help of Wairimu, she snatched him, casting a time spell on him to keep him a boy. Then ordered an Axehead guard to throw him into the dusty cells of Caligo Dungeon. After droning on for hours, she came up with a mean curse that went halfway to breaking his spirit.

'This boy will forget he ever saw the sky.' In a fury she ground her teeth until they were stumps and the gums bled. To this day, Judd dreamed of the sky, not knowing what it looked like, yet longing to see it. As he carried the lamp for Bazilia he wondered if the new prisoner, Ms Alayah also dreamed of the sky and whether she minded awfully that she couldn't see it. He wanted to say to her, 'Can you tell me about it? Is the sky still there?'

His thoughts and daydreams helped block out the sound of Bazilia's heavy flat feet behind him, the ominous click-clack of the unhappy worry beads that dangled around her neck and that deadly voice. The flat, most hated voice in Caligo.

'Stop dragging your feet, you dunderhead or I'll give you six of the best with my knucklewhack.' Bazilia's smug unhurried whine reminded him that she had forever to break him.

Meanwhile, on a bed of stone, Ms Alayah huddled under a scrap of old blanket. Determinedly, she went on with her joy list. 'I love my nephew Eddie and the gang, the Mason twins and all the other kids at Brightday High. I love my little house and the archway in my garden covered with coral vine and blue bush. Red for the earth and blue for the sky. But oh dear, these are the things I have lost. What do I have now?'

Like clippings from a bad movie awful 'what if' questions flicked through her mind. What if she died of starvation here in this cell? What if she never saw her family and friends again? The sky? The sun? Or the lovely light of the moon? Before she could stop it, an anguished cry of sorrow and fear rose from somewhere deep inside her.

I'm still alive, she told herself between sobs, with a strong body, and until now, an unbroken spirit. I must remain my best self...I must...I must....

After falling into an exhausted sleep, Ms Alayah was wakened by a voice that made her blood run cold. A bat-like creature, pug faced and pale-eyed stood over her. A moment passed before she realised it was a woman wearing a shroud of dark cloth. Around her neck, a set of worry beads clicked against each other uneasily. Unhooking a wicked-looking stick from her belt, the creature prodded the person who held the lamp – a curly headed boy of thirteen or so with a fair face.

His eyes were glazed, like somebody half-broken, but he managed to mouth a silent message. Ms Alayah mouthed a 'yes' in reply (years in a classroom had made her an excellent lip reader).

'Slave Judd, inform the prisoner,' the woman demanded and the boy spoke by rote.

'This is Bazilia (he bowed), Chief Scare person of Caligo Dungeon. You must call her Mistress Bazilia (he bowed again), and be sure to bow when you say her name.'

For a terrible moment Ms Alayah felt, not like a grown woman at all, but a very young child, uncertain of what powers this bat person might have. From Judd's question, she guessed he'd lost all memory of the sky. Not a good sign. If you defied Bazilia, surely, she'd turn you to stone.

Mistress Bazilia? I know that name. Ms Alayah gulped too much air. She wanted to throw up. Think…think Alayah…why do you know that name? And why is it important to remember? If only I could stop shivering. If only I could feel like a grownup, instead of a scared little girl. A girl who does what teacher says. A girl who never dares tell tales out of school.

Granny, if only you were here to comfort me. If only you were here with one of your happy ending stories.

'You, bold-as-brass hussy, open your eyes this minute.' The pupils of the woman's own pale eyes contracted to pin points. She grabbed Ms Alayah's wrist, digging in with sharp nails, leaving a trail of bright blood.

Staring down at her wrist, Ms Alayah remembered once again, what it was like to be a child. Something she had vowed, never to forget.

When Ms Alayah was young, her mum had been a busy doctor and her dad, a fly-in fly-out mine worker. It was her Gran who was there to comfort her when she was sad. Gran who told stories about her own childhood. *But there is no Gran here*, she reminded herself, *only me, and I'm no longer a child.*

'Look at me!' The bat woman demanded. Taking her time, she ran her hand over the edge of her stick and then teasingly swished it. Back and forth. Swish, swish, swish. It set up a rhyme in Ms Alayah's head. *She's the sorceress…*Gran had told her an old chant…how did it go? A few of the words came back to her.

'Bazilia was a sorceress, never called to account, never found out…never found out…'

'How dare you chant without my permission?' With an angry hiss, Bazilia threw back her cape, baring brawny arms and the stumps of her teeth. But as Ms Alayah began her chant, the bat woman stopped as if frozen.

Bazilia is the sorceress

Who was never found out, never found out

Haunted the halls of Burnwood

And never found out.

18 The Sorceress of Burnwood
A Holding Cell in Caligo

Ms Alayah longed to be safe in Gran's arms. Bazilia was the sorceress. A bad one who went to Burnwood City and was never found out. What was the rest of Gran's story?

'Watch out!' Again, Judd warned.

'Judd…I know you.' Ms Alayah barely felt the first swipe of the stick across her knuckles. 'I know you, not from my own time but from my Gran's. I know the name Judd and Bazilia…she…she…' Again, the stick struck, but instinctively, Ms Alayah drew her hand away. Enraged, Bazilia struck again. Ms Alayah gasped and then blew on her fingers to ease the pain. Her knees sagged. Her mind was fuzzy from lack of food but her gran's story came back to her in a rush.

Bazilia had tricked her way into Burnwood School by posing as a mortal. She ruled by fear, wicked magic and her knucklewhack for years without anyone stopping her. Again, Ms Alayah felt the edge of the stick – this time, around her legs. Bruised and bleeding she leapt out of the way to avoid the next strike. At the same time, she remembered the whole story. Judd was the boy who disappeared on the very day Bazilia left the school with gifts of flowers and fake tears. *One good thing has come out of this crime*, she thought. *Judd is still alive and as young as the day he was taken.*

'Gran told me about you,' Ms Alayah said. 'She was so sorry neither she, nor the other kids ever stood up for you. They were all too scared of Bazilia I expect.'

Bazilia snarled. 'Don't you know how powerful my magic is, stupid girl? See these beads of mine?' She shook her body and the long necklace of worry beads hummed like strung wire in high quavers. 'Can you hear the beads at their lessons? If I say, *chant,* they chant. If I say *sing,* they sing. Do you know what that means?'

'Only too well,' Ms Alayah flashed back. 'It tells me you are a wicked sorceress and child beater and you should have been stopped.' She quaked at the knees, but anger drove her on. 'Inside those beads of yours are the broken spirits of children who were struck down by you. *Release them at once.* I shall warn Mr Brown, the Big Boss of Schools that your wicked magic isn't dead and we must all guard against it.'

Ms Alayah breathed in a whiff of air. It was stale but the sick odour of bad magic was fainter. 'Don't *dare* touch me again,' she said. "Nor this boy with that knucklewhack.'

Judd shook his head as if waking from a dream. *Ms Alayah spoke up for me and kids like me,* he thought. *Nobody has ever done that for me.* Something strong stirred inside him. A small part of himself he kept for himself, always. *I might so easily have given it away. I might so easily, have become what Bazilia wants me to be…a worm…a mouse…a helpless thing.*

Mean eyed and dangerous, Bazilia watched Judd mouth, 'thank you,' to Ms Alayah. She watched the dawning of light in his eyes.

Enraged, she screamed, 'Hold out your hands…knuckle side up.'

'I will *not.*' Judd saw, not the powerful sorceress he had feared for so long, but a twisted creature. Demented and angry. Even so, he gaped, astonished when the knucklewhack shot out of her hand. It dangled in front of her just out of reach with Bazilia chasing after it. Red faced and gasping, she spat out her fury. Round and round in a circle, she chased the stick. As if drawn by a magnet, it leapt out of reach until its handle linked with an empty lantern hook on the ceiling above.

'What sorcery is *this?*' screamed Bazilia.

'Leave it be, Mother,' Wairimu called loudly from the viewing room. 'I'll see to the prisoner myself come morning…I need a drink.' He couldn't wait for a swig of black wine.

'But I want to whack him,' Bazilia screeched.

With a faint hiss, the lamp light died. Ms Alayah heard the thud of Judd's footsteps as he raced up the flight of stairs in a bid for freedom. Bazilia's enraged screeches filled the air as her anger turned inwards. With no knucklewhack and no one to beat, she tore at the worry beads around her neck.

'You should have stopped him with your chant,' she screamed. But her blood curdling wails were drowned by an explosive crack like gunfire. With her own hands she had snapped the necklace. Beads fell in a shower across the stone wall with ghostly cheers, hoots and hurrahs. Small ghosts of children released, Ms Alayah fancied. Now, the prison was silent and dark as pitch except for a faint gleam along the length of the knucklewhack, swinging slowly in the stale air.

19 Scare Persons
Caligo Castle

Ironbar!' Wairimu shouted, angry as a Tasmanian devil with rotten teeth. 'Get your daughter to take care of Mother while I work something out.' He clenched his fists. 'There's been a leak somewhere.'

Was it the pesky Justice Ants from Rhizanthella Forest?

'I should have burned that stinking orchid while I had it in my hand,' he muttered. The rubbish site where he buried it was now full of half-baked wizards…rejects from the mortal zone and their menagerie of so-called endangered species, many with a fondness for digging. Next, they'd be digging at the very foundations of his chiefdom.

'Oh, why do bad things happen to poor ol' me?' Angrily, Wairimu yanked Djak's lead. 'I need you to hear me, smart bird. Mother's lost her knucklewhack and Judd's run away. Meantime, we must put in more scare-persons.'

The dozing bird nearly fell off his perch. 'Awe, gosh, Master, you mean you want me to let in the hungry Grums to scare the prisoner half to death?'

'Who else have I got? The Axeheads think they're too grand for scaring now days. Selfish beggars. Lift the latch to the Grums' cage and don't try to cheat me. I'll know if they're not let in. I had 'em rounded up, locked up and kept hungry for days. They're sure to scuffle about in the dark looking for old bones to gnaw and fight over. There'll be a lot of sniffin' and squealin' if I'm not mistaken.'

'Not a nice sound to hear in the dark.' Mandel stopped herself from saying more. To say more, made it worse for the prisoner and herself.

'I'll remember that,' said Wairimu with a vengeful look. He turned to his hand mirror to smooth his hair and examine his teeth. 'Shut your mouth, woman, and go fix my dinner.'

With a fearful look behind and fluttering heart, Mandel picked up the tray of used crockery and left-over cake. She hurried through a draughty passage towards the kitchen. The trapped Wind of Ice chilled her bones and the invisible rope that tied her to Wairimu chafed her ankle. It reminded her of the ghastly pirate, Zagan. She was sure Wairimu kept the ghost of his ancient ancestor as a prisoner to be sure the old curses were kept alive.

'They are the source of his power,' she muttered, 'at the very heart of his hateful plotting.'

It was warmer in the kitchen. The currant buns were ready to be iced and the bread dough swollen like a lovely daytime moon. Mandel pushed the dough down and kneaded it one more time before dividing it up to make rolls with plaited knobs on top. When the bread had risen again, she popped it in the oven, enjoying a moment of ease with only the flickering wood stove for company. But Mandel's peace was soon shattered by the desperate screeches of Grums. Thinking they were about to be fed, the young one's scrambled over each other and snapped at the musty air. With high pitched squeaks and scuffles, they pounded along the narrow tunnel that led to the feeding trough in the dungeon.

A full tummy is what each of those creatures need to be nicer, Mandel mused. If she could wangle it while Wairimu wasn't watching, she would give them extra rations. And for Judd, she would add a few greens and cheese to a fresh bread roll and hide it in a pottery jar that was stored in the broom cupboard. *Poor Judd. Whatever happens, I won't let you go hungry.* It broke her heart and bruised her soul when all she had to offer him or anyone, were cups of tea and scraps from the kitchen. Judd might hide for a while, but how could he possibly find a way out of the castle?

When Wairimu returned to the enormous kitchen, he demanded a loaf of fresh bread, side salads and a great slab of roast pork, crispy brown with hot gravy and apple sauce. In between serious chomping, he muttered about the state of the prisoner.

'Too clever by half, is Ms Alayah. Far as I'm concerned, she and the whole dang lot of the cross-zoning mortals can slide down thte big slippery dip…not to the bottom of any weird ladder they like to talk about, but into my net and under my thumb.'

Ah yes, he'd scare the living daylights out of Ms Alayah come morning. Now the Grums had gone in, he was tempted to taunt the prisoner himself or to simply watch her crumble, but the black wine made his head too queer and wobbly.

'Methinks I need a little lie down on my day-bed,' he told Mandel. 'So, top up my tankard of wine and then stay right where you are in case I need you to fetch something for me.' He wound in the invisible rope, carefully counting the number of turns before holding it to his belly. 'I'm sure I counted right,' he muttered. 'It must be the black wine messing with my head, but it's like my end of the rope has shrunk over the years.'

Between yawns, he told Mandel a story about his friend Villiam-Von-Vampire who kept his wife from leaving the kitchen by turning her into a teacup and hanging her on the shelf. 'A good idea,' he said, 'but then who would bake the bread?'

'Who indeed?' Mandel gained another half turn of the slackened rope and wound it round the flat middle of her message stick. She had gained quite a bit of rope on that old message stick.

'He's scared of it,' she whispered to Djak. 'I don't know why.' It reminded her of Sunny Isle, her heart country. That usually saddened her but tonight it was a comfort.

A groan, a roll-over and Wairimu slept. Though broad shouldered and powerful, his body was growing quite lumpish and ugly in its natural state, rising and falling with his drunken snores. A wink from the bird and Mandel moved, very fast and light footed for a nicely rounded lady. She unhooked *Djak* to free him and then grabbed a bit more rope from Wairimu 's grasp for herself.

With a basket of bread in one hand and an oil lamp in the other, she tripped down dark passages to the viewing room above the dungeon while the bird fluttered overhead. First, she dropped crumbled bread, the ruins of a cream cake and well cured scraps into a feeding chute for the Grums, then after the squealing and munching subsided turned back to the bird.

'You know what to do, Djak.'

20 Pointing the Way: Lori & Cade
Aberash Castle

'A mortal boy, a mortal girl…eyed by a wizard…must fall to his spell or pass the test.' Cade mouthed the words as Lori completed the chant, 'Yet, with a coin and a key, may prove the best…the prisoners of a wizard's bind to free.'

'Oh brother, one of those prisoners is Ms Alayah.' It was a sunny day in Aberash but Lori shivered.

'We need to learn more,' Cade said. 'But with the Mage and Samuel behind us, we'll find a way to Ms Alayah…now let's go eat.' He clattered downstairs, ready for whatever lay ahead. Lori bit her lip. She followed with a growing sense of uneasiness. They needed to learn the rules for travelling in a land of magic…true, but was she brave enough to do it?

After breakfast, Samuel led them to a place of learning within the castle.

'We call it Raz Nehyer.' His goldie-brown eyes were distant and thoughtful. 'It's a kind of learning from ancient times.' They were standing in a central courtyard where honeybirds dived and splashed in an overflowing birdbath. Several doorways led to different mentors.

'Raz Nehyer…I've read about it,' Lori said. 'It means the Secret Way.'

'Yes?' Samuel eyes sparked with interest. 'You choose your own mentors here.' He told them of the poet who would explain the wisdom behind riddles and rhymes and the story teller who might warn of hidden dangers in Caligo. There was a map maker, a potter and others but it was Fortune Teller Alice that made Lori put up her hand.

'Ah, that's for me,' she said, even while a core of fear in her belly made her wonder why she was doing this. A timid knock on the door, and Alice ushered her inside. A tall woman with a swathe of dark hair and leaf green eyes. Her room smelled of cedar wood, perfumed oils and smouldering incense.

'Well now, I suppose you are looking for a pretty little story about yourself. And I suppose you want the answers in a trice.' The woman's earrings and necklaces swayed as she moved. Layers of sapphire and opal, aquamarine and moonstone. 'Isn't that what mortals usually want?'

'It's not…not…about wanting anything,' Lori stammered. 'It's just that…I need to know…what I need to know…if you know what I mean…'

'Is that so?' Alice's searching eyes probed her's. Her thick dark brows twitched. 'In that case, don't look at me…look at the *bola de crystal*.' She placed an enormous crystal ball on a small table and they sat on either side of it. With thick lashed eyes half closed, Alice chanted, her words rushing on like an anxious stream. Lori prickled against it as she shifted her gaze from Alice to the crystal. It was framed by her long beringed fingers.

'Concentrate,' Alice demanded sharply. 'Tell me what you see.'

'Ahh…eh…I can't see any…thing…but, yes.' Lori turned her gaze back to the crystal ball. 'There is…a path with a muddy kind of blur on all sides…and there's…oh no…it's kind of like…a movie with two kids. That's Cade…and me! It's me. We're walking along a path.'

'And?' Alice drummed the fingers of one hand on the table.

'We come to a split in the road…but this is wrong. Cade goes one way…I start to follow him, then I turn, and go the other way…no…no…no.' Blood rushed to Lori's face. She choked up, unable to speak. Her eyes filled. 'Cade and I are twins. We stay together always.'

Alice picked up a silk cloth that hung over her arm and rubbed the crystal ball, rubbed until something showed. Was there a glint of pity in her eyes? Lori dropped her own eyes from the fortune teller to the image…it was a picture of herself with large frightened eyes, an open mouth and a nose long and narrow as a bird's beak.

'You have a long way to go, little girl,' Alice said with a guarded look, even if you do…have….'

'Thank you. I need to find my brother.' Lori rushed from the room, away from the woman and the sickly smell of incense. She sneezed violently and it shook her whole body. *Little Girl, was she?* A beaky nose, she might learn to live with…but a journey without Cade? That was unthinkable.

Lori didn't wait to see the woman's eyes soften. Didn't wait to hear her murmur. 'Poor child, she has the gift.' Lori wanted to yell, rage or simply burst into tears but she almost laughed when she found her twin…of all places, with his nose in a book inside a room that was just like a regular library. She breathed in the familiar smell of books, art supplies, chalk and reams of paper. Close by, Samuel was sorting out a travel plan for each of them, with water proof maps and pictures.

'Whatever happens, you won't be alone,' he said, comfortingly.

'We won't?' Lori touched the end of her nose with her fingers. It was fine. Everything was fine. Alice just happened to be a mean cow. *We are coming to find you, Ms Alayah,* she vowed. *So please don't give up.* With this resolve, she settled down to read her travelling guide, snuggling into a beanbag. It was a bit old and worn. Just like her favourite one at home.

Cade left Lori to her reading. He wanted to explore more rooms on offer in Raz Nehyer – to hear the stories, to understand the riddles and rhymes. He wanted to know every detail of the landscape between Aberash and Caligo Castle. To learn with his hands by moulding clay – the mountains, the desert and the swamplands over which they would travel. What drew him most was the river. Mia called it The Tricky. Why was that? The question remained in his head, like a pesky fly.

Excitement and fear churned inside him. Cade couldn't wait for the adventure to begin. When he returned to the library he knew Lori had taken in every word of her guide book. Book smart…that was his sister, and though shaken by whatever she learned from Alice, she knew how to look for her own answers. *What was One Rock Desert and why was it sometimes called The Forgotten Sea? And what about The Land of Dream? What did it mean to a traveller like her and Cade?*

'Rhizanthella Forest,' Samuel reminded them, 'is a place of refuge and friendship. You'll find a door into it on the southern side. A door you'll know the minute you see it but not before you both see. Remember, if you're separated that's where you meet.'

'Rhizanthella Forest…' Lori chanted the name like a mantra. 'And there's a door we won't see until we both see it…weird. But why would we be separated? It's not going to happen.' With eyes blazing and hearts thumping, they studied Mandel's map and worked on a rough travel plan. At the same time, they knew that in a land of magic nothing was certain.

Leaving the twins with their growing confidence and high hopes, Samuel climbed the stairs to the roof-top garden. A see-through day-time moon hung low in the sky. With fingers stroking the cloth of the Mage, he wove another protection spell for his cousins.

'While I have the magic of this Mage,' he whispered, 'I won't let them down.' For long moments he thought about their impossible quest. With a growing sense of uneasiness, Samuel's intuition told him that Ms Alayah was in desperate need of light. Though it was only days since he opened the way for moon magic, he did so again, as if to remind the great Spirit who guided all, that time was running out.

21 Facing the Wall: Ms Alayah
The Dungeon of Caligo Castle

Is it part of the punishment? To be taunted by the smell of freshly baked bread while you starve? Ms Alayah looked for a chink of light in the pitch-black cell. All around her, unseen creatures chomped on old bones, or they fought over scraps, with irritable snarls.

'There must be a way out.' Alayah tried to remember what she had seen of the holding cell in the lamplight. A musty drop toilet in one corner. A rusted tap dribbling brackish water. A stone bench for a bed. The crudely built room divider. *Ah yes, the room divider.* A loose network of rungs, some broken. Here and there, a strand of barbed wire. Even if she could climb over it, what living creature would show her a way out? Surely not those hungry creatures scuffling about in the dark.

Another sound came to Ms Alayah. Something less angry. It was the gentle rush and hush of wings. Dreamily, she inhaled the smell of poppy seed loaves, warm kitchens and kindness. For a moment, the bird brushed its body against her outstretched arms.

'Don't be afraid,' said the bird in a voice, soft and deep. It led her to a basket of food in a corner of the cell. Ms Alayah guessed some person had tied it to a rope and lowered it through the air vent.

'You are so kind.' Tears of gratitude pricked her eyes.

'It is Mistress Mandel who is kind,' said the bird. 'She fed the Grums but the young ones are half starved and desperate, so do take care.'

After the bird left it was quiet. Too quiet. Uneasily, Ms Alayah raised a fresh bread roll to her mouth, only to have it snatched out of her hand. It was a signal for raucous screeches, fighting and childish name calling.

Greedy pig…you bit my ear…did not…did so…did not…did so… Animals with young human voices hissed and snarled – scratched, bit, and kicked. Though weak with hunger and suffering from the effects of Bazilia's cruelty, Ms Alayah knew what to do.

'Stop your fighting this minute!' she commanded in a firm but kind school-ma'am voice. It rarely failed in a tight situation. A shocked silence followed – and then a squeak.

Somebody yelled, 'We're gonna be in trouble with Ma and Pa…let's get out o' here.' The bread was pushed back into her hands and the creatures scattered. Ms Alayah stood perfectly still, trying to calm her breathing. *They've gone now and you need to eat,* she reminded herself. Touched by a weird Grum or not, Ms Alayah held tightly on to the food. She ate a little, trying to swallow down a sudden desire to be sick.

I must learn to eat again, she thought. *Take a little at a time.* It helped that the air felt warmer. Kinder. Friendlier somehow, and after eating a little of the bread, she was surprised by the warmth creeping into her cold fingers. Slowly, it spread to her toes and along her veins. With the warmth there came a faint glow of light from her skin.

'I'm in the realm of magic.' With this understanding, Ms Alayah opened herself to words that came in to her mind. *'While here I must stay…gentle light of moon, light the way'.* Chanting the words brought calmness. Ms Alayah stroked her own shoulders and extended her glowing hands. She was unsurprised by the magical light, but shocked to see how much body weight she had lost. How many days had she been without food?

'I don't understand,' she whispered to the unknown magician who must be at work. 'Whoever you are, thank you…for this gift of light.' But the lingering sting of Bazilia's beating and Wairimu's threat to 'deal with her come morning' filled her with dread.

I can't stay here to be tortured by Wairimu and Bazilia. If I climb the barrier it might be the death of me but I need to take a chance.

Until now, Ms Alayah had avoided the knucklewhack but the moonlight emanating from her skin made its long shaft glow. Its curved end had been hidden until now. Without Bazilia, it was simply a stick. Could it be used as a tool? Alayah studied the dividing wall that stood between her and the unknown darkness of Caligo Castle. Was she fit enough to climb it?

Not so long-ago Ms Alayah was agile and bendy as a twig. Nifty as a bird. Not so long ago she was a student herself. She had climbed King Karri to stand in the tower at the top. Foresters used it to spot bushfires, but Ms Alayah had climbed the silver trunked giant for a different view of the world she loved.

I am that same girl and I must do this…I can do this.

She kicked off her shoes, stretched and concentrated on her body. Every muscle of every bone. Every cell of every muscle. She started to climb the wall. Her eyes focussed, her fingers gripped. *One and two and three. Three rungs. Now three rungs more. One, two, three…and again. You slip now and then, but you save yourself. You begin a counting cycle. That's how you reach the top. One, two and three, and again. And when you get there, it's not the end. You need to stay steady. Cling with your bare toes. Use your calf muscles and thighs so that your hands are free.*

You can do it, Ms Alayah told herself. Just like you did as a student when you trusted your feet. When you trusted your whole body. At last, from the top of the barrier, Ms Alayah looked higher to the knucklewhack.

'It was Bazilia who did the beating,' she whispered. 'Now you can be my friend.' There was no time to lose. The giants were up and about. One was heading for the holding cell. Its heavy feet tramping…thump, thump, thump. Ms Alayah had no other choice but to grab the knucklewhack. It almost leapt into her hand and she gripped it tightly. *Now, hook the handle over a sturdy rung and slither down the dividing wall. Cling to another firm rung with your feet, and use the stick again to the same tune. Again, and again.*

A furious shout and Ms Alayah's heart leapt. It was an Axehead. *Oh dear, the moonlight will give me away. Hurry girl, hurry.* The giant was now shaking the unwilling rusted door at the top of the stairs to the cell. At the same time Ms Alayah leapt from the barrier and tumbled down. Finishing in a head roll, that softened her fall, she scrambled to her feet and ran for her life.

When Axehead Faradale lumbered down the steps to deliver a watery bowl of porridge to the prisoner, the holding cell was empty.

'Oh, dang and blast,' he muttered Now, there'd be hell to pay upstairs, and another death on his conscience. He believed there was little hope for anyone lost in in the lower reaches of the Dungeon.

With a beam of moonlight leaping ahead of her, Ms Alayah explored the musty halls of the prison. The first and second corridors led to more cells, the third to a wider passage. Covered with a mix of sand, sawdust and ash, the ground was soft under her bare feet. With the knucklewhack as a tester, and guide, she discovered the imprint of a giant hand on the path. Beneath it the cruel jaws of a trap had been hidden. Worked on the spring principal, the sharp metal teeth on either side of a delicately balanced metal plate told all. It was a person sized trap. One that might have left Ms Alayah badly injured.

'Without you,' she told the stick, 'I might have lost a leg and even my life from loss of blood and shock.'

As she walked on, the stick pointed to several more of the traps until the softer dusty surface of the passage changed to hard stone.

'*Good…no more traps,*' Ms Alayah sighed but within moments a metallic clunk prompted her to raise her eyes. From a burnt-out old stairwell above, a claw like cage hurtled towards her. Later, she would remember, the rounded end of the knucklewhack pushing her gently but firmly to safety.

A fleeting backwoods glance showed her the stick. It was crushed to a pulp. No time for goodbye. Ms Alayah had to keep running to stop herself falling down the steep slope ahead.

'I can't stop,' she shouted, as she stared at somebody in the middle of the path. A small person somebody. *Oh, not a child? My worst nightmare…to hurt a child.* Ms Alayah was thrown into the air…saw stars…and then nothing.

22 The Grums: Ms Alayah
A Maze of Dark Passages

A tribe of little people? They stood in a circle above her…with ears alert, long tails and twitching noses. Grums? Alayah knew of such creatures.

'Is she dead?' asked Thud, the largest and toughest Grum. 'I saved her from falling into the pit, but I'm afraid I've killed her.'

'She is a child of the moon,' said Da Grum in awe, 'And alive, if not altogether well.' The young Grums had never seen the moon, and never, until this moment seen a person blessed with its light. They stood in a circle around her, for once not squabbling or kick fighting, for it was a privilege to be in her presence. Amidst soft murmurings they helped her into the sitting position and urged her to move to a safer spot.

'I do hope you're feeling better,' said Ma Grum. Then seeing that indeed, the extra-ordinary being was feeling better, introduced Da and her family of nine. 'This is my dear husband, Da and these are our young. Introduce yourselves to Ms…?'

'Please call me Alayah,' she said and the Grum family beamed – daughters – Briony, Sparkle, Tammy and Twill along with sons – Thud, Limber, Percy, Shaver and Nib.

Between them, Briony and Nib gave her a rundown on the family history. Grums in general were thought to be distantly related to a person kind of species.

'Our relatives came to Terre Australis in 1504 with Captain Gonneville,' said Nib, the family historian. 'The crew were starving, the rats all eaten, when the crew turned to the Grum slaves. So of course, our esteemed relatives had no choice but to jump overboard.'

'Unthinkingly, they leapt right in to a realm of magic,' Briony went on. 'And we gained this human-like shape…if you can call it a gain.'

Ma beamed fondly at the eldest and cleverest of her brood while Da gave a little pep talk. 'Now my loves, Ms Alayah is a moon child. She has the protection of that heavenly body and we are duty bound to help her. The rule was made in very ancient times. Long before we came to this land.'

'I think you made that bit up,' Nib cried. 'Where is your evidence?'

'Wairimu will kill us if we help her,' Percy hissed. The others nodded their heads, echoing: 'He'll kill us, for sure.'

'Enough!' Ma glared at Percy.

Da bowed again to Ms Alayah. 'Our family is at your service. I assure you, there'll be no bun snatching or bone grinding in the middle of the night.' He turned then to stare down his offspring but a faint sound echoed through the passage from above.

'It's Wairimu in a terrible rage,' Percy yelped. 'Let's get out of here.'

'If we run for it with no regard for consequences,' said Briony in her ponderous way, 'one of the cages will fall on us. We must go to ground immediately.'

'To our hideout,' Thud added. The hefty young Grum pushed away a knot of feathers and fur, uncovering a hole between the sloping floor and the wall. With the help of the Grums, and the advantage of her skinny frame, Ms Alayah managed to squeeze through. They entered an air-pocket that had been secretly fixed up by Mandel as a refuge from Wairimu's worst rantings. A cosy hand-woven mat lay on the floor and a pretty curtain covered a fake window. It disguised a map of the castle Mandel had etched into the rammed earth wall. It showed various bumps and hollows, corners and steps, cage traps and black holes.

'More than a few prisoners have been saved with the help of that map,' said Da, 'but they needed strong magic to make it outside.'

'Are you telling me there's a way out of here?' Ms Alayah asked.

'That's a difficult question.' Da gazed thoughtfully at the wall.

Briony shook her head, 'There are many ways out of the Dungeon, but you're still locked up in Caligo Castle.' She paused, meeting Ms

Alayah's gaze with an expression of concern. 'Too many prisoners end up sliding down the chute into Zagan's domain.'

Even Shaver, known for his risk-taking ventures, shivered. 'I've been there…seen the old ship…and Zagan.'

'Don't speak of Zagan,' said Ma. 'Not to a Moon child.'

'Apart from Shaver, we haven't made it past the wine cellar,' Percy removed a wooden peg from his mouth (it was to stop him grinding his teeth away, Ma Grum explained).

'I almost made it outside,' Shaver snickered. 'I saw the door when Wairimu took Mandel out for her once a year ride in the Hellican. But it was gone in a flash.'

'I heard a whisper.' Wide eyed, Twill, the youngest girl, turned to Ms Alayah. 'They say Wairimu put a curse on that door to keep us locked in forever.'

Briony raised her hand to protest. 'That's not the full story at all. Don't you know Zagan added a clause to that curse?'

'Best not to dwell on it,' Da said, gruffly. 'It'll lead to arguments and then you'll be squabbling.'

'Anyway,' Shaver said with a sly grin, 'I've sniffed around in places nobody knows about. I reckon I could find another way out.'

'You mean along the old Grum-runs?' Tammy asked, uncertainly. 'You can't take a Moon child along a Grum-run, it wouldn't be nice.'

'Oh, but the Grum-runs are lovely,' Twill sighed. 'They smell so Grummy. Why don't we go there anymore?'

'Let's go there now!' the others chorused. The young licked their chops and Da sniffed the air.

'Ah yes, delectable, are the Grum-runs,' he mused. 'I remember when I was a youngster. We picnicked amidst the rubbish where mushrooms and truffles fed on nicely cured scraps from the kitchen. Oh, those were the days. We were never hungry before Wairimu's reign and there were no family fights at meal times. Do you think we could risk it again, my sweet?'

'Have you no memory?' Ma exclaimed. 'It was Wairimu's ancestor, Zagan, who started it all. He's been a wicked pirate from cradle to grave! Now tell me what happened the last time we made it to the Grum-runs?'

'Enough harping.' Da stroked Ma's cheek. 'We were trapped.'

'At the mercy of Zagan and his heir for the rest of our lives,' Ma cried, and then explained more quietly to Ms Alayah. 'We've been slaves ever since, locked up in the Dungeon and half starved. We had no choice but to sign an agreement for the sake of our young.' She couldn't go on for the break in her voice and welling tears.

Da nudged her gently with his nose and then turned to Ms Alayah. 'As Zagan's heir, Wairimu keeps us as scare slaves and we're bound under oath to serve him. But our allegiance to you goes back further. You are a child of the Moon, blessed with her glorious light.'

'I guess I am.' Ms Alayah lifted a glowing hand.

At this, Ma leapt up, her eyes wide. 'It means…it means…that our agreement with Zagan and his heir is null and void! It's not worth the paper it was written on. We're free…I mean…what I mean is, that we would be free, if only we could.'

'With a moon child to help protect us, we could all escape,' Briony said, softly.

'We should make a plan.' Eagerly, Tammy leaped forward but Da waved her down.

'Don't be too hasty.' The elder Grum wasn't known for doing a lot. He yawned. 'Thanks to Mandel our tummies are full tonight and it's been a long day. I think we should sleep on it.'

Her new friends gave Ms Alayah the only cushion they had and then curled up together to hear a long-winded story from Da before sleep time.

'When my kind first came to this land, it was full of Stick Nest Rats. The stick houses they designed were a marvel…truly grand.'

'Oh yes, dear heart,' said Ma, sleepily, 'Grand were those stick houses, as they are today with a soft grassy middle.'

Very soon, all was silent as the Grum family dreamed of distant days when tall sailing ships were carried by the wind – their holds plump with bales of wool from the land Downunder or spices and sweet-smelling incense from a mysterious land called The East. A time when sailors and Grum folk alike swam for their lives from ships wrecked by raging seas. 'Oh, those were the days,' Da murmured.

When all was quiet, except for a few whispers and Ma had settled her young, Ms Alayah studied Mandel's map of Caligo Castle, layer upon layer of darkness. The layer closest to the earth was called Deep.

'It is haunted by the ghost of Zagan.' Briony uncoiled herself from the others, bowing faintly. 'Ms Alayah, gracious child of the moon, Ma says I should be your guide. It's only right for a mortal to have one in a land of magic.'

'A guide is just what I need.' Ms Alayah smiled.

'Oh, I'm pleased to be of service.' Briony explained that Wairimu's spell was too strong for anyone to get out of the castle. Even *Zagan* in his ghostly form was a prisoner. 'There is just the one door to the outside and Wairimu has made it invisible.'

Together they examined every detail of Mandel's map. 'This looks like the kitchen with the wine cellar beneath it,' Ms Alayah said. 'And below that, a basement?'

'A basement…yes, where Wairimu does his deadliest transformations.' A flicker of fear crossed Briony's face. 'Below that, is the Arena where he plays blood sports with his ghoulish followers.' Her small body stiffened.

Briony and her family are putting themselves at risk for me. Ms Alayah's head spun with the enormity of Wairimu's hold on his kingdom. He was clever in a cunning way but childish, greedy and vain. How was it possible to escape from that kind of dumb oppression? What terrible things lay ahead? Her light flickered. As if, whoever gave her the gift of moonlight had lost a good bit of magic.

23 In Praise of The Mage
Aberash Village

In Aberash, the townsfolk went about their business. It was mid-morning and Renana was deeply asleep. The day seemed like any other except for a thick fog that hung like a frown over the low lying *Moyootj*.

'I don't like it,' said Aren. He and his brothers left the village with their Lightfoots. They were heading for the grassy plateau beyond Rocky Barrier while Mia fished in the bay with her *yoondoordo*. As promised, she sent a message with a tiny mirror-flash across the peaks: flick…flick-flick…*mind how you go brothers…and hold tightly to our Archie.*

Their reply flicked back: We are through the worst of it… take care yourself, sister.

In the market place the air was abuzz with mixed up smells and sounds. A delicious whiff of stir fries redolent with herbs and spices, sweet smelling flowers and freshly baked bread. Magicians and wizards were busy preparing for a day's trading. It went on until midmorning when the clock on the town hall struck the hour. At once, the villages downed tools and were silent. They turned as one to watch Samuel's rooftop garden. Between them, Mr Caius and Ms Cora pinned out the Mage to shine like a kite on the skyline while everyone sang its praises:

Lovely as a raven's wing — is the Mage, gold are its threads.
With its magic and Samuel, we are safe from the Scorpion.

The song told of the villagers' pride in the Mage and their affection for Samuel, a humble boy who blushed easily. A boy who was able to unlock its magic for the good of all.

'The little ravens sound uneasy today,' said the purple-hatted wizard.

It reminded her of a past raid by Wairimu. He had come in the half-light to burn a precious field of wheat that was ripe for the harvest. The alarm was raised and Samuel had come running. Thanks to the magic of the Mage, he was able to defend the crop with a counter-spell and Wairimu fled.

Old Sailor also remembered. 'Bless the Mage.' He looked up from his work bench that was laden with his scrimshaw etchings.

The purple-hatted wizard smiled. 'Bless Samuel for his pure heart that opens the door to its magic.'

'To the Mage and Samuel!' cried the Master of Bees as he poured a good measure of mead for a customer. 'Remember when the old chief died? The flowers closed up on my bees and they were trapped inside the petals with their leg sacks brim full of nectar – until we put the Mage on Samuel's shoulders. My word, that first nature spell our Samuel did was something! Only a very young lad, he was at the time, barely fourteen if I remember rightly.'

'Yes, yes, yes….' Others agreed, and then the fiddler played his first rousing tune for the day.

While the villagers went on with their trading, on the rooftop garden of Aberash Castle, Samuel helped Healer Ingrid set up a trolley of medicines, ointments and bandages. Between them, they treated the ailments of a dozen or more shipwrecked orphans who lived in the village.

'You're a natural healer, Samuel.' Ingrid went on bandaging a young boy's grazed knee. 'I'm grateful for your help.'

'I learned everything I know from you.' Samuel smiled fondly at the wizard who had raised him. Ingrid had taught him the art of healing from an early age. For this work he didn't need the Mage. In fact, he was happy for the villagers to enjoy the sight of the magical cloak fluttering in the breeze. The pair worked steadily until one patient remained, a young boy with bad dreams and a rattle in his chest. Samuel gave him a healing tonic and then rubbed decongestant in to his chest telling him a story at the same time.

'I like that story best of all,' the boy said, 'because it's about you when you were an orphan child like me.'

24 Mischief in Aberash
Aberash Castle and Village

When the orphan ran off to play with his friends, Ingrid returned to her work in the village and Samuel turned his attention to the rooftop garden. He placed a kneeling mat beside a spinach bed and was about to start weeding when the peaceful day was shattered by a loud thump of something falling into the shrubbery. It was followed by an agonised scream.

'Be careful,' Ms Cora warned from the far end of the garden where she was planting seeds. 'It could be a devil bird…a mawk spy.'

'Devil bird or not, that's a real cry for help.' Samuel hurried to the spot. One look told him that yes, it was a very young mawk lying in a pool of its pale blue blood. The creature – half bird, half beast, stared at him with pain filled but defiant eyes. It had been shot in its chest with an arrow.

Who could possibly have done such a thing? Surely not a citizen of Aberash. Samuel grabbed what he needed from the trolley, though he did so with a hollow feeling inside. *No good can come out of this but I am a healer – and under oath to heal.* Working quickly, he washed the affected area with a cleansing solution and applied a special paste to blunt the pain and stem the bleeding. This enabled him to see more clearly, a tell-tale brown stain.

'The arrow is tipped with poison.' He stared into the eyes of the young mawk. 'It will hurt, but I need to remove it as quickly as possible.' The creature stared back. Not with alarm, but a look of triumph. He grabbed Samuel's extended wrists with a huge muscular claw, applying enough pressure to remind him, *I could crush your hands to pulp if I chose…so leave me die for my master…for Wairimu, Chief Wizard of Caligo.* Immobilized, Samuel could do nothing but wait for the young mawk to die.

Within a hidden part of the lowland behind Aberash Castle, Wairimu lay down his bow and quiver. His slave and follower had fallen and the shadows of night had lifted. A time when Renana was deeply asleep. Set in open-top mode, the Hellican was primed for this moment. A mirror image on a screen reflected back all Wairimu needed to see both inside and outside of the aircraft. The parking extensions were folded back and the hatch in the aircraft's underbelly was open. This, he would use, to suck his victims into the hold while the open cockpit gave him the space to attack.

I'll soon have Samuel and the Mage in my power and Aberash will be mine. With these thoughts, Wairimu 's transformation began. His eyes rolled in their sockets as he summoned the Wind of Fury. In his mind's eye, he willed himself to become a creature that would hold a hurricane in its fist, one that would suck up or sweep away whatever it pleased. As the spell kicked in, he took off in the Hellican, with the hood down, screaming out his wish. His voice didn't just blend with the wind. It was the wind.

From you, I claim the myth
Of my forefather's wrath
An inward breath with which to take
An outward breath with which to break
A fist with which to strike and slay
A claw to snatch my due today.
The Mage and Wizard Samuel.

Wairimu's fingers tingled as the rogue wind entered his veins transforming his arms and hands into knotted coils of darkness. With the aid of a hook-like thumb he spun the Hellican around and made his first attempt to snatch the Mage with his free arm, but he hadn't waited long enough for the transformation to be complete.

The stream of power to his fingers was slow enough to allow Mr Caius to flip the Mage out of harm's way and to release magic of his own. It was a transformation chant from long ago. Cawing furiously, he willed the Little Ravens to increase in size. Their shoulder feathers shot out, giving them the appearance of giants with fearsome beaks and steely silver-white eyes. Answering a call from Ms Cora, some of the Little Ravens formed a circle around the castle to prevent it from falling. Others flew off to guard the villagers and the granaries. Nobody knew where Wairimu was likely to strike.

'A fist…a fist…I need a fist.'. With a snake-like tongue hissing flames from the open cockpit of the Hellican, Wairimu struck again. This time, his powerful clenched fist, king-hit Mr Caius from behind, and the Castle Keeper fell. Snatching the Mage away, Wairimu screamed triumphantly.

At the same time, the mawk he murdered with a poison tipped arrow, stiffened and died. Released from its vice-like grip, Samuel made the emergency call. It was taken up by the Little Ravens and passed on again throughout the land: *Wairimu is striking the very heart of Aberash. He has king hit Castle Keeper, Caius and he's taken the Mage.'*

Samuel clutched his heart, gasping. For surely it would break in two. *I was so busy with healing, I didn't attend to the magic. I didn't guard the Mage as I should.* Always so calm and strong, Samuel now shed tears for the people who trusted him and for a much younger self. The orphan – a small frightened child dressed in rags and half starved, waking at the foot of Renana's *mangatj* tree with the big bird in its branches, keeping watch. Now as a chief wizard he had lost the Mage. *Without its magic, will Renana die? And what will happen to the people of Aberash? Oh no, it must not be…*

In the reading room Cade and Lori heard the alarm. Bells rang all over Aberash. The villagers cried with dread. A no-good spirit lurked in the air they breathed. The words of Wairimu rang in their ears.

From Cruel Mistress of Time, in her tower sublime

Enchantment and Trance, my cause to advance.

Lori's eyelids were closing. 'Somebody's messing with my head,' she cried.

'Mine too,' Cade groaned. 'Everything looks so weird.'

Letters leapt out of books - metres high with grinning clown heads. Dancing demonically, they formed themselves into mocking words: **Wanted – smart boy and girl for traineeship with powerful wizard in possession of the Mage. Free tuition in transformations, jinxing,**

torture and treachery. Cade snapped himself out of the trance and shook Lori hard. Her glazed eyes cleared and she came to with a start. 'Hear that? The Little Ravens are going crazy but there's another sound.'

'Something terrible on the rooftop garden.' Her brother slid into his backpack and she slid into hers. They scaled the stairs to the rooftop in time to see a streak of darkness billowing from the open cockpit of the flying machine…and for a moment, Wairimu's face. Distorted and hideous. With an open mouth, he howled like a feral dog turned killer. *Winds from north, south, east and west…come snatch the Chief Wizard of Aberash…snatch him now.*

Lori and Cade, along with Ms Cora tried desperately to hang on to Samuel, but the hot sting of the killer wind's breath made their legs fold beneath them and he slipped from their grasp. The Chief Wizard of Aberash was pulled by the iron grip of a claw and the heat of a tightly coiled whirlwind that sucked him into the Hellican. He was then trussed up and thrown into the hold. Wairimu 's success came with another scream of triumph.

Dazed, Samuel looked back through the open hatch to see Cade on the rooftop, unprotected and in the open.

'No,' Samuel cried out as Cade dared to shake his fist at Wairimu. 'Don't draw attention to yourself.' But it was too late. In an about turn, the Wind of Fury streaked towards the boy who staggered and then fell. With a protesting heart and flaying limbs, Cade was caught and held by an indrawn breath, so fierce and strong he could do nothing but go with it.

25 Wind of Fury: Cade
Aberash Heartland

When you can't fight it, go with it…flow with it…but look for a way out. Beneath the belly of the Hellican, Cade struggled across the current of air like a weak swimmer in a raging river. In passing, he reached for the lip of the open-mouthed hatch. Closing his fingers firmly around the large rivets of its movable cover, he hauled himself into a groove behind it.

'Oh…no,' Cade cried out as the outward breath of the wind gouged him from the groove. So, began, the terrifying drop, the drag, the slap, the desperate reaching to safety, only to be torn away and dropped yet again. With raw fear in his belly, Cade realized the flying machine was moving away from the castle towards the estuary and he was dragged along with it. How much longer could he hold on?

Once in a 'drop' Cade saw what looked like a picture in silk. Streaked blue of water. Orange sail of boat. A girl with her long hair streaming. She waved and his heart lifted. This was no dream. It was Mia. The River girl was tacking, and the boat turned.

'Quee…quee…quee…tchip, tchip, tchip.' She mimicked the high-pitched call of her fisher birds, the *yoondoordo* and within a short time, every *yoondoordo* flew in from north, south, east and west. Lone pairs that usually kept to themselves were coming together.

'Oh…ah,' Cade groaned with pain and shock as he slapped against the lip of the Hellican's hatch.

'Trust the Mage and the power of wings,' Mia called.

Inside the aircraft, Samuel pleaded for Cade's life, 'You have the people's Mage and me, what can you possibly want with the boy?' He sank into himself. He knew that to show mercy for a prisoner, Wairimu would see as weakness, and a reason for more cruelty. There was only one thing he could do before Cade's strength gave out. Taking a terrible risk, he called on the forces of nature. It was the first time he had attempted a really big spell without the Mage.

Through determined lips, he chanted, 'Mia, queen of the *yoondoordo,* my magic is yours. Take what you need to save the boy.'

'No, no,' screamed Wairimu. 'Give your magic to me. Me! Me! Me! I want it. I want it *all.*' Spitefully, he used the whirlwind to keep Cade in mid-air, neither up, nor down, with the terrifying rush and roar of it howling in his ears. Then in an instant the noise of the wind stopped.

'Take this lifeline, boy,' Wairimu's voice became soft and hypnotic. A rope dropped down, such a safe looking rope, with a neat handle. 'Come on, lad, take it. You can trust me.'

Cade groaned. 'Oh, oh…nothing could be worse than this. I feel like I'm gonna die.'

'He lies,' Samuel yelled. 'Resist his spell.'

'Forget your cousin,' *Wairimu* went on in a kindly way. 'I will take care of you.' Cade was sorely tempted to grab the rope, but then through the open hatch, he glimpsed Samuel's stricken face. His cousin's lips formed words that gave him hope. 'I call on all good wizards in Aberash for a spell that will save Cade and the Mage.'

The Mage that had been flung into a corner, slipped across the tilted floor of the Hellican, into the stairwell. Pulled by gravity, it fell through the open hatch with a whooshing sigh. Once in the air, it opened like a kite in the sky and in an instant, thirty-six *yoondoordo* zoomed in to catch it.

'Cade,' Mia yelled. 'Free fall, now.'

'I can't, the wind is sucking me up,' Cade yelled back. 'Aah! Now it's spitting me out.' His body was surely no longer a boy's but a scrap of paper, a leaf or a twig. Yet somewhere inside him was a voice telling him, *You can and you will free fall!* He counted carefully, the in, the out and then the pause. Now in the pause!

His heart, his lungs. Everything burned as he leapt far and wide, away from the Hellican and the devil wind's fearsome grip. Rushing air swallowed his breath. For a second or two, he passed out. Then he was staring down at a rim of jagged rocks leering at him from the water. Cade gulped, his eyes growing bigger and the rocks closer, until – whoop. A flutter of many wings brushed his skin. Thirty-six *yoondoordo* scooped him up in the Mage. With capes of brown, white suits below, each proud warrior bird wore a necklace of shining black gemstones. They gazed at him with fierce eyes, their hooked warrior beaks gripping the edges of the Mage.

When his strange rescuers came close to the orange sail, they bowed their heads and then promptly tipped Cade from the outspread cloak into the waves. He rose to the surface spewing sea-water from mouth and nose, gasping for air.

'At least you're alive.' Grinning, the queen of the *yoondoordo* pointed to a boat ladder. 'Hurry up. I need a deckhand urgently.'

Cade didn't see what happened to the Mage and had no time to ask. Shivering and spluttering, he clambered into the rocking boat while the girl grabbed the tiller.

'Mind your head,' she yelled as the boom swung towards him. The raging devil wind had roughed up the waters. The boat dipped and heaved.

'Don't just stand there,' Mia gasped. 'We're being pushed out to sea.' While the furious wind howled, Cade leapt from one task to the next, hanging over the water to keep the sail upright. It was a bumpy ride with the chop of waves and wind roaring in his ears. In an eye blink, a wall of water rose before them and Cade prepared himself for a ducking. But the little boat dipped and then rose on the crest of another wave. He was still alive and oh the air rushing into his lungs was quite unexpectedly delicious.

They rode the storm until late afternoon and then limped into a bay. Numb with cold and weariness, they beached the boat and then flung themselves onto the sand.

26 A Message: Cade
The Estuary and River.

Mia blew on the sulking embers of her *karl*, feeding it with dry leaves and twigs until it flared into life. She built a pyramid of sturdier branches above it while Cade looked on. As if in some kind of trance, he lost track of time as he focussed on nothing but the leaping flames – blue, yellow, red.

'Hey!' The fisher girl startled him. Grinning, she waved a spray of gum leaves in his face.

'For…for me?' Cade stammered. He wanted to thank her for saving his life, but the right words evaded him.

'Yes! They are for little old you…cos you're my guest. Pinch the leaves and throw 'em into the fire for a treat.' She laughed.

Before each leaf melted into the flames, for a second or two it became a leaf of red-gold. Shining and beautiful. Then it was gone. A pungent swathe of smoke drifted from the campfire. Brownish at first and then blue. A thin squiggly line. Like writing, Cade thought.

'It's a message,' Mia said, in an awed whisper.

Slowly the smoke formed words that spread across the sky. '*Cade, mortal boy – Keeper of the Mage*'.

'The Mage!' Cade yelped. 'What happened to it?'

Mia's eyes glinted. 'The Mage is here.' Calmly she ruffled through her belongings. 'It's safe and sound in my tchield.'

'Tchield?'

'That's what I call it.' She helped him into it. The tchield with the Mage safely inside was supported by a separate harness that eased the weight of Cade's backpack while sitting comfortably across his chest. Neat. Mia flipped up a hand hold in the centre.

'Slip your hand into it and lift it from the harness…easy…see?' As though crafted for Cade alone, the tchield was a perfect match for his hand and for the shape of his body. It was light, tough, pliant and flat like a shield. He'd never seen or felt anything like it.

'This is the one thing I have from my past…and very precious.' Mia gave him a long steady look.

'It means a lot to you.' Something stirred in Cade's soul. 'But why am I the Keeper of the Mage…and not you?'

'Because your name was written in smoke…and it's part of an unfinished story.' Sadness filled her eyes. 'For we who live in Aberash, our stories are everything and we must be true to them.' She tossed her head proudly before striding away. *As if she doesn't want me to feel sorry for her…I know how that feels.*

Mia was soon hidden by paper barks with gnarly white trunks and overhanging branches. It was lonely without her. The silence eerie. He jumped in fright when a young *yoondoordo* squealed – a high pitched plaintive cry. An alarmed shriek from the parents of the chick and the shadow of a much bigger bird hovered.

Cade shivered with apprehension as its shadow passed over him and then it was gone. He sighed with relief soon after when Mia arrived and was able to grin when she showed off her catch. Two nice sized *nyola*.

'These fellows hang around in weed near the shore,' she said. 'Easy pickings.' With swift, deft strokes, she cut off the stings, scaled and gutted the fish, feeding the entrails to a rogue gull.

'I should be helping,' he said.

'Fishing is what I do, remember?' Her white teeth flashed in a grin. Her long sure fingers smeared each fillet with a little oil from her supplies and then placed them on a *muller*, the large flat stone, now piping hot from the red-hot coals around it. When they were done, the *nyola* were served with purslane leaves on hand crafted pottery dishes.

They sat on a log by the fire and ate with their fingers, relishing the comfort of hot food. After washing up at the water's edge, Cade opened his bag of chocolate with Minnie's words running through his head. A piece for himself, a piece for a friend and a bit for the bag.

Later he told Mia about the shadow of a large bird or glider that had frightened the *yoondoordo*.

'It sounds like a mawk.' Her head shot up in alarm. 'It's not a true bird and not to be trusted.'

Dread caught in Cade's throat, taking his words.

'I've only ever heard whispers,' Mia went on in a low voice. 'Devil birds that change their shape to suit. The one's in Wairimu's domain are kept by a person called Dame Grey from the Land of Bad Dreams. Nobody really knows how they came about.' She went on to explain they were thought to be a distant cousin of the pterosaur, a throw-back to the Jurassic era or more than likely, invented by bad magic. A few mawks had the power of human speech. 'The one you saw would be long gone by now.'

'What's it doing here, then?' Cade shivered.

'Keeking for Dame Grey, I reckon.'

'Keeking? What's that?'

Mia laughed, a rippling sound that surprised and warmed him. 'It's a word for spying. Came from an old Scottish sailor who lives in the village. But that's another story. To get back to the mawks…news travels quickly in this land. Dame Grey is one of many who will know that the Mage is now in your possession.'

'And she wants it for herself?' Cade watched the camp fire flare. Then it died and he helped Mia build it up again with more branches. In the circle of light that lit up their faces with a warm red glow, Mia offered him a feather quilt, while hugging one to herself.

'A gift from my brother Nyan. Sorry, it's not magic.' A teasing smile played at the corners of her lips. 'Of course, you could always use the Mage to keep you warm. You might even make magic from it…what's to stop you from trying?'

Cade shook his head and pointed to his heart without a word. He didn't tell her about his own blanket, a featherweight with a certain magic of its own.

'Imagine having power over fields and wild creatures, like Samuel,' Mia said.

The thought scared Cade. He didn't know enough. 'I'd probably mess up,' he said, feeling stupid again.

'You really care, don't you? But what if somebody else got the Mage? What then?' She sat down on a carpet of sheoak litter, with the quilt around her. Cade picked up a hefty log and heaved it on the red-hot coals of the campfire. It landed with a thud. Tiny red sparks flew and for a moment pungent blue smoke blew in his face. He took a drink from his flask and then hunkered down, the quilt warm around his shoulders.

'The Mage belongs to Samuel.' He looked at Mia, steadily. 'I'm going to give it back, no matter what anyone says.'

Mia let out a rippling laugh again. 'I know that. Sorry, I was teasing. But how are you gonna do it ah?'

'I got a map.'

'Sure, and it will take you to Caligo. But what about the tricky places in between…huh?'

'The map and pictures make it look doable,' Cade murmured but he was troubled. According to legend, it took two mortals to break Wairimu's curse – a boy and a girl with a coin and a key. So, what should he do? Go back for Lori or trust her to find him? And what about the key in those old chants? As far as Cade knew Lori didn't have one and nor did he.

Mia yawned. 'You should trust more and worry less.'

Moodily, Cade gazed at the smoke from the fire curling into the night with those words again: *Cade, mortal Boy – Keeper of the Mage.*

27 Finding Renana: Lori
From Aberash Castle to the *Moyootj*

Cade, Mortal boy – Keeper of the Mage. Lori saw the words in the gaps between the clouds. 'Oh, my brother…surely this means you are safe.' During Wairimu 's raid, she had struggled to save him, but Ms Cora held her so tightly she was forced to look on while the devil wind snatched him away.

'You are the Lorelei,' Ms Cora had whispered fiercely, 'and you have the gift…you must not be taken.' The mournful cry of a raven brought Lori back to the present. To Ms Cora weeping over the dead body of Mr Caius.

The Castlekeeper placed a small stone on each of his eyes to keep them closed and gently kissed him. With tears still wet on her cheeks, she told Lori, 'You and your brother are the children of our legend and destined to free the prisoners of Caligo.'

'But we are only kids.' Lori swallowed words of protest. I am not a Lorelei, she thought, and I don't want to be one. The Lorelei belong in some old fairy tale from the other side of the world and should stay there. Nothing good ever came from it. The scary creature had the power to lure a sailor to his death with its song…or so the story goes.

She stared into the silver pupils of Cora's eyes and saw in each diamond of light, a small picture of Renana. In a land of Magic, you look for signs. Surely this was a sign that Renana would help her understand about the gift and lead her to Cade and Ms Alayah.

'I must go to Renana…but will you be all right?'

'Yes, dear girl.' Cora held her for a moment and wished her a safe journey. *A safe journey?* It didn't feel very safe. As she ran downstairs, Lori's footsteps echoed around the empty rooms of the castle. Without Samuel it was hollow, like a run-down old mansion that didn't belong. For a moment she wished it was a comfy old farm house with a tin roof and veranda.

Lori headed for the *Moyootj* with her mind firmly on the big *mangatj* tree. It was her only hope of finding the big bird. As she drew nearer, Lori stopped to listen to the soft creaks and squelchy sighs of paperbarks bound together with entwined branches. But there was something else. Somebody was chanting: *A boy with a coin – a girl with a key…*

'Hello, hello,' a bell like voice called. With long, loping strides, he came to her, leaving a silver spray of water along the way.

'You may call me Bello,' he said. 'And in case you're wondering, I'm your guide for today.'

'I…' Lori couldn't keep her eyes off him. Bello wore some kind of jumpsuit in dark silky cloth with a purple-blue sheen that shifted each time he moved.

'Boys can be beautiful too,' he told her.

'I…I didn't say they couldn't.' Lori stammered uncertainly.

'You wish to see Renana? And you have a question for her?'

Lori tried to explain. She wanted to see the giant bird. Of course, she did. Firstly, because Renana was her Dreambird. The magical creature who once saved her life. As for the question, she wasn't sure that it was a sensible one. Something about a gift Lori didn't really believe that she had.

'Come.' Without another word, Bello sprinted ahead and Lori followed with the soft pink tips of shrubs brushing her arms, filling her head with a musky wildflower scent. Faster and faster, the boy ran.

'Can you please slow down?' she gasped.

Without answering her, he chanted. His low croon blending with the soft patter of hammer frogs – the *koorni*.

Trust me, Lorelei,

Our stories don't lie.

Trust me Lorelei

With Renana, to fly.
A boy with a coin – a girl with a key
Must save The Mage
And the prisoners to free.

'I'm not a Lorelei,' Lori protested. 'They're weird singers that don't belong Downunder.' *But will I really fly with Renana?* The idea spurred her onwards. 'Oh, do wait for me, Bello.'

Bello stopped by the edge of a pond where a giant duck stirred the water with strong webbed feet. At the same time, a fierce looking red pouch rose alarmingly from beneath its bill. Its tail feathers spread in a gigantic fan shape, each one, tipped with a sharp claw.

Bello pointed to a skinny log that arched over the pond. 'That's the only way to go.' He was shaking all over.

'Are you sure? It looks pretty wobbly to me.' Lori felt pretty wobbly herself. The giant duck stared – mean eyed and dangerous while her guide looked the other away.

'Over to you,' Bello shook his head. 'This isn't the shy brown musk duck you might know. It's a mawk in disguise, working for Wairimu.'

A sharp arrow of fear entered Lori's heart. Her nerve endings cringed. She wanted to run. But there was no turning back.

'You'll need this *wadi* to defend yourself.' Bello handed her a club like weapon made from wood. Gripping it tightly, she stepped on to the log, reeling against the suffocating stench of a filthy rookery. Lori looked back with longing to Bello and safety.

'What do we do now?' she asked.

'Not we, Lorelei girl, what do *you* do now?' An ear-splitting squawk drowned Bello's words as the duck creature flew at her. The motion of its sweeping wing sucked the breath out of her lungs. Once, twice, three times, she felt the sting of a vicious raking. Bleeding and gasping she clung fiercely to the curve of the log with her feet. The winged creature fell back to shake itself and then with shrieks and snarls attacked again. And again. Scared and baffled by its venting, she beat it back with the *wadi.*

On the third strike, Lori saw, not the weird creature of a wizard's invention, but the face of a bully. The leader of a gang who teased Cade when he stumbled over his reading, always with an audience. The hurt expression on her brother's face would bring tears to her eyes. Helpless angry tears. This creature was like him. Amidst a chorus of hideous snarls, the mawk flew at her.

'Oh Bello…Mum…Dad…it's going to kill me,' Lori pleaded, but she stayed on the log, pushing back with the *wadi*. More onslaughts, more needle-sharp pecks that left a poisonous after-sting. *Like words. Like the words of Trent and his gang.*

The brush of swooping wings flapped and swirled while Lori swayed back and forth before an ugly open beak. Its eyes were like Wairimu's. The probing stare was his. The wizard who wanted her in his net. *No, you can't have me.* Lori straightened her spine. She bent her knees and clung to the log with her feet, opening herself to whatever might come next. It was an explosion of sound. Not from that creature, but herself. It was a cry of protest, a song and a chant in one, and it came from somewhere deep inside herself. It was a feeling, not the words that drove her.

Sticks and stones may break my bones

But names will never hurt me

Go to your grave, angry mawk

Buried in the names you call me.

Lori drew in a raggedy breath and chanted the same words again. Something strong burned inside her. *Too bad if you kill me*, she thought, *I'll stay here and fight you.* At the end of the third chant, she was shaking and desperate until a shadow fell over them all and then, a sudden silence. Bello's steadying hand was on her arm.

'It's over,' he said, softly. 'Look!' A smaller duck, one that might have been a real musk duck, landed on the water with barely a ripple. It stared at her, eye to eye. It's was like seeing a mirror image of her own eyes.

You are me and I am you it seemed to say.

For reasons, unknown to Lori, the angry mawk, still in the shape of a giant duck sank into the water and disappeared with barely a ripple.

'It's like somebody cast a spell on him.' Lori waited for her thumping heart to settle and her breathing to even out. Her voice trembled. Only when she and Bello were safely on their way, did she ask. 'Was it the presence of a real musk duck that stopped the mawk's attack?'

'You were brave.' Bello smiled. 'You did well.' It was no real answer. But somehow, she knew it was all she would get.

'I didn't feel very brave or do anything special, except chant an old chant. I learned it from my mum and she got it from her mum.' An expression on the swamp boy's face made her think he knew more than he would ever tell her. Lori shrugged. She didn't understand why, but Bello's praise put a spring to her steps.

When the next hurdle came it was Bello who knew what to do. They were blocked by a wall of tea-tree overgrown with myrtle, mistletoe and rogue blackberry brambles and so he chanted a request.

'I call on the magic of all good wizards in Aberash to please let us pass.' A single strand of mistletoe untangled followed by another and then another. Even the stubborn blackberry parted. More shifting and murmuring and the swamp plants coiled over to form a tunnel of green.

'Let in the light,' Bello murmured, 'for the mortal who has the gift.' Flickering gleams of sunlight shone through the spaces between the leaves. Lori breathed in the earthy smell of ground water and the heady aroma of swamp loving boronia. The gold and brown blossoms brushed her as she passed. Faster and faster they ran until overhanging bushes fell away. Ahead lay a splash of sunlight.

It was the first time Lori had smelled the colour gold, but it was here. In the sunlight and the earth. In the spring that gently bubbled from the ground. In the bark of the mossy tree she sensed without seeing. With cupped hands, they scooped up water from the pool to drink.

'I can taste the colour gold,' Lori said. 'Not hard like metal but soft and earthy.'

'This is the real taste of water,' said Bello.

Lori bathed her wounds and the stings eased. As she leaned close, her submerged gem stone gleamed. Thankfully, she placed her hand beneath it and for the first time, felt a strong connection to the stone and to the tiny mudfish that swam between her loosely held fingers. A faint stir, and a small swamp-turtle nudged her hand with its soft round nose.

'You're blessed by the wild things,' Bello said, 'and that's some moonstone you have there.'

'A moonstone? I didn't know.'

'Now you do. And there's something else you need to know. You have earned the right to open the door to the *mangatj*…Renana's tree. But do be careful how you go,' he warned. 'You may never want to leave it and if you don't, you stay a child forever.' Their eyes met. *He will go now*, she thought and was sad. Would she ever come to know him? The beautiful Bello. The boy who led her to Renana's Tree and to Renana herself? He raised a hand to her and then sprinted through a shrinking tunnel of green.

28 Renana's Tree: Lori
The Moyootj

It was lonely for Lori without Bello. Even the fish and the swamp-turtle had gone. But what was this? A tiny shadow flicked across her face. A butterfly. A Golden Wanderer. Behind this tiny creature, the blue sky and a close-up view of Renana's tree. It was like coming home.

Lori had read about other famous trees but none like this one. She had seen other *mangatj* trees but none like this one. It had a broad sloping trunk covered in a soft blanket of moss. It looked easy to climb with branches that spread like a bridge to another world. Bello was right. You might easily forget to go on with your journey in this tree. Lori touched her gemstone and remembered her mum, her dad and Cade. She didn't really want to remain a child forever.

Yet when she reached over a barrier of bull rushes to touch it, she was thrown to the ground where she lay amongst bruising seed cones and fallen feather shaped leaves.

'What is it that won't let me in?' With tears in her eyes she waited, and then, as if in answer, the soft wings of the Wanderer brushed her hand. It led her around the tree to where the reeds grew even thicker. Here she found a door, set back from the tree. It was bendy and strange with no key hole and no handle. Nothing except a smooth circle at its centre. It appeared to be made from honey coloured sap that had hardened into amber.

Lori clutched her gemstone. 'Oh Mum,' she whispered, 'why is this door made without a key hole? And where is the key everyone keeps talking about?' Her gemstone was warm and smooth in her palm, but why did her mum give it to her?

It must be a key. A different kind of key. Lori lifted the gemstone and held it to the light. It was still wet and shining from the spring water. As she moved it, the light caught a hidden flash of blue within the stone. 'Why didn't I guess?' A thrill of excitement coursed through her. It was a tiny key symbol in the form of a bird's head and neck. Using the gemstone like a mouse on a computer pad, she scanned the amber circle on the door until she found a matching symbol. But something wasn't right, the gemstone had turned cold. Did that say something? Of course, it did! If you are in a land of magic, then you need chants and spells.

'With respect,' said Lori at last, 'I call on the magic of all the wizards in the *moyootj* to open this door.' Her words sounded frail and tinny in the bigger silence and the door remained stubbornly closed. With tears building behind her eyes, she waited. Waited, until from far away, she heard the clear throated song of a mud-lark.

'How beautiful you are,' she whispered. Then, as its song closed on a high clear note, the same note rose from her throat. Words came without effort.

With love from a mortal
I call on the magical
Moyootj, the moor
I call on the magical
To open this door.

Lori was startled when the door swung open and there was Renana's *mangatj* tree waiting to be climbed.

29 The River Girl: Cade
The Tricky

Cade woke up to find Mia leaning over him. 'We need to go – before another mawk comes to stalk us.' Wasting no time, they launched the boat and with a snappy 'whoop', the sail cupped with wind. A stiff westerly pushed into their backs and they sailed upstream across the estuary to the mouth of the river. As they moved on, Cade looked out for a landing with the idea of finding the track that would take him through Rocky Barrier to the Plateau of Wild Grasses.

'That will take you ages,' Mia said. 'If we head for Tricky Falls, there's a short cut that'll fool any mawk on the prowl.' Her voice trailed away as she muttered to herself. 'A risky business…but it must be done.'

'What must be done?' Cade waited but Mia simply shook her head as if to say *please don't ask*. When the sea breeze dropped, she pointed to a punting pole clipped to the side of the boat and Cade hopped to it. Punting was something he knew from a school camp and it pleased him to be moving the craft upstream along the shallows.

'The river flows from a mountain in the Land of Dream,' Mia said 'And I can tell you it's not called The Tricky for nothing.' Slowly, the distant purr of the falls turned to a roar. Cade drew in his breath at the sight of it. Brushed red by morning light it sprang from a great hole in the cliff, fanning and falling in a cauldron of white foam. Broken here and there by islands of granite, the rushing waters swept on. Eddying waves, swooping and curling into giant whirlpools before brushing the banks and sliding swiftly downstream to the sea.

As they moved closer, the little boat spun in a circle and then wobbled from side to side. To evade the worst of it, Mia steered it behind a horse-shoe shaped rock of granite. But they were in deep water with a powerful backwash building. What could she be thinking? Cade tried to read her face but it told him nothing.

'I never tasted chocolate before last night,' she said, calmly. 'I wonder if that fragment you were so careful to leave behind grew while we slept.'

Cade gulped, and then covered his surprise at finding the chocolate had indeed grown.

'Well?' Mia laughed. 'What are you waiting for?'

He grinned uncertainly, hoping she wouldn't notice how scared he felt. They gulped down their 'breakfast', not forgetting to leave a bit in the bag. Within seconds, a surging current, forced them from the shelter. Pushed to the outer rim of another giant whirlpool, Cade felt the blood drain from his face. *How long would it take for them to be sucked in and drowned?*

'Trust!' Something in Mia's voice made him drag his eyes away from the whirlpool. The girl stood tall with her long hair blowing in the wind, her eyes half closed. Her lips moved in a chant.

Turnabout water. Go, go, go

Turnabout water, 'til uphill you flow.

Cade's voice came out in a croak. 'You are queen of the *yoondoordo* and a wizard in one.'

'Call me any name you like. It makes no…' her voice was lost as the boat lifted. A suck and a roar, and the current turned, taking the boat upstream. She grabbed the tiller and steered it towards the bank on one side where it slapped into the shore.

Before Cade could speak, Mia leapt onto the bank. An unearthly silence followed. Her lips curved in a slow uncertain smile like somebody waking from a dream. Cade swallowed his disappointment and sorrow when her eyes told him – *this is as far as I can go.*

'What about your boat?' he hung onto the hope that she might stay with him.

'The boat will take care of you and then it will come back to me. But right now, you need it more than I do. You're *Keeper of The Mage.*' For a moment, she looked sad. 'Just follow the map and trust yourself.'

'Will I…will I see you again? What if…what if something happens to me…what about Lori?' For a moment, he wasn't the Mage's keeper but an ordinary boy. A very shaky one.

'I don't know if we'll see each other again…as for Lori, she has the gift…'

'What did you say?' Cade called but his words were drowned by the indrawn whoosh of a river. *Turnabout water, go, go, go, turnabout water, til' uphill you flow.* Mia's words played in his head as a wall of white foam came from behind. Like a warm friendly hand, it coiled around the boat holding it firmly while Cade put his own hand on the tiller. The white water stretched and grew, like a team of horses with massive heads and glittering eyes bearing the boat-chariot. Bucking…surging, but never letting go of the boat.

It seemed to Cade the power of all magicians in Aberash were in this one place, turning the Tricky back to its source. He gripped the tiller more firmly. *Is this really me? Is this steady hand mine?* As the boat soared upwards, his heart told him, *'Yes. That steady hand is mine.'* The boat sailed through a giant hole in the rock, descending on the other side in a long slow glide. The galloping waves dissolved with no roar, no churning – just a gentle shifting and then only stillness and silence. Finding himself in a large backwater, Cade unhooked the punting pole and headed up stream. A three-way split lay ahead. Which one to choose? The map told him to look for a sign, so what did that mean in this strange land of Aberash? *It means I think outside the square. A sign can come from anywhere.*

His ears tuned to the secret sounds of still water and the answer came. 'Perweet, perweet, perweet…tchip, tchip, tchip.' High above him a pair of *yoondoordo* darted forward with bowed heads to the north. At the same time a tiny circle of deflected sunlight flashed a message from the estuary towards the plateau.

Current and gravity pulled the boat to the bottom of a ravine and then nosedived, tipping Cade onto the base of a cliff. He stood in a mush of quicksand with the tide rising swiftly and his hiking shoes filling with water.

'Have a safe journey little boat and say hello to Mia.' Cade watched it disappear into a cave. There was nowhere to go now but to climb the steep cliff. In a seam of shining obsidian on its surface, Cade saw his own pale face reflected…his dark brows and startled eyes, telling him, 'You can't do magic…you're just a boy and you're stuck.' But somebody was yelling at him. *Kaya-Kaya!* Upstairs…look up here.' The River brothers peered down at him from the top of the cliff.

'Mia sent us a message with her mirror,' Aren hollered. 'If we sling you a rope, you can climb up…okay?'

'Ah…um…okay.' If he could sail in a boat up a waterfall, of course he could rock climb…with a bit of help from his friends.

30 Danger: Lori
The Moyootj

Tread carefully little Lorelei. The wind whispered a warning as it brushed the feather shaped leaves of the *mangatj* tree. Lori didn't want to hear. She soaked up the sun so sweetly warm on her skin, the rustle and stir of birds happily feasting. Dreamily, she munched on some chocolate, not forgetting to leave a bit for the bag and some for a bright-eyed pygmy possum that peeped at her from behind a twig.

Lori didn't think it unusual or strange when the fragment of chocolate in the bag grew back. Nor did she flinch, when the delicate feet of a tiny wren tickled the palm of her outstretched hand. A playful wind ruffled the seed-bearing nuts of the tree – each one a golden candelabra. Lori breathed in its scent, as she bent close to observe a tiny marsupial busily sucking on nectar between the stamens of a flower spike.

Again, the wind warned her. Move on mortal girl, or you'll stay a child in this tree forever. Don't you know the danger of staying too long in such a tree?

'But I don't want to leave.' While in this tree, Lori didn't think scary thoughts or sad ones like a journey without Cade. She didn't think about a difficult promise that couldn't be broken. The big *mangatj* was beyond her understanding and it spread too far for her to see its end. She just wanted to be there. To touch its mossy bark. To taste the honey of its flowers.

'I may be a mortal,' she told the wind, 'but I belong to the earth too, just like the creatures in this tree…and those creatures in the *moyootj*.'

Beneath the tree, a shining blue dragonfly skimmed the water. A flock of swallows dipped and dived. With giant claws, a busy crustacean worked on its mud house on the bank. Lori lost track of time. Only when the shadows lengthened, did she remember why she had come to the tree.

Renana – how could I have forgotten I had to see you? Lori needed to move on, but her legs refused to budge and her arms fell heavily by her sides.

This is the tree of memory and childhood. You must not stay too long. The wind's song had a sharp edge to it. 'I can't move…I can't think.' Lori clasped her hands together, distressed now. 'Which way will I go? Where will I go?'

'Hark…hark…hark!' It was a Little Raven's warning that cleared her mind. With a sense of urgency, she climbed further into the network of branches. On and on, until, exhausted, she huddled into a mossy hollow between two branches to sleep. Unbeknown to her, a troubled Renana looked on from the branch above. *Without Samuel and the Mage, I am lost and broken, but I will find a way to help this girl, somehow, I must.*

31 The River Brothers: Cade
Plateau of Wild Grasses

The River boys kept a neat camp with walls and a roof made of woven brush, the ground spread with rushes. Nyan had his own working area where he laboured with reams of cloth, needle and thread. It was Aren's job to tend the Lightfoots. He herded them into their night enclosure to be sure they were safe from wild dogs and then, with Archie by his side, he stoked the campfire.

Cade was thankful for a sleeping space and chance to spread his maps on a table. Like the chairs and stools, it was cut from fallen timber and lashed together with twine, its surfaces sealed with resin.

It feels like the roof of the world here. He looked towards the skyline, where a mob of *Marloo*, stood – still as statues, resting on sturdy haunches, small ears upright, pointy faces questioning. Nervously, the russet coloured roos watched a flock of emu's sprint past, with feathered rumps rising and falling.

'This is my heart country.' Nyan had joined him to take in the cooling breeze. Nearby, Aren tended the camp fire, now and then lifting the lid of a huge caste-iron pot, stirring a stew – a delicious concoction of chopped tubers and greens in a rich gravy. It had been hours since Cade had shared that small portion of chocolate with Mia and so he didn't argue when he was given the first serving.

'Guest's privilege,' Aren said. Before tucking in to their own food, the older boys watched him like a couple of eagles feeding their young.

'That'll give you an extra bit of punch…you're sure going to need it,' Nyan blurted. A stern look from Aren and he closed his mouth. *Archie* was served next and then Nyan. The eldest brother ate after the others had eaten, savouring each mouthful, closing his eyes now and then, as if he inhabited another world.

Night came down with purple tinted shadows and a trillion stars. Cade used his backpack for a pillow and curled into his blanket. Close by, Aren settled his little brother murmuring, 'Sweet dreams, Archie boy.' And then he too fell asleep. Under the glow of an oil lamp, in his working space nearby, Nyan went on with his stitching, sometimes murmuring a low chant.

From far away, Cade heard the song of a dingo, melodious and strange. Surely the loneliest sound in the world. It left him with a sense of longing he couldn't explain, even to himself. He thought of his family, of Lori…where was his sister? He thought of Samuel and Ms Alayah. *We can do this. Somehow, we must.*

32 Brumbies: Cade
Plateau of Wild Grasses

Cade woke up with a stream of sunlight on his face. New clothes lay beside him – two sets of loose-fitting pants and tops with hoods.

'For you and Lori,' said a sleepy Nyan from the depth of his swag.

'You worked all night? For us?' Cade remembered feeling so alone, yet all the while Nyan had been working on the clothes. He wanted to say thank you, but a weird kind of shyness stopped him and the words just wouldn't come.

Nyan sat up and fixed him with an eye to eye stare. 'Put them on after you swim in the Hot Springs of Now. Not a minute before. Do you understand how important that is?'

'I do…I do now you mention it,' Cade stammered. 'We swim in the Hot Springs of Now, before we put on the new clothes.' He pretended to check the map, though he knew every inch of it. The Hot Springs of Now were in Rhizanthella Forest. The door into the forest wouldn't be visible until both he and Lori saw it. So where was Lori right now? How could they possibly do this?

Trust more and worry less. That's what Mia had said. But sometimes you needed to know. At least a boy did. An ordinary kid like me who is weirdly too shy to thank a friend.

'With these suits you'll blend in day light or any bright light,' Nyan went on earnestly. 'Handy if you're in a tight spot.' He gazed at Cade intently with brows knitted. 'You simply pull the hood over your head and chant. See that your sister does the same. You need two words – *Blend Now.*'

'It will work, just like that?' Cade chewed on his bottom lip. He was about to stammer out his thanks at last, when they were both startled by the drumming of hooves on the earth.

'Brumbies!' Aren crawled out of his swag, bright eyed and ready for action. Close behind, a tousled *Archie* followed.

'They're on the move by the sound of it,' Nyan said.

'Brumbies? They're horses that run wild, aren't they?' Cade had read about them. Horses brought by ship from across the sea in the early days.

'Yep. Came from the first horse slaves,' Aren said, his voice muffled as he pulled a jumper over his head. 'I bet they got a whiff of our sandalwood fire.'

'It's made them curious.' Nyan was up now, helping Archie with his clothes and dressing himself.

Nervously, the horses moved to the outskirts of the camp with a half dozen of the leaders coming close to stare at the boys. Emboldened, the others followed. Some were rugged ponies with sturdy limbs, shaggy manes and long tails that swept the ground. Others, streamlined with high arched necks, sleek bodies and gleaming pelts. Still others were sturdy draught horses with heavy limbs and broad backs. Cade could feel the heat of their bodies close, along with their strong horse smell.

'It didn't take you long to find us,' said Aren. 'Curious, were you?' The reply came with whinnies and snorts but the meaning was clear.

'Why shouldn't we be curious?' The racehorse with a long slender neck, tossed his fine head. 'Why have you been stalking us?'

'We wanted to know where you were, that's all.' Aren waved a hand towards Cade. 'As you can see, we have a true mortal here, and he needs a lift to cross Big Rock Desert and the Land of Dream.'

'Hah! We heard about the mortal.' The racehorse turned his head sharply with an air of contempt. Cade leapt up from his swag. Catching a ride on a horse seemed like a smart idea.

'I'm not asking any favours. I could lend you my lucky coin. You don't get to keep it, but I'd say it'll bring you luck while you have it.' He held it in the palm of his hand for the horse to see. He flushed when a tough looking beast with a shaggy coat and big ears laughed. Another one snorted while the racehorse simply stared. A frisky mare leapt back with a high-pitched neigh, joined by others in the same tone. So many horse voices; Cade struggled to make sense of the meaning.

'We don't do transport.'

'We don't do anything that involves having a mortal on our backs.'

'We won't have mortals pulling the strings.'

'You mean reins, Mother,' said a big brown gelding.

'Strings, reins, does it matter what you call 'em?' said the mare. 'The point is, we don't want mortals in charge of us.'

The racehorse tossed his head. 'We won our freedom and we aim to keep it.'

A flighty palomino sniffed derisively. 'Give mortals a centimetre and they take a kilometre.'

'Yeah…' A fiery young Arab sneered. 'Remember how they used us to fight their battles? I had an ancestor once…rode with that murderous Alexander, the so-called Great. Thousands of horses killed, cities sacked and burned, people slaughtered all over the place and they called that, success.' His shoulders rose up in a weird horsy shrug.

'Even up to World War Two they used us,' said a Bay mare. 'Ha! Don't even mention the word mortal to me.' She tossed her shiny black mane and stamped her pretty black tipped feet. 'They took us off to the battlefield, and then left us to die or drown when we tried to follow their ships home.'

'They sent us down mine shafts to do their dirty work,' said a tough-looking pony, 'and they made us haul logs…dangerous work, that!'

'Then when machines took over, they dumped us.'

'Kill us for pet meat when it suits 'em,' grumbled an old retired racehorse. 'And even today, they've been known to eat us. Not to mention using us for their experiments. How do you think they make their anti-venom for snake bite, eh?'

The young foals stared with wide frightened eyes. An awkward silence followed, and then the tough young pony with bold eyes and big ears, noticed by Cade earlier, spoke up. 'Ah forget the past, you guys. Build a bridge, will ya? I'll take the mortal.' He grinned and his big yellow teeth gleamed. His eyes challenged him with a twinkle. 'I'll take you, but only if you can stay on my back for one hundred breaths. No rope or saddle though. I'm nobody's slave.'

Nyan and Aren smiled nervously, secretly wondering what would happen. How would this mortal get on? He wasn't what you call tough. In fact, he was quite small for his age, and timid, even after eating the herbals.

Aren drew Cade aside. 'Are you sure you want to go through with this?'

At this, Cade's courage vanished – leaving his heart as hollow as an old tin can. He touched his lucky coin. He slipped his hand inside Mia's tchield and stroked the silky Mage.

'I will ride the wild horse,' Cade said – too loudly. 'I'll ride it for Samuel and Ms Alayah. But I want to know your name, horse. If you don't have one I want to give you one.'

'Oh no,' said the gelding, 'I'm getting out of here.'

'You don't let a mortal do the naming,' the racehorse said in a clipped no-nonsense voice and a stiff upper lip. 'Next, they want to own you like they own everything else; the sweet earth and everything on it, even the ocean. Some even speak about cutting up the moon! Great galloping clod-hoppers, you can't count on a mortal to know when to stop wanting things.'

'No naming.' The young horse, stared boldly at Cade. 'Matter o' fact, I have a name already and watch out anyone who takes it away. Now let's see what you're made of.'

'So, it's agreed?' Aren looked from Cade to the horse. 'If the mortal can stay on your back for a hundred breaths you take him?'

'I take him to the gateway that leads to the swamps of Murruk and no further. After that he's on his own. I'm not going near no mawks.'

'You won't have to go near any mawks,' Aren promised, while the horse and Cade eyed one another.

'Would you let me climb on your back before you try to throw me?' Cade bargained.

The animal gave a horsy grin. 'I'll give you ten heartbeats after you're seated, then you'll hit the dirt.' Obligingly, he sat on his haunches like a dog so that Cade was able to grab onto him. *I won't hit the dirt.* Something strong beat in Cade's heart – a stream in his blood that made him feel as bold as any wild brumby.

Nyan flashed a worried look at Aren. 'The special herbals you added to his stew must be kicking in,' he whispered. 'I hope you didn't overdo it.'

Aren shrugged. 'I gave him the witchetty grub special along with the usual herbals – no more, no less. The rest is up to him.'

Cade had never been on a horse before. It felt extremely high-up and pretty shaky. *I will ride this horse,* he vowed while breathing deeply, then – whoop! His body and feet were in the air. It was only his firm hold on the knotty forelock of hair between the horse's big ugly ears that saved him. There followed a bodily shaking impossible to forget.

Again, and again, the horse reared up. It was like being hurled about in a washing machine or dangled over the edge of a cliff and shaken by somebody big. Eerily quiet, all that could be heard was the hollow ring of prancing hooves. Now and then a horse fart or furious snort. And to Cade, his own heart thumping away like a two-stroke engine. His own gasps and gulping. But somehow, in the terrifying timeless space, Cade picked up a rhythm. He leaned more closely into the horse, tuning in to the rise and fall.

I'm getting it, he thought, until the horse kicked up his legs and lowered his head. A surprise move that threw Cade off balance. He slipped forward along the horse's neck, his face so low, he got a whiff of sun-baked earth. The horse shook his head from side to side as if wanting to be finally rid of something nasty. Suddenly the animal flung his head back. Cade lost his hold and he was riding back to back, clutching air.

With clenched thigh muscles and flexed spine, he dragged himself into a sitting position and then dived for that tuft of hair between the horse's ears. In an instant the air was somehow delicious. A bolt of energy and power rushed through Cade's veins. A dark cloud in the sky lifted. Boy and horse were splashed with light as they sped over a wide yellow field of everlasting flowers, the beautiful *mooljool.*

'I'm still on…still on…still on,' Cade gasped. 'I can't believe I'm still on.' *You do have to trust. Trust yourself.* They pelted along, leaping over a huge fallen log, that was taller than the horse, landing on the other side in a long wet-mud skid. The rider and horse. Both let out gasps of relief. Then the horse chuckled loudly. Cade had never heard a horse's belly laugh and it set him off. He laughed until tears streamed down his face and his tummy hurt.

'Okay,' said the horse, at last. 'I take you as far as the gateway to Murruk and no further, but you haven't won anything. We're equals on this trip, so don't start anything.'

Aren and Nyan raced over to them with Archie hanging on their shirttails. They had big grins on their faces. Aren hooked a leather water bag to a strap he put around the horse's neck. Then added an extra water bag to Cade's backpack.

'Looks like we'll be seeing you, when we see you,' Aren said. 'Now we'd better check on our Lightfoots.'

Cade leaned down from the horse to palm touch, first with the two older brothers. 'Thank you…thank you.' He looked at each one in turn and then to Archie on Nyan's shoulders. The little boy whose soft brown eyes told him, *everything will be okay…and you are okay.*

The horse wheeled around and they flew across the field until the three young wizards were tiny specks on the horizon. When the horse finally spoke, he did so in a grave and lofty tone.

'You'll learn my real name when the right time comes, but for now call me Bb. It's short for Brumby.' Instantly, the agreement took effect and their journey became a story about a boy and a brumby, to be told and retold among the wild herds and leapers of Aberash.

33 Renana: Lori
The Moyootj

Lori woke to a birdcall, rich and full. Renana's large body flared with heat and then slowly cooled as she squatted low on her perch. Unable to resist, Lori touched the green-gold outer feathers and a soft inner layer of creamy down.

'So, you are awake.' Renana spoke with a friendly smile in her voice 'Shouldn't you get on with it and ask me a question?'

Lori raised her face to the bird's starlit eyes and knew the answer before she had spoken. *Your gift is the gift of song.*

Her voice right now, felt clumsy and uncertain. 'If I…I really have this gift, how…?'

'Will it help you? Or hurt you? Will it make you go gladly or sadly? Isn't that for you to find out?'

'I thought…I don't know what I thought.' Renana had answered a question with more questions. In her confusion, Lori heard herself over-explaining. 'You see…Cade, that's my twin, well, he's not with me right now, but I need to stick to our plan. I need to meet him at the door to Rhizanthella Forest you see.' She felt so stupid she wanted to cry.

Renana bent her head. 'I am willing to take you as far as I am able, but the truth is, without Samuel and the magic of the Mage there are risks.'

A long silence followed with just a faint stir of wind ruffling the stiff leaves of the *mangatj*. The honeyed scent of its flowering filled the air. From somewhere in the *moyootj*, a bird-called. A mournful wail. Lori shivered. What if Renana died far from her home? *My gift wouldn't help her. How could it? Come to think of it, how could it help Ms Alayah or anybody?* The worries crowded in, yet in her heart, Lori was sure of one thing. She wanted to be with the big bird. Her fingers closed around her gemstone and she thought of her mum and dad. *Trust…I must trust myself – and the magic.*

'I have my own key.' Her words fell over themselves too eagerly. 'And this gift…if I really do have it…might help Cade and me do…whatever it is we need to do…if you know what I mean.' She closed her mouth and let the silence grow.

'While my strength holds, I'm willing to take the risk,' the big bird said, softly, 'but I can only lead the way.'

'Of course,' Lori whispered. She had to do this thing herself but somehow a gnawing fear of not measuring up fell away from her.

'Climb aboard.' Renana squatted lower still and without another word, Lori clambered onto the broad back. The big bones shifted allowing her to sit comfortably in the protective hollow behind the strong neck and the ridge of bone behind. Cosy within a down of ruffled feathers, Lori snuggled close.

'We fly by night and rest by day,' Renana said, 'for as long as my strength holds.' As they passed over Aberash Castle the big bird sighed.

With warm feathers around her, Lori welcomed the inky night with the wind cold on her face. *What more could I want, than to fly with the Night Protector?* She hummed to herself in tune with the wind and then she slept. When Lori woke up, the moon was a golden ball in the sky and a girl was singing. Her voice was clear, strong and it was beautiful. It took Lori a moment to realise it was her own voice she heard. *Is it really me? Am I that girl?*

Fully awake now, she sang to Renana, her dreambird. She sang to the moon, to the stars in the Milky Way and unknown worlds beyond.

'Trust,' said Renana to herself. 'Even a bird of magic is nothing without trust.'

34 A Whiff of Water
One Rock Desert

From the burning red sands, the fossils of star fish, shells and the bleached bones of unknown creatures stared up at them.

'My guide book says we're in the Forgotten Sea.' Cade blinked. There was grit in his eyes. He licked dry, chapped lips.

'Harrumph…a forgotten sea is a desert in my book,' said Bb. Their water supply had dwindled. At first glance the giant rock formation looked like a mountain made of pink candy with a clear blue sky behind. But as they came closer, each stone-head turned into a scowling face.

Cade muttered into the horse's ear. 'We can forget the idea of finding a *gnamar* hole full of fresh water here.'

'Yeah, it's too scary,' replied Bb. 'Even if my tongue does feel like a wrung-out old saddle cloth…how much further is it?'

Cade stroked the horse's cheek, 'Not far. You're doing well, my friend.' He hunkered down, trying to forget the carcasses of animals they had seen along the way. Dead from starvation or thirst, he supposed.

Dull eyed and with swollen tongues, they passed the huge rock formation that gave One Rock Desert its name. It was guarded on its northern border with a ridge of razor-sharp corals and the air bristled with uneasy spirits.

'Powerful magic is here.' The horse whistled through his teeth, showing the whites of his eyes. 'Hear that?' A whispering sigh rose from the secret tunnels and caves within the rock.

'Voices singing,' said Bb. 'Ghosts I think.'

'It might just be the wind,' Cade said. Though he tried to sound brave, he shivered with apprehension.

The brumby's nostrils dilated. 'That's no wind, but we need water. Hush your lips and smell the air.' He snorted.

'What is it?'

'Water – further north. That's what.'

Cade looked across the land. 'All I see is a mirage.'

'I didn't ask you to see it.' With his long mane flying, Bb bolted while Cade clung on with his thighs and clutching hands. A hot easterly wind pushed them along until without warning, Bb pulled up, snapped his big yellow teeth and let out a shrieking kind of horse curse.

'Damn and blast, I lost the scent.'

'Of what?' Cade puzzled.

'Water. That's what. I lost the scent of water.'

Cade sniffed the air. 'I can't exactly smell it…it's more than that…I can feel it in my bones.'

'Now you're talking like a water wizard…I say we go with your hunch.' Bb whinnied softly, trotted slowly around in a circle. With Cade waving him on, Bb cantered over another rise to a tell-tale sign of a dry creek bed. It was marked by a winding ribbon of white trunked gum trees that grew on its banks. The horse stopped too suddenly, sitting on his tail like a dog.

Taken unawares, Cade tumbled to the ground with protesting groans and moans.

'Awe come on, it can't be that bad.' Bb looked on.

'The bloody thing hit my shin!' Cade held up a wooden stick. He was about to heave it as far as he could, but as he caught the two arms of the *y* shape in his hands, pins and needles shot into his fingertips. The tail of the *y* pulled down sharply.

'Go with it.' Bb pawed at the ground. 'You've found the spot.'

Between them, with Cade using a sharp edge of the stick and Bb his hoofs, they broke through a deep crust of hardened clay to a sloppy mess of grit and water.

'Stop now,' said Bb. 'Take a breather.'

Cade wiped sweat from his sun burned face, breathing hard. He squatted in front of the hole they had made. A clear throated mud lark sang its song…up and down the scale. From the shade of a low hanging branch of a white gum, a mother roo with a joey in her pouch thumped her tail, eyeing them curiously.

After their rest Cade looked at their diggings. A small trickle of water had pooled into the hole and slowly the mud cleared.

'You first,' said Bb. 'Put your head right in.'

Lowering his hot face, Cade slurped up clear fresh water finishing with a refreshing head dip. Next, Bb gulped down his share, lifting his head to swallow. He too, finished with a head dip, spurting water through his nose. Grinning, they stood back to watch the bird take a drink and then the mother roo and the joey.

Horse and boy crossed Big Rock Desert in this way, looking for the signs and digging for water.

'This is how we brumbies live through a drought,' Bb said. 'We…and the leapers of Aberash, like the very first people who came to this land. We look for the signs, we smell the water and we dig.'

Led by their noses, they found a pool left by the wet season in a dry river bed. Thankfully Cade and Bb sank into it, washing off days of grime. On the banks, in a cluster of paper bark trees, a flock of white cockatoos fluttered like flags, their shrill cries rising and falling. Cade crawled out and then jumped back into the pool making a huge splash.

'There's a bombie, for you.' He laughed and then laughed even harder when Bb did the same with his gawky legs spread. Snorting and blowing out water, Bb rose to the surface. They swam and dived until Cade's skin goose bumped and Bb's stomach rumbled hollow. After drying off in the warm sun, the horse chomped on wild grass while Cade was satisfied with a piece of chocolate. Lazing by the pool, Bb told Cade the story of his ancestor – the first tiny dawn horse, who adapted and changed along with the climates of the world.

'We have travelled far.' He sighed, taking in the warm sun and they dozed. Their shadows grew long and the velvet night came down. But before turning his head into the pillow of his swag, he thought of Ms

Alayah…of Lori…where was she? Of Samuel. 'I'll keep this Mage safe,' he murmured.

Cade woke up with a heavy feeling of sadness and worry, but smiled when Bb tried to jolly him along. Lowering his head to the ground, he wobbled from side to side, pretending to throw him. Then, with a neighing laugh and chuckles from Cade, they took off at full speed with the earth spinning beneath them. After hours of travelling in this way, clear mountain air brushed their faces. They had come to the Land of Dream.

35 Amber: Lori
Big Rock

After riding a hot desert wind, Renana slowly descended.

'I'm sorry,' Lori sensed the big bird's distress. 'You should be at home, resting.'

'It is my choice to be here,' said Renana.

As they neared Big Rock, Lori drew in her breath at all she saw.

'It's so…so…grand,' she whispered. Layer upon layer of coloured stone rippled across the cliff face. Seams of red, purple, orange, pale gold and white. Here and there, fingers of sunlight glowed through long fissures to the ground.

From within the rock, there came a whooshing sound like the sea…and something else…voices more beautiful than Lori had ever known. Who were they? What were they? Unwanted questions and memories of stories about the Lorelei tumbled about in her head. With heart thumping, she pushed aside her own fears. The big bird was exhausted and needed to rest.

'There's a tree not far from here…see?' Lori said, 'with a sturdy branch for you to perch on.' The old rivergum straddled a cliff face with its roots embedded in a pocket of debris and soil. Renana's landing was wobbly and uncertain, but Lori was able to sit tight and then slide safely to the ground. When the bird failed to leap high enough to perch, Lori put on a brave face.

'Just a little higher and you'll be there.' The smile on her face when Renana finally succeeded hid her dismay. 'Sleep well, dear friend,' she called. How much longer could Renana go on? *If she dies far from her home it will be my fault....*

Without Renana's presence Lori looked around uneasily. There were strange others in this place. She put her backpack down near the base of the tree and walked towards the rock. From where she stood she noticed movement along a ridge. White gowned figures, merging with the pale wall behind.

'Ah yes, I see you,' Lori whispered. 'There against the cliff...and I hear you.'

The voices rose and fell, sometimes fading and blending with wind song and the swishing of a forgotten sea. At the end of their passage, one by one, the singers disappeared into the sunny entrance of a cave. Puzzled and shaken, Lori ran back towards the tree. There was no sound now, but the crunch of her sturdy hikers against the gritty red sand.

As the day went on, the merciless sun, beat down. Sweat poured from her brow and an ache between her eyes made Lori reach for the water bottle from the pocket of her backpack. Water gushed into her mouth too quickly, choking her for a second or two. She coughed and spluttered unhappily. *People die in the desert*, she thought.

Only when Lori breathed more easily, did she look with concern at Renana. Birds usually sleep with their heads under their wing, don't they? Why are her wings spread and her beak open as if gasping for air?

'Even a bird of magic needs water.' A wild looking girl leapt from behind a rocky outcrop. Dark skinned and quick, with a crazy head of uncombed hair, the girl barged past Lori towards the tree. A shoulder bag bobbed about on her back. It didn't seem to hinder her. Quick as a possum, she scaled the cliff, and then leapt from a jutting slab of stone into the tree. From there, she scampered towards Renana. *My Renana*, thought Lori.

'What are you doing?' Surely this weirdo girl couldn't be trusted, yet a little voice in her head told her: *She is Aboriginal and knows what she is doing.*

'I said...what *are* you doing?' Lori yelled again, though less stridently.

'Following the ants to the sap...that's what.' The nameless girl used a stick from her bag to tap the trunk of the roosting tree. 'Ah...here it is

– an ant hole. See?' She turned to Lori, triumphantly. 'I use a hollow straw to suck up the sap, right? Then I blow it into your bird's big gob.' Time and time again, the girl repeated the ritual until Renana closed her beak, nodded her head with a gesture of thanks, then tucked her head under her wing.

The amount of sap was small for such a large bird, but somehow Lori knew the magic was in the giving.

'I could have shared my drink with you, if only you had told me you were thirsty,' Lori said, too softly for Renana to hear. At the same time, she silently scolded herself. *I should thank this strange desert girl, instead of being jealous and angry because I didn't think to give Renana a drink myself.*

The girl scrambled down, leaping from one of the lower branches of the tree. She stood close. Eye to eye. Green-blue to green-blue. Like matching jewels.

'Your eyes are like mine,' Lori said, too loudly, 'even though your skin is so dark.'

'My name is Amber and I am a Lorelei like you.'

'I'm not a Lorelei,' Lori reddened with sudden anger. Stories about the Lorelei had never lost their power to scare her and right now, she really didn't want to be one.

'I bet you're thinking of those old stories about sailors who smashed their ships on hidden rocks and drowned.' Amber's eyes flashed. 'It was their bad seamanship that made their ships break up. It had nothing to do with the Lorelei and their songs luring them to come closer.'

'That's not right.' Stubbornly, Lori shook her head.

Amber folded her arms. She scowled. 'The Lorelai were trying to warn those sailors *away* from the rocks and that's the truth of the matter.'

Lori didn't want to believe it. 'So, what do you and your sisters do in the desert then? Wait for travellers so that you can fool them with false promises and then watch them die of thirst?'

The girl rolled her eyes. 'Yes, people die of thirst in the desert. Their eyes play tricks on them when they see a mirage that promises water. But please don't blame us.' Amber went on to grumble about the visitors that came by. Loners, runaways and fortune hunters looking for treasure. 'Only yesterday, a boy and a horse came by.'

'Was the boy just a bit shorter than I am, with dark hair and deep-river eyes…I mean…'

'I know what you mean,' Amber said, impatiently.

'I think that was Cade, my twin.'

The girls looked towards the north where desert oaks and white gums appeared like tiny brush marks on a huge canvas washed in red.

'That horse was scared and he bolted.'

'Did Cade stay on his back?' Lori asked worriedly. 'We never learned to ride. It cost too much to have lessons.'

'He stayed on all right…like glue. My sisters and I knew they were water wizards as soon as we saw them so we sent them on their way.'

'You sent them on their way? How?'

'With a spooky song of course,' Amber laughed. Her teeth flashed white. Again, Lori heard singing from many voices.

'You're thinking my sisters voices are like fool's gold…a sweet bate to trap travellers?'

'I didn't…I didn't like to say' Lori admitted.

Amber stepped towards her, belligerently. 'As a matter of fact, you are privileged to be listening to The Lorelei School of Song and don't think because you have the gift you haven't anything to learn.'

'I…I know…at least I don't know…I don't know anything…I have a gift…but I don't know how I use it or when to use it…It feels like 'pot luck' when it works…like when I chanted to open the door to Renana's tree.'

'Oh that…'

'How come you know what I'm thinking before I even say it?'

They were silent for a time and then Lori said quietly, 'I do want to learn more about my gift. That is, if I really have it…do you think it would be safe for me to go to your School of Song for a bit?'

'There's no danger for you…you're a Lorelei, but whether we'll have you or not is another story.'

The girl was sweating a little. She wore a kind of shift made of woven fibre of some kind. Her teeth were very white and her light-brown hair, although uncombed, shone in the sunlight. She had a smoky bush-tucker breath.

'We'll talk about it later. Are you hungry?' Amber asked. 'Can I give you food?'

'You mean bush tucker?'

'Of course.'

'I do have some chocolate…but yes please.'

'Good. Then we can share.' Amber led the way. 'Like you, I'm a Lorelei, but my link to this land goes back further.' They clambered over a small rise to a *gnamar* hole. The covering was a heavy flat stone. The two girls worked together to lift it. But it was Amber who climbed into the well. She passed up refreshing cold water in a cup that had been made from a boab nut.

'Now we'll see what my daddy's tribe have left for me.' Amber clambered towards the desert scrubland and Lori followed. They passed spiky spinifex grass, stunted wattle and sheoak. The red earth shelter was cut into the side of a sandhill, away from the hot sun. Hanging on the skimpy desert oak outside was a little package of dried meat and inside, a wooden dish piled with walnut sized fruit. The flesh was bright pink and juicy.

'Bush peach?' Lori asked. The girl nodded and they squatted in the dust to chew on dried strips of meat, finishing with the fruit and the chocolate.

'I wonder how it was when the real sea was here,' Lori said.

'We'd be under water.'

'Yes, and there'd be tropical fish in rainbow colours and the corals too.'

'And the tide swirling into secret caves where my sisters and I have our concerts.'

Lori warmed to Amber and they talked together with no sense of strangeness or time passing. It was like being with a girl cousin, sharing secrets.

'I can still hear the ghost of that sea and your sisters' beautiful songs, so when do I get to meet them?' Lori asked.

'You won't meet them,' Amber said.

'Why not? I got to meet you.'

'I told you, I'm different. I have the eyes and the voice of a Lorelei from my mother but my link with this land is stronger. My brown skin and everything that is not a Lorelei comes from my father who was born in the desert.'

When the day cooled, they emerged from the earth shelter to climb a nearby hill.

'Up ahead, see?' Amber pointed to a smooth boulder at the top where they sat, cross legged to look at the world through their blue-green eyes.

'So,' Lori began, 'maybe your sisters don't want me....'

'Yes, they do.' Amber looked into her eyes. 'You are already in the school and I am your tutor. I was supposed to begin right away...then...I just loved having a friend.'

'Me too,' Lori said. 'But I do have a lot to learn and I need to learn it quickly.'

'Okay then, you can start by listening to my sisters' song carefully. Notice how clear it is? It's made with the outward breath alone.' Amber's lesson began with the breath and then the voice. From there to the art of listening and making music from minions of sounds. From the stealthy movements of small animals and their calls to the wind sighing against the leaves of a desert oak. The lesson ended with a game called Where am I?

'If you hear my sister's song, where do you think she is?'

'It's from the east one minute and then the west...how does she do that?'

'My sister is throwing her voice. It is what we do when danger is near.'

'Can you teach me that?'

'Yes, but there's a knack to it – a secret way and it takes practice.' The lesson went on while Renana slept.

36 Pearls: Lori
Leaving Big Rock

Beware the Far Away bird, the choir from Big Rock came faintly at first with the sound increasing. It was a warning. A warning Lori did not wish to hear. All she could think about was the sadness of leaving a friend. When Renana flew down from the moon-dappled tree, refreshed from her daytime sleep, it was time to move on.

'I'll never forget you.' Lori linked arms with the desert girl.

'You're my friend.' Amber's white teeth flashed in a smile. 'You're my very best friend.'

'And you're my first best friend.' It lightened Lori's heart. She wanted to sing. But not about any *Far Away Bird*. What could the Lorelei sisters mean?

Amber's words followed her as they left. 'I like being with you so much I forgot to tell you about the *Far Away Bird*...I should have warned you...'

'I don't care about some *Far Away Bird*.' Lori laughed and waved again. They waved to each other until Big Rock looked tiny. Lori thought no more about Amber's last-minute warning but held tightly to the notion of having a best-friend...like a treasure in her pocket.

At the same time, Renana came to a moment of truth. Before the moon reached its quarter mark, her failing heart hammered in her chest – too strongly – and then it faded. For a few seconds, she lost flight. It was a warning. Hot needles of pain shot through her great thighs to her feet. As she flew, they hung limply beneath her, the talons chalk like and broken. The splendour of her gleaming feathers faded. Even her mind betrayed her with fog and confusion.

Renana told herself, I am the mother of all birds. I am the Night Protector. Surely, I can find the strength to take Lori through the dangerous Land of Dream. But there was a voice within her saying, 'Without magic you are nothing. Your tomorrows are running out with every breath you take – every wing stroke you make. When Lori goes to the Land of Dream, you won't be there to guard her…especially from the Far Away Bird.

The big bird waited for the tears that beaded her own eyes to melt away and a deeper sorrow to enter her heart. But instead, her tears hardened into a number of pearls that melded together to form a bracelet.

'For you,' she told Lori and a fresh surge of energy entered her body making her wing strokes stronger. In a half dream, Lori slipped the bracelet onto her wrist and then crooned to Renana softly, 'You are the Night Protector…but after I leave you it will be the magic of a white daytime moon who helps you return to Aberash.'

In Lori's own heart she was sure that was the way it would be.

'While Samuel is away, you'll be at home, Renana, and you'll keep the night safe and you'll sing in each day like always.' Lori barely remembered her own words and she wondered at the pearls around her wrist. They were like something from a dream.

'Keep them,' said the bird. 'They are yours.'

'But they are precious, and I'm just…I'm just a girl.' Lori knew that soon she would be alone, and like those pearls, she must harden herself against hurt. *Sometimes you only have yourself.*

'If I have to be alone a little sooner than we thought, it won't matter, I'll be alright.' Gently, she stroked the bird's neck, knowing there was strong magic in the pearls. It frightened her a little. *Trust – I have to trust that I will know what to do with the magic I have…that I won't ever disappoint myself or let Ms Alayah or Renana down.*

Perhaps she did have the gift of a Lorelei, but she was an ordinary girl too, one who needed to eat and sleep and go on being a girl. *It just so happens I have these magic pearls from Renana and my gemstone that keeps me close to Mum and Dad.* The thought made her feel strong…strong enough to go on until she and Cade found their teacher just like they planned.

As dawn broke they came to well-watered farmland with fields of ripe corn between irrigation channels. 'Do stop here, Renana,' Lori begged. 'The air here is good.' Renana stumbled when they landed, leaving Lori unhurt but shaken.

Making light of it, Lori picked herself up and quickly gathered grass to make a cosy nest. It was a lovely round dome with a large hollow centre. Gratefully, Renana crawled into its cool interior while Lori spoke to a farmer who gave her a great armful of ripe corn. The corn seeds looked like tiny suns waiting to be eaten. Before they parted, Lori left Renana a stash of the seeds and water, adapting Amber's idea of storing it in hollow straws and blocking each end with soft clay.

'There is magic in every seed and every tiny drop of water, that is gifted in this way,' Renana told her, gratefully. 'Go now but remember your brother is riding a pony so look for its tracks in the Land of Dream.' It was something to hang onto in the lonely days ahead.

37 Temptation: Cade
The Land of Dream.

Cade looked towards a maze of paths in the Land of Dream. Each one pulsed with light. Each one beckoned, whispering…*follow me…follow me…*

A long valley offered up sweet green grass beside crystal clear pools. Bb shivered with anticipation while Cade stared into the distance, his heart hammering. He saw a towering peak of jade, another of pearly opal topped with slabs of lapis. Closer at hand were rocks seamed with gold and crusted with diamonds.

'Fool's gold and cheap glitter, I reckon,' Bb snorted, 'and besides, even if it's real, what can you do with it? You can't eat it.'

'Hush your lips, horse.' Cade feasted his eyes on all he saw but he didn't protest when the horse moved on. Bb trotted briskly until they reached a lush valley where fruit trees and berries grew like weeds. Where butterflies with shimmering wings sipped on the nectar of flowers. One path led to a pretty stone cottage and a hay shed with a loft.

'Why go to the Swamps of Murruk?' said Bb flatly. 'It's a flea-bitten wretched place – smelly and dangerous.' Cade breathed the aroma of spring flowers. Further on, there was a clear pool filled with leaping fish and hovering dragonflies with scarlet wings. Beneath shady trees several dappled ponies feasted. They whinnied and Bb's nostrils flared.

'It's horse talk,' he said. 'Every word, sugar coated.'

'Wondrous boy, Keeper of the Mage,' said a proud looking trotter. 'You cut a fine figure on your horse *slave*. But how much finer would you be, if you wore the Mage and kept it for yourself? Before a bat could blink you'd be King of Dream.'

'So, why don't you?' Bb mocked. 'Are you scared?'

'I'm not scared.' How could Bb do this to him? 'I choose not to do it, so there.'

'Why?' Bb teased.

'Because it would be wrong, that's why. Ever heard the word?'

'Means nothing to me, but wrong it might be. Still, if you did rule over Dream, you'd be rich with all that shiny treasure and I'd be fatter.' On and on, Bb harped about the advantages of staying in the valley. It was a long speech for a horse and they were both tired at the end of it.

For the rest of the day and into the night, they were silent, with nothing between them but angry twitches and black looks. At the same time, Bb tempted Cade by choosing paths that lead to wondrous things. Each time they come to a fork in the road, he acted like a dumb horse, saying, 'Where to now, mortal?'

'You know very well, where I wish to go.'

At this, Bb shied, galloping away without heed, and then stopped suddenly as if to throw Cade – though he swore later he was only kidding because he was so bored with the place. At this, they laughed.

Bb's pace quickened. Following a path chosen from the guide book, they watched a corroboree where Aborigines sang songs and told stories from long ago, where children danced by firelight to the sound of didgeridoos and tapping sticks.

They saw a city of spires, domes and steeples where the sun shone endlessly. There were no smelly cars, only gardens and fun fairs where laughing children played on awesome slippery dips; where for a lucky coin, you could buy almost anything you wish, where people walked on their own two legs to get about or on foot mobiles equipped with tuneful warning bells.

Once they saw a grand building with words across it: Hall of Fame – *Welcome, Cade, Keeper of The Mage*. It was full of cheering people. From its windows there came a delicious smell of food. The inviting doors swung wide open.

Bb's eye rolled upwards as Cade tapped his heels against his flanks, saying in a husky voice, 'Let's get out of here, Bb.' They chose a broad straight track pushing on until afternoon. As the shadows grew long, so the track became steep and narrow. It passed over a causeway between two mountains. Cade almost fainted with dizziness when he glimpsed the bottomless void on each side. He gripped Bb's forelock and spread his arms around the animal's strong neck.

Only when they reached the other side of the causeway did Bb allow himself a head toss and snort. 'Whew, Cade boy, we made it!'

The light faded fast and, against the darkness, shadows fluttered across the ground. An icy wind clawed at their hearts.

Bb pawed the ground. 'Mawks…devil birds, they're checking us out.' Again, and again, the shadows flicked over them, then without warning, a clap of thunder. Lightning rent the air. A sheet of cold rain spattered their faces. Within minutes water poured from the sky to pool around the horse's hoofs.

'I have a feeling this rain was sent by a friend,' Bb said. Mawks can't fly in rain. They'll not worry us tonight.'

Bb went on with head down until he was up to his middle in flood water. He dug hardened hoofs into the sticky mud, unknowingly leaving footprints in spite of the flood water. While Bb struggled through, Cade became the watcher, hoping to find shelter in the rugged ranges on either side of the path. At last, he spotted a cave.

'It looks high and dry – and it feels right.'

'It is right for you,' Bb said, thoughtfully.

At the entrance Cade slipped off the horse's back expecting him to follow, but Bb threw back his head and backed away.

'Aren't you coming?'

'No.' The horse looked at him with wide fearful eyes. 'It isn't right for my kind.'

He's going to leave me here. With this thought Cade entered the cave. Inside was a smouldering hearth. A place to dry his clothes and then to lie on a bed of stone at full stretch before falling into a dreamless sleep.

38 Bb and The Stranger
Southern Border of Murruk

The smell of rain lingered in the air. Bb put his nose to the ground and it led him to a thermal spring. After a long warm soak, his weary body was rested but his mind was troubled. What was to become of the boy? As if in answer he heard the far-off whinny of a wild horse and then the drumming of its hoofs. Tall and prominent, a stallion pulled up and then stood waiting – a gleaming figure in the starlit night. With a snort and a head-toss, the animal pawed the ground. It galloped a little way, bucked, then turned back towards Bb with a nod.

'You want me to follow?' Bb trotted behind the horse at a respectful distance. Increasing in speed, they paced it out and then thundered over the wide field. Ungainly as he was, Bb was the fastest galloper in the brumby pack, but out of politeness, he stayed a little way behind the older horse. Bb knew the horse was a loner, one of a kind that chose to live apart from the herd.

It wasn't usual for such a noble beast to notice a shaggy, long eared pony. What did he want? Nervously, Bb gulped the night air to clear his head before pelting across the ground with the wind tossing his mane. They came to a rise where flaking stone scattered with a sharp, ting – ting. At the summit of the peak, they stood in the cold night, blowing hot air through their lips and nostrils. They saw below the rise, a curving stone wall and beyond, to the land on the other side.

'There you see the Swamps of Murruk.' The stallion butted his head towards a brown coil of smoke. Even from this distance it gave off a sickening smell. 'It's to keep the devil birds away.'

'The mawks?' The young horse allowed his gaze to wander from the Swamps of Murruk to the stallion. Even by starlight the loner's dark eyes showed the mystery and strangeness of a life lived apart.

'Ah yes.' The loner's voice was soft but insistent. 'I see you have a problem with the Swamps.'

'Not I.' Bb snorted too loudly. 'After tomorrow, I'm out of here. The poison milkers and the mawks don't bother me. They're none of my business.'

'Hmmm…if you say so,' came the reply.

For quite some time there was no sound except for a desert oak singing. A song about a horse that perished in the desert while helping its human master to find new land for his cattle and sheep.

'Huh!' Bb snorted at the soppy story, but two warm tears sprang from his eyes.

'Are those tears for a stupid horse that trusted a mortal?' the loner asked, 'or could it be you've gone soft on the boy?'

'I'm not soft on anyone,' Bb snorted. 'No way…that's a step into slavery.'

The older horse moved closer until their heads almost touched. Together they gazed into the land beyond the wall where the shadows of wings darkened the white mist.

'A mawk spy,' said the Loner. 'Soon your boy will be fending for himself among creatures like that.'

'He'll be ready for them. 'I'll teach him to defend himself before I leave him. I need three more nights with him. That's all.'

'You're sailing close to the wind, my friend.' The loner's eyes flashed. 'Have your three nights, but I reckon you're very close to losing your heart to that boy.'

'Ah! Get away from me'

'You're thinking of going with him, aren't you?'

'Hmmm…it did cross my mind, but how do you know?'

'Never mind how I know, but if you're soft on the boy, you know what that means.'

'It means…I lose my freedom.'

'You lose more than that, brumby. Now go back to your herd before you're lost.' There was no sound for quite some time except for the high-pitched crooning of a dingo and the faint rustle of wind in the grassy field.

'Who are you?' Bb gulped down a wave of awe for he'd never met a horse with such a noble presence…one who read him so well. 'I mean – from what herd do you come?'

'In horse talk they call us traitors, slaves, bootlickers, horses who get their fame from selling out to greedy mortals who want the earth for themselves.'

'Yes, yes,' Bb said, sharply. 'I know all about it. It's been drummed into me from my first gallop in the field. You don't go soft on a mortal. They'll use us and kill us, then stuff us for their museums, like they did to poor Phar Lap. I've heard the story a thousand and twenty-one times until I'm sick of it, but, tell me, did you go soft on a mortal?'

The horse lowered his head. 'It was a woman in the near Long Ago.' His ears flicked back. 'She was droving cattle when I met her – a loner like me. They called her *Red Jack* cos of her long red hair, but her kind were not kind to her.'

'You mean she was rejected by the human herd?'

'Yes, and for that, she rejected the human herd,' said the horse. 'She couldn't abide their rules.'

They were silent for some time, there senses sharpening. Alert to possible danger from mawks, they were startled by their own shadows. From faraway there came the sound of a whip being cracked.

'That's Dame Grey,' said Bb, 'News travels quickly. Maybe she heard about the boy carrying the Mage and wants it for herself.'

The older horse sighed. 'A pity that woman ever came over from the mortal zone.'

'Yeah,' said Bb, 'but they'd be glad to be rid of her. They say if she gets her hands on a victim, she'll force your jaws open and shove bad magic down your throat.'

'And she laughs while she does it?'

Bb turned to reply, but the older horse was moving away.

'Is that all you've got to tell me then?' Bb called.

'Asking you to think is enough,' the older horse flung back at him, and then he whinnied softly and disappeared into the night.

39 The Allies
Caligo Castle

Dame Grey had indeed, 'cracked' her whip. Oh, how the axeheads loved to bate her when Wairimu summoned her to his castle.

'I'll show those dumb guards not to mess with me,' she muttered.

'Do be careful, Ma'am,' said Mo. He was her personal servant, one of the few mawks with human speech and the only trustworthy one in the pack.

'Your passport please, Ma'am…and we'll need your whip,' the guard snapped. It was Chief Axehead Ironbar. They met eye to eye with mutual dislike. He handed back her passport and slapped a consent form in front of her, then ordered trainee Trixie, to tie Mo to a security bollard.

Mo was one weak spot in Dame Grey's armour and it offended her mightily. Wordlessly, she followed the young axehead across the bridge and up the ramp to the castle rooftop. Wairimu appeared and Dame Grey was blindfolded while he cast a long tedious spell with much chanting and arm waving. Only then was she permitted to enter the one and only door into his castle.

For long moments, she lost track of time, waking with a headache and a nasty taste in her mouth. As usual, Wairimu explained why he put his guest through the door spell – as if she didn't know.

'Nobody…and I mean nobody, gets to see my secret door. I'm sure you understand.'

'Of course.' She forced her lips into a smile. 'Oh, how lovely, you have decorated in that bilious green since I last visited. But then you always did like those murky shades.'

'I'm glad you like it, Dame. Ah…this is nice, having you over. It almost calls for a glass of Black,' said he. 'And of course, when I get the Mage we can come to some agreement about the land in Rhizanthella Forest.'

Dame Grey's eyes sparked with greed. It was stronger than her irritation with the evil wizard. 'Oh yes, we are neighbours after all.' She followed her host through the wine cellar down a stair case to the basement where a sorcerer's fire burned dimly. It gave off a putrid pall of smoke.

'I'd call you a subject rather than my neighbour.' Wairimu smirked. 'You are one of my workers, aren't you, Dame Grey?' Thinking he'd scare her a bit, he transformed his hands to flames. Blue and red fire sprites danced before her eyes and then zap – the flames were gone.

An illusion of course, thought Dame Grey. A common street magician could do the same. But wanting to keep on the right side of him, she smiled a sickly smile and accepted a small glass of his ghastly wine from a cabinet in the corner.

The blue flames from the fire flared and then cleared. Looking into them, Dame Grey saw an image of Cade, with his hands clutched over his chest.

'So, he keeps the Mage close,' said she. 'I can't believe he hasn't nabbed it for himself.'

'Such loyalty…he'll make an excellent slave once he's been trained…and with a transformation spell…I might even lure him over to the dark side.' Wairimu spread his hands, closed his eyes and muttered mean magic. With malicious grins, they watched mosquitos swarm around Cade's face.

'Oh, I wish I could do that,' she gushed. 'You're so clever…where as I'm just an old thing, come in from the realm of mortals.'

'Ah, but of course, I'm a true wizard. '

'So, you're not planning on snatching the boy yet?'

'I'm leaving that pleasure to you,' said Wairimu. You and Captain Ironbar with help from his daughter…what's her name? Hooksie or Hoopy…what does it matter? The bottom line is that you'll deliver the boy to me the moment he steps into your realm.' His eyes now were pin pricks of malice.

As soon as she might do so politely, Dame Grey asked permission to leave. It meant a repeat of the tiresome "invisible door spell" but at last she was out of there. She unhooked her mawk and hurried away. Mo, once a powerful wizard in his own right with a human shape, was supposed to be her slave, but he'd been with her so long, she relied on his wisdom.

'Wairimu is such a boaster and a loud mouth,' she muttered.

'He drinks too much black wine,' Mo observed quietly (very quietly, for Dame Grey rather liked a nip herself).

'That too,' said the dame, virtuously. 'But tell me, what's he planning when he gets the Mage? Does he do away with me as Head of Murruk or what?'

'Hmmm, it's true he only keeps the people he can use, but Dame Grey, look ahead, the guard is waiting.' They had reached the gate to the bridge and thankfully Captain Ironbar was no longer on duty.

'Your passport please, Ma'am.' The guard's jaw jutted like a veranda with no roof. He opened a big hairy hand for her little black passport.

She snorted, 'As if it hasn't been seen already today.' To be treated no better than a snake-milker by Wairimu's guard cut deeply.

'Rules is rules.' The ignorant guard studied the small print on the passport, taking his time. Then he hit his helmeted head with a gong and shouted, 'Let the dame through, boys, but check the passport at all points.'

'The dame's passport to be checked at all points…the dame's passport to be checked at all points….' The dreadful bellowing across the bridge sounded like a herd of cattle stung by a nest of case wasps.

Dame Grey fumed at the humiliation. 'After I've nabbed the Mage, Wairimu will be the one showing his passport to those dumb-headed guards.' They trundled over the bridge, only to be humiliated again.

'If you want your whip back,' said the bored guard at the exit gate, 'You sign for it, here, here, and here.

With a rasping breath of fury, Dame Grey scribbled her name three times and marched off. Once on her own turf, she wheeled her whip round her head and – crack!

The nearest guard yelled: 'I've been shot,' while the others ducked for cover.

'Mo!' the dame shouted. 'Keep the mawks locked up and hungry, but tell them whoever captures the boy and gets me the Mage can have him for their dinner. Send a message to the Poison Milkers – tell them there's a price on the boy's head.'

Inside the castle, Wairimu smiled vindictively. Soon he'd have the Mage and the boy…even the girl…and without him lifting a finger.

'Mandel,' he shouted, 'I want bread and some of my vintage wine and I want it now…I said now, you dithering fool.'

40 Preparation: Cade
Near the Entrance to Murruk

An odour of stale mud wafted over their faces. Cade slipped from Bb's back and they stood side by side looking down on the vast swampland. The horse held his head high with ears laid back. Every muscle of Bb's body quivered. His eyes narrowed.

'What is it?' Cade asked.

'There are mawks down there.'

'If only I could use Nyan's blending hood I'd be okay.'

'Those birds are dim-witted, but they're not blind. Forget blending when it comes to birds, beasts, ghosts and swamp folk– they're sharp as tacks when it comes to seeing.'

Cade had to admit the guide book warned it might be so.

Steely eyed, Bb stared ahead. 'You'll need a shield.'

'Pity I don't have one.' Cade shivered. Evil coiled around them – an invisible serpent gripping tighter.

'See that tchield of Mia's?'

'It holds the mage and keeps it safe.' Cade caressed the tchield that almost felt like an extra layer of skin and kept him warm.

'What do you notice about the handle?' Bb's words challenged him.

'It fits my own hand like a glove.'

'Have you ever taken it off and held it like a real shield?'

Cade reddened. 'I have sometimes…just for fun.'

'I've seen you do that when you thought I wasn't looking. I want you to do it now. I boot you with my hoof and you defend yourself with the tchield.'

'But it belongs to Mia and I promised to take care of it. Besides, the Mage is in there.'

The horse laughed. 'Trust me, that tchield is harder than the wood of a *kardil tree*. It's tougher than any hoof or boot in the land.' Bb tossed his head and pushed his nose to the ground, then kicked with one leg.

Without thinking, Cade lifted the tchield. He fended off the blow, but tripped, falling back on his bottom. 'Are you sure it is that hard?' He still felt uncertain.

'Imagine a material as flexible and hard as graphene.'

'Ooh…really? I learned about graphene in science.'

Bb chuckled. 'Now let's try again. Keep your eye on me.'

Quicker to respond to Bb's next kick, Cade stayed upright.

'Very good,' said Bb. 'But tell me – how did you know I was about to strike?'

'By your ears,' said Cade, thinking he had been quite smart. 'They twitched before moving back towards your tail.'

'My ears!' mawks don't have no ears…not ones you can see.'

'Okay…okay…Mawks don't have ears like yours. I get the message. Let's try again.'

'Now, watch my eyes. And other bits of me, too. Pretend I'm a mawk.' Bb bared his big teeth.

'Are you telling me mawks have teeth?'

'I don't know about any others, but these do. Teeth, claws and eyes as big as oranges.' Bb kicked out again.

They practised all afternoon with the horse kicking and Cade defending. They practiced until the watching sun brushed them with coppery light – casting their long shadows on the grass. The shining moment passed and they went on until darkness stroked their skin and the stars shone white.

'Enough!' said the horse. 'Drink some water from the spring and have some of your chocolate. Then we'll find a spot to sleep.'

It was comforting to hear the horse's stomach rumbles and snorts, his gentle breath rising and falling through the night.

For three days Bb went on with the instructions. He attacked the boy from all sides, from above and below until he couldn't get past the tchield. On the last night Bb and Cade were so weary, they didn't even say goodnight. In the early hours Cade sat up. He heard Bb drink from the spring and munch grass but instead of settling for the night beside Cade, Bb trotted away. *He's a wild horse. Of course, he must go.* Cade lay down with silver starlight soothing his wrinkled brow. He tried not to give way to the tears building inside him.

From a rise close by, the horse looked back to the boy. He waited for Cade's heaving shoulders to be still and for the even sound of his breathing in sleep.

'Travel safely, Cade boy,' Bb whispered and then swiftly galloped away, moving over the wide field in search of sweet grass.

41 Enchantment: Lori
The Land of Dream

Lori was filled with uneasiness about Cade. 'I'll be with you soon, Brother,' she whispered, 'and I will follow the footprints of your horse just like Renana told me.'

After leaving the big bird, Lori joined a line of passengers to go by ferry across the lake to the Land of Dream. She had no money but was told by the ferryman, 'You can earn your ticket if you promise to sing…yes?'

Lori was about to agree, when somebody screamed, 'No Mathilda.' Clasped by a slim brown hand, Lori froze. 'This naughty girl is my younger sister. I have a ticket for her…look!' A masked Kiwi girl had an iron grip on her wrist. She wore a pale-yellow sundress embraided with a line of brightly coloured wahine dolls around the skirt. 'You're in big trouble,' she scolded, 'running away from our mother like you did.'

'Come on board then, little sister.' The ferryman smiled at the girl over Lori's head and they were swept along by the crowd across the gangway to the ferry. In the crush, Lori stood to one side while Kiwi-girl mingled. Among the many musicians on board, a girls' choir famed for its sweet harmonies, performed, Kiwi-girl among them. While the others sang, she danced freely with her eye-catching skirt swirling, the line of wahine dolls spinning. With her long dark hair streaming, she drew the crowd. But, not once did she utter a sound.

While the other passengers cheered and clapped, Lori turned her back on the crowd and especially the girl. She longed to be with Cade like always…or to be flying with Renana. She didn't want to be with strangers or to lose another best friend like Amber.

As the shoreline receded the wheeling gulls fell away, leaving only three black swans in the sky. With sweeping wings and long necks extended, the birds flew towards a gleaming city across the waters to the mountainside. For a magical moment Lori saw the ferry with its crew and passengers as if from above – the ferry pulled through jade water by the soaring swans with threads of gold attached.

How beautiful. Lori forgot the strange girl. Without any thought of an audience, she sang the delight and awe in her soul. As her voice swelled, she didn't hear the sudden hush among the passengers. She didn't see Kiwi-girl cover her ears with her hands. Didn't hear her distressed cry,

'I must not be bound by her spell.'

The air felt lighter in the Land of Dream. A train carried them up the steep face of the mountain. It stopped at each level of the staggering streets where musicians performed. There were instruments of every kind: shell trumpets, flutes, reed pipes and keyboards. Everywhere, the visitors were welcomed by families of musicians. Aborigines played didgeridoos and tapping sticks, beating the earth with strong dark feet. Minstrels sang ballads while street performers shimmied and danced to the beat of kettledrums.

Lori was drawn to a performer who called for volunteers to sing on stage. 'You there, young lady,' she thrust a microphone at Lori. 'This is a talent quest. Show us what you can do. If you can *throw* your voice, all the better.'

Gladly, Lori opened her mouth to sing when Kiwi-girl stopped her. 'Oh no, this is not for you, little sister…not here.' Her masked face came towards her. A grinning mouth, too close. She avoided the girl's eyes gleaming through slits in the mask. 'Beware the *Far Away Bird*, little sister,' she hissed in a whisper. 'The Land of Dreams is full of dangers for a Lorelei.'

'No!' Lori cried. 'I've changed my mind…I don't want to be a Lorelei. I'm just a girl…don't stare at me like that. Don't come near me…I don't want to know you.' With fear and suspicion giving her wings, Lori ran as if for her life. On and on, this way and that through the crowd, but no matter how hard she tried, the Kiwi was not far behind.

With the surging crowd between them, Lori stopped to face the girl and to shout. 'I don't want you near me.'

'What is it with you?' The girl shrugged and then reached with her arms, palms up.

'What is it with *you*, Kiwi-girl? Leave me alone.' Lori turned and ran on, past a large gathering of the girl's relatives at their *marae*. It was redolent with the smell of wood smoke, barbecued sausages, hot tea and toast spread with butter. Lori's stomach rumbled. She was hungry for hot food, for people and kindness. It was here in the clan's *whare-hui* – their meeting house. *But I can't give into it,* she told herself. *I don't need Kiwi-girl or her people.* She slipped through a hedge and finding an overhanging peppermint tree, flung herself on the ground beneath it. She slid out of her backpack, using it as a pillow. As the sky darkened, Lori lost the will to move on. Wrapped in quiet despair, she curled up under the tree, without bothering to cover herself or to eat a piece of life-giving chocolate.

It was a bird-call that wakened her. Gentle and lovely as the rising sun. It blocked out any other thought or wish. Was this the *Far Away Bird?* How could anyone warn her against something so perfect?

I must have that sound – I must find that bird. Like a magnet, the birdsong pulled her. Near, yet far – she ran after it. Ran through lightly timbered mallee with smoke bush and fields of pink and white everlasting flowers. The flowers and the shining mountains that had attracted Cade were of no interest to Lori. It was the bird and birdsong that drew her. She ached to hold the sound close, to stroke and love the bird. But each time she came close, the sound leapt ahead. Behind the next clump of trees, around the next corner, in the next field. Like a see-saw, the song rose and fell deliciously. As Lori moved on, so did the sound, always ahead of her. On and on, she followed it from one place to another – searching with no thought for anything else but that sound. Sometimes Lori threw her voice after the bird, hoping to attract it, and then disappointed, ran on, blindly.

Before she was ready for it, the bright day was swallowed by the night. A biting chill crept over the land. A hoar frost – a thick white fur, covered every blade of grass, every tree and every shrub. Lori felt a pang of loss and then fear as a voice in her head overrode the birdsong. It was the voices of Amber and Kiwi-girl telling her: *Beware little sister…beware the Far Away Bird.* Half delirious with exhaustion and cold, she sensed Kiwi-girl's presence. Her hand on her wrist, leading her back to her people's warm fire. Kiwi-girl – Amber, both with blue-green eyes like her own telling her, *Just as the Lorelei binds with her spell, so she is bound…beware the Land of Dream.'*

You tried to save me from myself and I refused to see. Lori choked back tears. When next she wakened, she was wrapped in her own blanket and alone. She reached for a fresh chocolate from her backpack, gulping it down, remembering just in time to leave a fragment in the bag and to sprinkle a few crumbs on the ground. 'How could I have forgotten I had that chocolate?' she whispered to the scurrying ants. 'I must never forget to take care of my body again as long as I live.'

Lori bathed in a thermal spring that reflected the blue-green of her eyes. When again, she heard the *Far Away Bird,* she asked herself: 'Why did I want more, when I already have the sound of its song in my heart?' Refreshed and warmed from the thermal spring, Lori dressed hurriedly and then studied her map before heading north. Over several hours she padded over a criss-cross of tracks that rose steeply. They broadened into a clearly marked passage. Its soft clay surface had hardened and it bore the clear footprints of a pony. Like a friendly face each one stared up at her. The loneliness and uncertainty of days fell away.

Swiftly, the night came down – black velvet with no moon or stars. Yet the prints of the horse glowed white. Pulling her jacket close, Lori trudged on. Within a short while, a cluster of bright stars broke through the darkness – leaving silver threads of light. They revealed a narrow causeway across a deep ravine. One false move and she might hurtle into a void. Yet the engraved horse's prints went on.

'Cade has been here and I can do it, too.' Lori touched the pearls around her wrist and then held the gemstone that fitted snugly into her palm. *I have these precious things, the pearls from Renana and the stone from Mum, and I have the footsteps of a brave horse to follow. I'll be alright.*

With these words, her bones felt longer…stronger. Though the way was dark, she never veered from the track. It was almost dawn when she found shelter in a cave. It was still warm from a smouldering camp fire. While snug in her blanket, she heard the gossip of travellers camping beneath a stand of sheoaks nearby.

'Pity any mortal child who has to go near Dame Grey,' an old woman sighed. 'Oh, how she loves to rattle the bones of children.' There were murmurs of agreement and more stories about the dame and how she secretly helped Wairimu even before she came across the waters. Their fearful words came to Lori in whispers. She cried a little, feeling very young and afraid. How could she possibly get past Dame Grey and her team of mawks to the safety of Rhizanthella Forest? Then a thought came to her: *If she's a mortal, surely Dame Grey was once a child herself. In the deepest part of her heart she will remember what it was like.* Trust…you had to trust.

42 Serval
The Swamps of Murruk

Pesky mosquito…get the hell away from me.' Cade slapped the back of his bare neck. A fierce red sun beat down from a smoky sky. Pushing through prickly bushes and a swathe of razor-sharp reeds, he stopped now and then to check his map. There were bogs further on, but there was something else he had to remember here. What was it? Something nasty. If only Bb were here to remind him. Oh, how he missed that brumby.

A sudden dip on the ground sent him sprawling. 'Ahh…my thumb…damn it, damn it,' he groaned. There'd be a bump on the left side of his head for sure, but it was his right palm that took the brunt of the fall. *Damn it. Damn it.*

Cade was still on the ground when he saw it. Any move on his part and it would surely strike. There in the shadows, pulsing with life. Sleek and black, gleaming silver. The long-flattened body turned back on it itself in a loose but tense curve. Head slightly raised. Mouth open. Tongue flicking.

Cade stared into strange reptilian eyes before it lunged. *I'm gonna die,* he thought. *I'm sorry Ms Alayah…I so wanted to find you…and Samuel…I so wanted to keep the Mage safe…you see I…well…*So why wasn't he hurting? Surely you couldn't die of snake bite without something hurting. Whose hand was that? A strong hand grabbing that snake by its throat.

'*Noorn,* my pet…don't waste your venom on a mortal. Sink your fangs into the mesh of my beacon instead.' The speaker was a boy of about sixteen.

With heart thumping, Cade scrambled to his feet. A dribble of poison from the snake's fangs fell into the boy's beacon. Only then, was the creature released with gentle strokes and kind words. 'Until next time my lovely.' Sluggish and sleepy as a newborn kitten the snake slithered away.

Cade was dumbstruck by the grinning boy. What kind of person could live in such a hell-hole as Murruk?

'My name is Serval, but my people call me Tigercat.' The boy grinned. 'So, what's it to be then, mortal? Do you take me on as your guide or what?' His skin was a deep reddish brown, like the swamp pools tinted with coffee rock. Serval knew the land well – every inch of it, he said.

'If you hadn't grabbed that snake it would have struck me.' Cade was grateful but could Serval really be trusted?

The boy laughed, as though guessing the doubts that crowded his mind. 'What choice do you have? There's a price on your head in these parts. Everyone wants a bit of you. But you know and I know, it's really the Mage, they're after.'

'Is that what you want, too?' Cade put his hand to Mia's tchield ready to guard it, but the boy laughed again.

'I could have grabbed it when you thrashed around in the mud.'

'You mean you were watching me all that time?'

'From the moment, you came into Murruk. You should have seen your face when the Joker Door wouldn't give up your coin.'

Cade tried to explain. 'It said on the sign, a lucky coin would release the catch and come back to its owner.'

'It's a Joker Door, so what do you expect? It didn't say when it would come back, did it?' Serval grinned.

Cade scowled. He was bleeding from the slap of reeds, mosquito bitten, filthy with mud and his thumb throbbed.

Serval's coal black eyes glistened. 'How much longer can you go on alone, huh?' His voice was a surprise…soft and musical. 'We need to fix that thumb. And besides, the land ahead is rougher still than this. Without a guide, you'll soon be a bog's dark secret.'

'I know about the bogs.' Gloomily, Cade remembered warnings from his tutors at Raz Nehyer – he was instructed to look out for pale grey patches of ground that looked solid. Step on one and you are swallowed by a bottomless pool of liquid mud. A moment of silence and then from a distance, the sound of excited chanting with loud whoops and bleating. The boy looked at Cade through narrowed eyes.

'Hear that? They're my relatives, Snake Milkers who work for Wairimu – Scorpion…and his ally, Dame Grey.'

'What is their problem?' Cade asked. 'They scare me.'

'Quite rightly too. They are baying for your blood…they want the Mage.'

'I can't give it to you or anyone.' He reached for the tchield. 'It's not mine to give.' He'd been warned about swamp dwellers. They had sold out to Wairimu for the right to live. Desperate people – who knew what they might do to him if they wanted the Mage?

'I'll guide you through Murruk, but not for any Mage. I'm not a cloak man, but times are tough and I expect some payment. What have you got that you can trade?'

Cade opened his backpack and peered in. 'There's my guide book but you wouldn't need that – and you don't need my water bottle or the clothes. The teeth cleaning chewie you wouldn't want.' The boys' own teeth dazzled with their whiteness. Cade didn't even consider the chocolate for trading but he took out a fresh one to share with Serval, explaining that he had to leave a bit for the bag.

Serval's eyes lit up. 'What strong magic! Just what I need for hard times. I'll give you a safe passage for the chocolate and the bag it comes in.'

Cade experienced quite a wrench when he handed it over, but there was no other way. 'It's a deal,' he said, and added, with a smouldering eye to eye look. 'But only if you promise me this: to give my sister a safe passage when and if, she gets here…and promise not to wait for a whole day before you bloody well do it.'

'Oh…err…sorry,' Serval mumbled.

Was he sorry for taking the chocolate? Or for leaving him to suffer for a day without help? With no more chocolate and no lucky coin, it looked as if Cade's own luck had run out…but maybe…just maybe, he could trust this boy.

Wearing nothing but a loin cloth and a carry-bag on his back, Serval led him to the village. Careful to stay hidden behind a curtain of low shrubs and reeds, they crept close. In a low voice, Serval explained how his people created a liveable space by heaping up mud. Their rambling shelters were built on the same lines as the mud mounds of fat clawed crustaceans. Each dwelling had various openings, curved ramps and viewing platforms, but never a straight line. Everything curved and coiled tipsily, like pottery pieces made by young children. Each dwelling was ringed with peat fires.

'The fires don't do much for the sky, but smoke and heat keep the mawks away,' Serval said.

Through a screen of rushes Cade and Serval looked on while a group of boys and girls in their teens formed a circle. Together they chanted, swaying back and forth – woodenly, as if controlled by a master puppeteer.

'Under Wairimu's reign,' Serval said, quietly, 'with no elders to guide us, they waste their time trying the old chants and spells…thinking it'll make us what we were…but it'll never happen while they're slaves to the devil scorpion.'

'Were you all nature wizards of some kind?' Cade was trying to grasp an idea…a whiff of light in the dark.

'We were indeed and very good at our jobs, too. But my brothers and sisters sold out to Wairimu.' With wide dark eyes, he stared into the smoke hazed landscape. 'My snake milk doesn't go to him. It's preserved for better times. I don't and won't belong to Wairimu. I belong to the swamp.'

They crossed the vast wetland with Serval leading. Often a smooth green 'field' turned out to be duck weed or pussy willows growing over the surface of icy black water.

'Keep wriggling,' the boy warned, 'or the leeches will have you.' They waded through a stretch of water to Serval's own small island. Bone-weary, Cade found himself in a cave-like mud shelter. Serval treated his thumb with a jelly like ointment that reduced the swelling and eased the pain. Like everything else, the bed on which Cade lay was rock hard sun-dried mud. On the ceiling above him the pale reflections of water from a pool within the shelter rippled in an endless play of dancing light.

Cade slept through until the early hours and then went outside where Serval worked. He stood for a moment beside the swamp boy, taking in the spreading warmth of a campfire, the soft whoof-whoof of leaping yellow flames. Serval handed him a mug of hot *mangk*, a rich herbal tea. He sipped it while the swamp dweller spoke of his craft.

'Small doses of venom can be injected into horses to produce an antidote for snake bite.' He explained how he dehydrated the poison to preserve it. Cade wondered what it was like to be born a swamp dweller and to be alone, like Serval.

In the morning, the boy dived for eel in a deep pool near his home. The eel, and two large crustaceans, were char cooked for breakfast, though Cade couldn't bring himself to eat food so fiercely tainted with mud. Serval simply laughed at the pained expression on his face and ate both portions with noisy relish. With a wry grin in return, Cade made do with *koolah*, the rather tasteless fleshy stalks of flowering emu plums, a hand full of oily *marda* nuts and crusty damper.

By day two, Cade's thumb was healed and it was time to move on. With Serval leading, they leapt over each of the dreaded Bogs of Despair.

'Tigercat passing,' the boy yelled.

'Keeper of the Mage passing.' Cade too yelled, surprised by the brave sound of his own words.

'We're through the worst of it,' Serval said at last. 'There is just this shallow stretch of water to wade through and then you are on your own.'

Cade paddled through the stagnant water. It smelled of decayed vegetation but that didn't stop the leeches from latching onto his bare legs.

'Get off me, blood-suckers,' he muttered.

'Don't try to pull them off,' Serval warned. 'Only another fifty steps and we're through.' Serval rushed ahead and was waiting on dry land with a vinegary potion to wash off the leeches and a poultice of ash to stem any bleeding. He explained that his own oily skin was resistant to the blood suckers. Before parting they sat for a while on the trunk of a ground hugging river gum, with its cool leafy canopy above.

Smiling, Serval shared some chocolate with Cade, promising to keep it for bad times only. 'It might well save my life in a drought.' When their eyes met and they touched palms, Cade knew he was saying goodbye to a trustworthy friend.

On his part, the swamp boy felt the rare ache of loneliness as he turned for home. To comfort himself, he sang an old chant and hearing it, Cade thought the low croon might be the wind in the trees, or the sound of some wild creature blending with the swamp's secret gurgles and sighs. But Serval himself knew it was a powerful protection spell, very like the one he learned from his mother as a young child: *By the power of all that breathe in the marshes of our homeland, protect Cade, Keeper of the Mage.* Serval's heart lifted, for in this land of mean intentions he detected a whiff of good magic. In the past two days, he had saved a mortal from certain death and given him a safe passage through the Bogs of Despair.

43 Treachery: Samuel
Basement in Caligo Castle

Trussed up with ropes, Samuel had been thrown into a cage that hung below the rafters of Wairimu's basement. He learned from the wizard's mutterings that Cade was quite near and would soon face Dame Grey and her dreaded mawks. *I need to stay calm,* he told himself.

'I'll get my basement slave to show you how nice I can be,' Wairimu said, his voice heavy with sarcasm. He rang a thunderous old bell and the captured Judd limped in with chains and shackles clamped to his ankles.

'Bring the holding cage down and undo the ropes that hold the Chief Wizard of Aberash,' Wairimu commanded.

With a sinking heart, Judd did so. After escaping from Bazilia, he was soon found by an Axehead, hauled back to Wairimu and set to work. Gently, he undid the ropes and guided Samuel to a chair decorated with ghouls and gargoyles. For a moment their eyes met. He mouthed a 'sorry' and shook his head while Wairimu placed a hideous crown on Samuel's head.

'I can make you a king if you say the right words.' Wairimu offered Samuel biscuits and lemonade. Oven fresh, the biscuits smelled deliciously of freshly ground ginger and the lemonade was like the brew Samuel made in his own kitchen. Though famished, the prisoner shook his head.

Wairimu 's eyes were strangely bright and green, but what Samuel saw in his pupils was like a film clip: Ms Alayah – lost in the dangerous underworld of Caligo Castle. Cade – surrounded by hungry meat eating mawks. Lori – about to enter the land of Murruk where she would face Dame Grey. Renana – dying. Sometimes it helped to look evil in the eye, Samuel knew but he tore his eyes away. *What can I do but guard the very last gram of my energy and magic?*

To Wairimu, the Chief Wizard of Aberash Samuel appeared to be in a trance – his eyes focused on a place nobody could know. There was no way to touch him.

'Take the crown off him,' he ordered. 'Lock him in the cage again. Tie him up with rope and make it tight.'

44 Battle Ground: Cade
Dame Grey's Domain

The Mawks are here. Cade knew by that strange animal smell. He'd been warned of their stillness before an attack. How they skulked between giant grey stones mottled with lichen. How they merged with monster shadows of ant nests or the stump of a tree blackened and scarred by fire.

Oh yes, Cade knew about the mawks from his guidebook. But the guide book didn't know about him. About his heart, beating like a trapped bird in a cage. A mawk just metres from him, opened its elastic jaw to let out a whistle-like shriek. It was a signal to the others.

Mawks everywhere. Moving as one. They could smell live meat. Cade saw a space between the birds and ran – but the biggest and scariest mawk cut him off, bellowing loudly. From the sidelines, others hissed and yawed. Before he was ready for it, the mawk charged. Caught off guard, Cade stumbled, but flicked out Mia's tchield and was on his feet.

Clang, clang, clang: beak and tchield clashed like cymbals. Again, and again the sound split the air while the giant bird attacked, its half open beak revealing rows of sharp pointed teeth along its edges. Again, and again, Cade fended him off.

Now, now, now – Cade paced himself, trying to read the mawk's every move. Somewhere in the fog of his mind, he recalled Bb's coaching voice. Clang, clang, clang – faster, faster. The thwacking iron hard beak against tchield. The salivating mawks swarming – jeering and sneering. And from somewhere across the way, a giant woman screaming. Screaming for his blood.

'Where are you mawks?' Dame Grey yowled into the fog. 'Can't you smell that boy? Why haven't you got him yet? I want that Mage. I want it now, and don't you forget: when I get it, I'm queen of the show.'

'Dame Grey,' said Mo, 'The young ones are baiting the boy, taking it slow because they want their sport.'

A second mawk attacked Cade's feet with a vicious jab of its beak. He jumped out of the way, only to meet another mawk with its elastic jaws wide open. Its sharp teeth clamped onto the tchield and then came a bellow of pain. The mawk fell back as though hit by a live wire.

Like a wounded bull, it returned for a revenge attack, this time with its beak firmly closed. Cade fended it off but his feet floundered as another mawk dived in. He rolled over and the two birds collided with screams of outrage. More yawing and hissing from the onlookers while the bullish pressure of three beaks pushed against the tchield in a deadlock.

It's all over. There's no way I can win. The thought was powerful, but Cade didn't let go of the tchield. He tilted it to one side and the beaks slid off. At least one neck was grazed by the tchield. The mawk crumpled and the others fell on top of him. Their baying howls chilled Cade's blood but when the sounds stopped without warning, the silence was unbearable. A voiceless scream rose in his throat.

In slow motion a mawk danced around him with fetid breath and drooling open beak. Others joined their brother. The unhinged bodies swayed with delight at the sight of live meat. If Cade stepped forward the mawks stepped in front of him. If he stepped back they come forward. With bulging eyes, they leered at him, gnashing their teeth.

Emitting a bark-like yelp, the largest bird signalled to the others and four attacked while others waited to take their place. The best he could do, Cade thought was to make a run for it or even throw the tchield in their faces to save his own life.

A flash of movement in his side vision made him look west. The sun flashed in his eyes, and then something big came at him…not a mawk. It was bigger than a mawk. It was Bb. With a clatter of hoofs and a snort, his friend leapt to his defence.

'Forget the back field,' yelled Bb. 'Three mawks coming in from the right flank.' They fended off the birds together. It was like having another four tchields. Poof, poof, poof. Each time a mawk came in, it was booted into air. Air that crackled with ear-splitting squawks and caws, the gnashing of pre-historic teeth, the ruffling of primitive feathers. Yet the dumb mawks came back for more.

With Bb near his back, Cade's vision sharpened and his arms were threshing machines, faster and faster. *We're winning. We're winning,* he thought. Yet something in his side vision worried him. Like an itch. A pale 'something' low on the ground. An anthill? A stone? Was it moving? Cade fended off another mawk. Surely it was nothing, just a variation in the rough terrain. But then came an agonized scream from Bb.

A small framed one eyed mawk had cunningly crawled on its belly, remaining still as only mawks can. He'd chosen his moment and pounced, clamping his beak around the tender knee joint of Bb's back right leg. It would not let go. The creature remained motionless with a cold glint in its single blood-red eye. In a terrifying moment of truth, Bb reared up then staggered about on his three legs.

'Ooh Bb, you came to the place you most feared and you did it for me.' With tears streaming and the tchield in front of him, Cade charged, pushing at beak after beak of excited and triumphant mawks. To save Bb from certain death, he needed to remove the stubborn 'One Eye' without delay.

'Bb,' he yelled. 'Watch your two front feet. Use your own big ugly teeth on those critters up front. I'll get One Eye off your back leg just as soon as I can.' He peered through the swirling dust almost fainting from the mawk's stench. Their orderly semicircle had given away to a stampede.

Cade's struggle to break through the mawks was like swimming in a sea of mud spiked with poison. The poison of sharp teeth and claw. How much longer did he have? How could he possibly save his friend among such creatures? How much longer could he go on fighting with the weight of sadness and despair pressing on his heart?

Cade struggled with the impulse to throw his arms around Bb's neck and to wait for the end. To his horror, the mawks yowling had increased to a deadly din. Half-starved for days, they wanted the prize on offer and they wanted it now. Not a skinny mortal boy but a robust brumby with flesh on its bones. A horse once fallen was fair game. There'd be a vicious struggle between individual mawks. A bloodied struggle to be the first to get to the kill and then to shred the carcass with tooth and claw into ribbons of horse flesh. Already they jostled for space with drooling beaks wide open.

I can't let it be, Cade cried inwardly but looked for a way out. In a flash he realised the creatures were fighting among themselves to be first in line for the feast and while they were distracted he was, by some miracle, given a small window of opportunity to get to Bb's attacker. Stumbling through the dust and swaying mawks, he honed in on One Eye who remained totally still with its stubborn beak firmly attached to Bb's leg.

Cade examined the offender quickly and thoroughly as a physician might, then finding the soft tissue on either side of its beak, he used his own finger-nails and dug in.

'Open your beak, you stinker,' Cade hissed. Seconds dragged. Any moment now, a wary mawk would spot him and it would be all over.

'Open up…devil-bird.' Cade dug in harder with his nails. At the same time, he positioned the tchield, using his knees to push the tip of it into the creature's mouth. Surely it would let go of Bb's leg now. So why did it remain there with its one eye closed? And its jaw? But something had happened. Though the mawk was still, its jaw was flaccid as an old rubber boot.

In an instant the sky fell on its head. Cade couldn't tell up from down. Was that really Bb? He was standing up on his two back legs and pawing at the dust laden air. Now he was sitting in that doggy position that allowed Cade to jump on his back and grab that tuft of hair between those big beautiful ears.

'Let's get out of here, boy.' With Cade clinging to his back, Bb pelted along as only a true bush brumby could. Meanwhile the dumb mawks fought on, until the voice of the one with human speech rose above the rest. 'Enough!' He bunted the most troublesome young birds and gradually the creatures understand their loss. The boy and the horse had fled. Mawk bones rattled. Their teeth ached. Some moaned and wept for the dusty quiet of Long Ago when dinosaurs roamed. Others wondered what punishment Dame Grey had in store for them.

'We've done it,' Bb said, as they watched the scene from the hillside.

'Thanks to you my friend.' Cade slipped to the ground and threw his arms around Bb's neck. 'Now for that door into Rhizanthella Forest. It should be somewhere quite near.'

'I can't see no door,' said Bb.

'Nor can I. There's only that vicious looking hedge that marks the border of Murruk and the forest.' It was dense and dark, prickly with thorns intertwined with poisonous nettles. Could the guide book be wrong? Just then Cade heard the shouting of giants on the floating bridge nearby. It was another way into Caligo Castle but guards were everywhere.

'The bridge is a no-go,' Cade said, 'And we need to rest up. We need that door into Rhizanthella Forest…if only we can find it.' Before they could move, a deep shadow brushed them filling them with dread. From somewhere quite near, came the spine-chilling screech of a giant woman.

45 Dame Grey on the Prowl: Cade
The Land of Bad Dreams

With bulging eyes, Dame Grey stormed through the land. Wham, wham – her razor whip snapped the air, the bushes, everything in its path. Now and then she emitted a high-pitched scream before bringing the whip down with an ear shattering crack.

'Huuuuuuuurrrr,' Bb snorted in horse talk he was so scared. 'Give me a dumb Mawk any day.'

Cade gasped, 'We need to find that door now.'

The dame headed straight for them. She was a threshing machine or an earthquake at nine on the Richter scale, Cade reckoned – and what's more she came with a newly-released clutch of mawks behind her, ready for the pickings.

'The dame is after the Mage and nothing is gonna stop her.' Bb's long ears flicked back. His eyes rolled and he hissed: 'Leap on my back and we'll make a run for it.' Cade didn't need a second invitation. One leap and he was on the horse's back. Instantly Bb reared up as the dame's whip cut the grass from beneath them. She raised the whip again and Bb froze as if confronted by snakes.

Surprising them, Dame Grey, too, stopped in her tracks. She stared at a slender girl emerging from the swamps of Murruk. Though covered in mud and grime, with uncombed hair standing on end, Lori appeared perfectly at peace with the world skipping along the path, singing her little heart out.

All eyes focussed on the girl, and then Cade yelled: 'Hey, giant lady, it's me you're after. Remember? He lifted the tchield above his head for her to see. 'That's only some girl from the mortal zone.'

'Who is it really?' Bb snorted and hissed at the air.

'It's my sister. It's weird. But look where she's heading.' The path Lori chose stood out clearly against the fuzziness of Murruk. It led straight to a door – a reddish gold beacon shaped like a pear with a line down the centre.

'Run for it, Lori, Bb and I will deal with the Dame.' Cade glared at his sister. 'What do you think you're doing? I said run now.' He wanted to slap her. Lori refused to look at him. From all around came the stir and swoop of wings on the move. The air filled with birds from all over, swirling and coiling, parting and meeting. Together they formed a protective guard above the path where his twin tripped so lightly.

Lori sang in a high clear voice…about flying with Renana to a forgotten sea and her journey to the Land of Dream. About the Lorelei and the Far Away Bird who almost destroyed her. She sang about finding the footprints of a pony to guide her. About clever Serval who saved her life many times over.

If Lori saw the mighty figure of Dame Grey, it didn't show on her face. It didn't show in the way she skipped from one foot to the other in the wind. Dame Grey forgot her wicked plan to snatch the Mage. She forgot about throwing Cade and the horse to the meat eating mawks. Here in the land of foul mists and nightmares, a frail-looking girl dared to come without fear. Dame Grey didn't notice the gathering of birds. She didn't notice the stir of wings or the unusual silence. Not one sound did they utter. Even the mawks were silent. As if they too, had no eyes for anything but the girl on the path: no ears for anything but the song.

The voice was sweet as a lark's, as far-away church bells or wind chimes. It carried high and far. It held the dame and all who heard it to the spot and it spirited them away. Something stirred inside the hardened heart of Dame Grey. Some memory. Oh yes. Once long ago she was a child herself.

46 Partings and Promises
Near the Door into Rhizanthella Forest.

Old Mo kindly led Dame Grey back to the Lodge and she was put to bed by a brawny Axehead nurse who was experienced in cases of this kind.

'She'll soon come to her senses,' said the Axehead. 'After all it was Dame Grey herself who taught me how to handle difficult cases of Flashback and Trance.'

'Are you sure?' Mo worriedly returned to the hungry mawks. Some of the worst meat eaters were yowling and prowling again.

In the meantime, Cade helped Lori onto Bb's back. With his two passengers, Bb galloped at full speed to the door. Moving high above them, a thousand and one birds wheeled. Vast flocks of tiny birds rode the thermal winds above. For the keeper of Rhizanthella Forest it was a warning to stand by. As they came close to the shining door, Bb sat on his haunches and the twins slid to the ground.

'Listen!' Cade whispered.

With the mawks close by sniffing at the ground, Bb's large frame tensed in readiness to bolt.

'Come with us.' Cade looked deeply into the eyes of his friend, trying to read him. 'Won't you?'

'I can't do that…sorry,' the horse said in a low rumble. 'But we will meet again.'

'When will that be?' Cade held his breath.

'When you see my shape in the clouds. That will be the signal.'

'What about your wounds?' Cade felt the soft bump of Bb's head on his shoulder and the warm breath of a horse's whisper. 'My real name is *Courage* and I'll be with you in spirit *always*.'

'I still don't want you to go.' Cade looked up with teary eyes. 'What if the mawks attack you?'

'I'll outrun any mawk.' Bb grinned. 'That's what horses do best. Like the leapers of this land, when we see the enemy, we don't attack unless we're cornered, we bolt. That's why we're still here after fifty million years.' He snorted in a horse like way. 'I almost forgot. There's something in my forelock that belongs to you.'

'*My lucky coin*,' Cade yelped.

'I found it near the Joker door into Murruk,' Bb said.

'But…how the heck did you pick it up with no hands?'

'A head butt…and a lip flick trick is all.' Bb grinned and then bolted, dodging one slow moving mawk after another. A tail wind pushed him along at top speed. Mawk after mawk charged him but he outpaced them. In Murruk, he found the Bogs of Despair marked out with burning chunks of peat, then heard a furtive whistle and there was Serval, leading him away from a party of swamp dwellers who lay in wait for him.

'They fancy horse meat as a change from eel,' he hissed through his teeth. 'I'll give you safe passage…in exchange for…'

'Sorry, I'll have to owe you,' Bb snorted. There was no time for bargaining. With minutes to spare he heaved himself out of the squelch and ooze of Murruk and cleared the dividing wall. At last, in the northern reaches of Aberash, Bb breathed in a lungful of clean cold air, a whiff of sweet grass and something else. What was it and why did it make his heart beat so wildly?

'I must go back to the herd,' he told the wind, yet deep down, he knew where he belonged. Not with the herd. 'That's what comes with losing your heart to a mortal,' he whispered. A sniff of air and again – the smell of horse, and in the distance – the outline of a noble beast rearing against the sky. The Loner waiting for him.

47 Gateway to The Forest
Rhizanthella Forest

Hurry, hurry, there is no time to lose. While the trees of Rhizanthella Forrest whispered and stirred, the anxious face of a small grownup person appeared at an open shuttered window above the door.

'I am Mari, keeper of the gate and the ancient book of Forest Law. 'Are you a mortal boy, Keeper of the Mage and do you have a lucky coin to open this door?'

'Um…yes.' The shadow of a mawk brushed over him and Cade flicked out the tchield. 'Yes, to both questions.'

'Are you a mortal girl with the gift of song, and do you have a key for this door?'

'I do have a key. But…about the gift.' Lori hesitated while Mari sighed rather impatiently, 'if you can't say it, then for pity's sake, sing it.'

And so, Lori sang:

A mortal am I

With the gift of song

With the gift of so…ong.

'Coin to the left and key to the right,' Mari cried. 'Now say a few magic words. Any will do.' Cade fended off two mawks and the ungainly birds reeled backwards. It gave the twins seconds to open the door.

'We two mortals enter Rhizanthella Forest for good, not evil.' They gasped out the words and shut the door firmly while the mawk staggered off to chomp on pine cones. As Mo would tell them if only they would listen. Pine cones and zamia nuts were a perfect diet for mawks and also the reason this particular kind of devil-bird was born with teeth in the first place. Mo could only shake his head at the wrong-headed ways of the world.

Within Rhizanthella Forest, Mari kept Lori and Cade waiting in a bough shelter while she wrote in her book with a feather pen dipped in plant-ink. Their visit had to be recorded and their signatures examined under a magnifying glass.

While Mari saw to the formalities, the twins looked at each and sighed. 'How are you, my poor brother?' Lori held Cade's face between her palms to be sure he was real.

'I'm alive, but I can't get the sound of mawks out of my head and their smell is all over me.' He gave her a brotherly hug and then looked down at her feet.

Lori followed his gaze. 'Yeah, I know, my hikers are falling to bits and so are yours.' She rolled her eyes. 'Just look at us, how are we gonna go on?

Cade held the tchield close. Was it enough to protect them? Bb's words spun around in his head. *My true name is Courage and I'll always be with you in spirit.* Was that it? He whispered into the blue air, 'So where is courage now, Bb?'

Beside him, Lori put her hands to her forehead in quiet despair. 'The trouble is, I still don't really know what I do, or when it will work.' They were equally paralysed by thoughts of what lay ahead.

Mari snapped her fingers and clicked her tongue. 'Before you do anything you need a good soak in the hot Springs of Now.' Marching ahead, she led them across a footbridge to a series of thermal springs screened by trees. Here, they were assisted in their preparations by a young giantess with skin soft and sheeny as black rose petals.

'Don't look backwards to all that has been,' the giantess chanted, 'nor forward to what lies ahead. You have come to the hot Springs of Now.'

Smokey blue, the waters lapped around their bodies. For Cade, floating weightless, he felt the bite and itch of his wounds dissolving. There was nothing now, no thought of anything but the deep blue dome of sky and the sweep of peppermints and sheoaks hanging low to the water. A safe cacoon. *Blue is bluer in Now,* he decided. *Green is greener.* And when Lori rose from under water, smiling, her hair looked like wet gold.

After bathing in the cleansing waters, they dressed in the new blending clothes made by Nyan. Gatekeeper Mari, who was waiting for them, smiled warmly. 'How beautiful you are, all shining and clean,' she said softly. 'I think the *Now* minder has something for you.'

The gentle giantess gave them each a pair of boots made of some kind of tough fibrous material. 'You'll walk faster in these,' she said. 'You'll run further and skate on hard surfaces if you need to.'

'And we have our blending hoods from Nyan,' Cade said. His friend's instructions on the art of blending came back to him.

'The sun is so warm and bright right now,' Lori said.

'A good time for blending?' He grinned because Lori already had the hood over her head and was peeping through eye slits.

'Blend now,' they said together. All at once, Lori experienced a strange lightness and clarity in her thinking.

'I could throw my voice and nobody would find me. Want me to show you how? Then hear this.' She yodelled, and the cheerful sound floated back to them from the other side of the bridge.

'I didn't know you could yodel,' Cade said.

'Neither did I, until now, but why are you looking at me like that?' She threw back her hood staring into his deep river eyes. His dark brows came together in a frown. He looked like a wizard.

'The voice trick…like a ventriloquist…it's so neat…but how do you do it? Or could it be you are part wizard…are you Lori?'

'I don't know, brother,' Lori whispered. 'Are you?'

48 Brodd the Smoke-Reader
Rhizanthella Forest

Tall even for a giant, he came with an oil lamp.

'I'm Brodd – the Smoke Reader.' He knelt on the ground to shake their hands. A boy of about fifteen with shining dark eyes, and a gleaming bob of black hair. He lifted the lantern to show them a lace of silver tracks that wound between the trees. 'That's where the Rhizanthella orchid has spread.' As they walked he explained how the orchid grew underground without sunlight, living in harmony with the honey myrtle and a special kind of fungi. 'They are pollinated by a wasp, a fly…or even our own Justice Ants in these parts.'

'Ah yes,' said Gatekeeper Mari, who bustled along beside them, puffing a little to keep up. 'It was your own plant wizards who named them Rhizanthella Gardneri. But my business is the story. A mouth to speak it – an ear to hear it. A prediction if you like.'

'A prediction?' Cade and Lori exchanged a look. They knew of one prediction that scared them out of their wits.

'No mortal ever sees our Rhizanthella bloom,' Mari said. 'But one day, they will, and when that happens….'

'Yes?' The twins spoke as one, eager to hear what the gatekeeper had to say.

'Ah…I must not speak of it.'

Brodd's face flushed. As if to fill an embarrassing lapse, he spoke of his people and how every living thing had a task and a place in the forest. With the lantern held high, he signalled to stand aside for a native cat.

It's white spotted coat, made it almost invisible in the dappled moonlight.

'Our *djooditj* doesn't have human speech,' he said.

'But some animals do?' Lori was confused.

'Only the ones who begin as mortal.'

They continued on a well-trodden *bidi* to an open sided shelter and meeting ground. The air smelled of wood smoke, camp fires and damp earth. More importantly, the delicious promise of something hot and savoury.

'Aha…who do we have here?' The man overseeing the food had twinkling dark eyes that made you forget the deep scars on his face. 'I wondered when you'd get here.' With a big wooden spoon in his hand, he waved towards the people now gathering around the fire circle. 'Call me Granda if you like. They all do.' He turned quickly to lift lids, stir and taste the contents of huge cast iron pots on their bed of hot stones.

A chunky dwarf grunted. 'Welcome to any mortal who can get past those mawks and still be alive.' With strong muscular arms, he pulled up a pair of heavy jarrah stools to a huge semi-circular table. Mari rang a dinner bell and then Granda spooned food into bowls.

'There you go, Nutsy…still on a diet, are you?' A patter of words as he served each one – 'Half a scoop for Gatekeeper Mari…and a goodly portion for the mortals…you're sure to be famished after battling those stinky mawks…how did you find it…eh?' He didn't wait for an answer. 'Now Brodd, you'll need an extra scoop of mushroom for your lanky frame.'

The twins ate hungrily – creamy mushrooms, caramelised carrot and best of all *yoork*, a native spud that flourished between the trees. There were side salads of forest greens, sprinkled with wild tomatoes.

'Help yourselves to damper,' Gatekeeper Mari said. 'I made it with grains you won't find in any mortal zone….'

'Mortals can only blame themselves for that,' said Brodd, pausing with a spoon in mid-air. 'It's the way they use the land…oh if only they would think before they *do*.' He glanced at Lori and then reddened, embarrassed. 'Oh, I didn't mean to be rude. Please…don't take it personally.'

'Not at all.' Lori was too busy enjoying his gorgeous soft voice and the sheen of his hair, to be offended.

'We tread carefully here and the land repays us with food that we can safely cultivate.' He spoke about the mosses and lichen that kept the ground moist and explained various drainage practises that ensured a healthy life style for all. Brodd was so handsome, Lori was quite sad to think that she must soon say goodbye, but the delicious food on offer, soon brought her back on task. She was famished, and by the way Cade tucked in to the stew, so was he.

'Ah lovely…delicious,' the diners murmured. After the main course, they sipped cups of *djoorla*, a refreshing drink sweetened with honey and nibbled on *mol* – red ripe forest berries. Lori enjoyed the moment, quite unaware of what trouble lay ahead.

It all began with a concert. Three brothers mimicking bird calls and animal sounds with coos, whistles, shrieks, and quiet murmurings. Twin sisters playing a thrilling duet on clay pipes and then a drummer with no hands played drums. Lori leaned towards him, fascinated by how easily he held the drumsticks in his flexible toes. But it was the hypnotic sound he made – like rain on leaves that held her captive. Until the will to sing was so strong she was unable to resist:

When the blooms of Rhizanthella, we see
A door, a secret door will open
The prisoners of Caligo to free.

At this, the drummer stopped drumming. All eyes were on Lori.

'What are you saying?' the drummer cried. 'There is no doorway into *Caligo*. The glitter veins all end here. That's why we made this our home-hearth. Besides, the Rhizanthella will never show us their blooms.'

'Why should they?' a voice from the crowd piped up. The others murmured the same sentiment. Some grumbled into beards, muttering about the dangers of allowing mortals into the forest, a place of refuge and safety.

'We live in peace here,' said one of the pipers. 'We don't interfere with the Rhizanthella and we have nothing at all to do with Wairimu.'

'Or his dark chiefdom,' her twin added.

'But there's no door as far as I know.' Everyone turned to Granda for a lead. He looked down at Lori and Cade from his great height. 'Unless the young mortals think they know more than we do.'

Lori's cheeks burned. She hadn't meant to upset anybody. The words had come to her with the music. A dwarf with a mop of unruly hair turned his gaze away as if the very sight of her offended him. He waved a hand at Brodd. 'Hey Smoke Reader, you're a scholar, what do you know?'

'I can only tell you what I read in the fire smoke.' The flames of the hearth-fire flickered. An uncomfortable moment of silence, and then Brodd went on. 'There's quite a bit of unusual magic about. It tells me a small person will soon come into our midst – an animal with human speech. She's a scholar and a thinker who will bring us a message.'

Gatekeeper Mari reminded the people about the bad deeds of Wairimu – the Scorpion, and how Chief Wizard Samuel of Aberash was now a prisoner and without the magic of the Mage to help the people who are, after all, citizens of the homeland. 'With our blessing and luck, this boy and girl will return the Mage to him. We all want balance in Aberash.'

At this, Granda stood firm. 'We are only obliged to shelter mortals when mawks are on the prowl. If they want to go to Caligo, they take their chances across the Bridge.'

Brodd's eyes blazed. 'You expect them to face the Axeheads on a bridge where there's nowhere to hide?'

Fearing trouble between the giants, Cade raised his hand, trying not to upset anyone yet needing to speak up. 'We'd take our chances if we had to, but the door in Lori's song is marked on my map. If we can find it, we're no longer your problem.' He unfurled a map from his guide book and lay it on the table while some of the giants and dwarfs strained their necks to see.

'Huh!' Granda tapped the map with his large index finger. 'There's a door here alright, but this map's out of date by years. I've heard of this door. It was used by Wairimu and his basement slaves to move back and forth to the lands south of here....'

'Ah yes, I see what you mean,' said the drummer. 'If you want to find that door you build a tunnel through Orchid Hill.'

Somebody in the crowd laughed. 'You wouldn't even know where to start.' Most of the others joined in, though Granda remained quiet and thoughtful. Lori met Cade's troubled gaze. So, what were they to do? Trust the answer would come?

49 Enter Briony
Rhizanthella Forest

Ouch! *A possum* landed on me.' An offended dwarf untangled himself from the possum and moved from his favourite resting place beneath a small tree.

'And something landed on me,' said the shaken possum. Nervously, he raised his black-ringed white-tipped tail. 'I was only picking a few ripe snotty-gobbles for my dinner.'

A weird little person slid from behind the possum onto the ground with a splosh of over ripe snotty-gobbles, flaky bits of red paper bark and sprays of elongated green leaves. To add to the confusion somebody yelled, 'I wanta know what one of Wairimu's scare slaves is doing in Rhizanthella Forest.'

'Oh…yes…yes…a scare-slave…a castle Grum.' Gatekeeper Mari was supposed to know about such intrusions. Her short arms flapped like a non-swimmer in deep water. Somebody had entered their fire-circle onto the tree from a crack in the wall above. That solid divide between the castle and the forest. More to the point, the person had come without permission and not through a door.

Beyond the fire and lamplights, there were open mouthed squawks and groans. If a Grum could come in, so could Wairimu.

'Rhizanthella Forest is a place of refuge for rare and precious things, said a sharp-muzzled animal with human speech. 'How dare a castle Grum enter our domain?'

'But isn't our home to be shared with whoever falls into it?' Brodd asked.

'If the Grum has human speech,' said Gatekeeper Mari, tetchily, 'have her come into the light to explain how she got here.'

It was a Grum all right, rather slow moving as castle Grums go, stopping now and then to gaze about her, as if to study all she saw for some greater purpose.

'My name is Briony and it's true my family and I were once Wairimu's scare-slaves. But thanks to Alayah, a child of the moon, we have escaped that ignominious occupation.'

'Ig-nom-in-ious?' cried the drummer. 'That sounds bad.'

'Indeed.' Gatekeeper Mari opened and closed her mouth like a fish waking up in a frying pan. She didn't know what an ignominious occupation was, but she knew every rule in the book had been broken. 'How did you get in?'

'I didn't mean to get in at all,' Briony replied 'My brothers and I were in Wairimu 's wine cellar hiding out with Ms Alayah (she's looking for a way out of Caligo Castle, you see). We found the entry point to an old Grum run and my brother, Thud, clumsy oaf, knocks me flying. Before I could pick myself up, I fell into quick sand and somehow ended up on your side of Orchid Hill. The weak spot was made by the coming and going of your own Justice Ants if my guess is right.'

Gatekeeper Mari blinked a hundred blinks to the second. She had no idea the Justice Ants were at it again, but she defended them. 'Naturally they have a grudge to settle. The poor things were poisoned by the likes of Mistress Bazilia just because she didn't like 'em.'

'True,' said Brodd. 'But we are getting off the subject here, Gatekeeper Mari. Spare a thought for Briony. She didn't mean to come here, so I believe we should waive the permission rule.'

'But the magic words weren't spoken.' Mari muttered about the pitfalls of letting one person break a rule. 'Before you know it, everyone's breaking the rule and it's a free-for-all.'

The Drummer drummed impatiently. 'Nonsense,' he rapped 'The rules may not have been followed to the letter, but we shouldn't close our minds. Maybe Briony being here is some kind of magic worked by Samuel.'

'But could he, do it?' Gravely, Mari searched their faces. 'Without the Mage, I hear his magic is weak as water.'

Brodd threw her a look. 'How can you say water is weak? That is a ridiculous old saying. Anyway, Samuel is a magician in his own right. You only have to hear about his cures and nature magic to know that. I bet it's his magic that brought Briony to us.'

'Come to think it,' said Briony, 'something helped me to breathe while I was stuck in quick sand, or it might have choked me.'

'It would have, for sure.' Brodd beamed. 'I've just realised what the smoke from our hearth fire is telling me. You being here is to help us help the mortals help the prisoners of Caligo – if you get my drift.'

'It is?' The tiny hairs inside Briony's nose stood on end. In that moment, she felt more like an everyday Grum with a keen sense of smell. Whether that would help the mortals get the Mage to Wizard Samuel, she didn't know. Whether it would help them save Ms Alayah, she didn't know, but her keen sense of smell urged her to find the source of a wondrous aroma that drew her to it in a most peculiar way.

It wasn't the usual Grum friendly smell, like last week's scraps – oh no – it was richer. Earthier. Like freshy risen mushrooms or chocolate coated truffles…or something….

Brodd observed the Grum person closely. Her twitching nose and dreamlike expression made him sniff the air himself. Something was about to happen – something marvellous and fantastical. Could it be that old legend coming to pass? The words long lost to the Rhizanthella Forest folk, were slowly coming back to him. *When the Rhizanthella shows its blooms to brave mortal hearts…it is time…the prisoners of a wizard's bind to free…*

For an instant, time stretched out. Past and present were there to see, if only anyone cared to look. The earth shimmied like a belly dancer. With the glow of the moon above, the silvery pathways crossed the forest in new directions, spreading like the branches of a tree. The ground shuddered and some of the older beings in the forest needed to sit and hold their dizzy heads.

'What does it mean?' Cade whispered.

'Oh brother!' Lori clutched his arm. 'Whatever it is, it's big.'

Mari waved her short arms and shouted: 'It's in the book. It's been predicted.'

When the Rhizanthella shows its blooms to brave mortal hearts, Caligo Castle will fall. Taking the words to heart, the Smoke Reader's pulse raced. Brodd feared for his new friends, Lori and Cade but also for a whole people. When a kingdom or chiefdom falls, whether for good or evil, people get hurt. A cold shudder ran down the length of his giant spine.

All eyes turned from Mari to Briony. Intent on one thing alone, she followed small veins of light that criss-crossed the forest to Orchid Hill. Once the castle rubbish tip, the hill abutted the darkness of Caligo Castle. Briony paused now and then, sniffing at the edges of it to pick up the scent. The forest people followed, keeping their distance, but now and then their curiosity got the better of them and they came right up to her. To the fore were eager digging animals.

'Dig here,' said Briony, firmly. She scratched at the earth, kicking up the first spray of grit towards softer earth beneath. The others followed, sometimes bumming each other out of the way quite fiercely until they cut through to a layer of rich black loam.

'This soil is so lovely, I could eat it,' said a kangaroo like person. 'It'd make scrumptious compost for my orchard. Can I have a few barrow loads?'

'Oh yes, Wally, my friend,' said Briony absently. 'It's quite remarkable how the stuff of broken dreams and misery can turn into something so rich and strange.'

'Friend is it?' said Wally in surprise, but Briony was too busy guarding her digging spot to reply. On all sides, earth-loving animals (some with human speech) nudged her while Mari called out their names in one of the local dialects.

With Granda leading, the giants propped up the earth roof and walls with tree trunks and cross beams of timber while strong armed dwarfs carted earth away. Barrow loads for Wally's orchard and their own growing fields. Slowly the hill became a tunnel and then a great cavern, tall enough for the tallest of the giants, to stand in.

'Cease the digging,' Granda ordered. 'This is nature magic, and we must flow with it. It's the life force of the Rhizanthella that has been driving us.'

The diggers stopped digging, sitting back while everyone beamed with pleasure and surprise. A warm haze of light filled the cavern while silver veins above and all around the walls shimmered from within, casting a luminous glow. The light seeped into the skins of watchers and workers alike and they all became drowsy from its beauty.

'Oh, just look at that…how strange…how wonderful,' Mari murmured. Enchanted by what they saw, everyone slept where they stood until they were well rested and ready for new wonders.

They woke in time to see the Rhizanthella unfurl petals with plosives of sound like bubbles bursting. Deep pink to orange to delicate reds and purple, the Rhizanthella spread rapidly over the walls and ceiling of the cavern. A network of pulsating jewels enclosed in pearl shell sepals. Rows and rows of blooms, never before seen by the forest folk or the mortals.

The pipers played their pipes and the drummer beat his drum. '*Kaya…kaya!*' Everyone sang in praise of the orchid's beauty but Briony went on scratching at the end of the tunnel. Slowly she unearthed it…first a glint of silver and then something richer. It was a jewel of a door, like the underground orchid itself, ruby red and waiting.

Lori nudged Cade and he nudged Brodd. Soon they all nudged each other and exclaimed, especially the busybodies amongst them, drawing in their breaths and whispering: *Ah yes, there's the door…I knew all along they'd uncover it…no you didn't…yes, I did,* they argued.

'But does this mean the young mortals have to go through it, into Zagan's domain? Will Wairimu nab them?' a dwarf whispered.

'Not right away,' said Mari.

'There'll be Axeheads about,' said the drummer.

'And the creepy pirate, Zagan,' a squeaky voice added. Others talked over each other with scary 'what ifs', until the Gatekeeper clapped her hands.

'Do hush your lips,' Mari scolded. She asked Lori and Cade to stand still and then bustled among her people, pushing and pulling, until they formed two long lines to wish the mortals on their way.

'Are you okay?' Lori whispered and Cade nodded. They straightened their spines. The glowing door beckoned with its beauty, yet it mocked them cruelly. *Behind me lie the darkest secrets of Caligo…are you up to it?*

Of all the forest folk, it was Brodd who most feared this moment. To ward off evil, he threw cleansing sprays of gum leaves into his own hearth fire. *I chose my destiny and I must accept it,* he thought. Yet he so wanted to stand with the mortals in their time of need, even if it meant breaking his vow never to strike or hurt anyone.

'Ah, Brodd,' said Mari in a raspy whisper. 'I know not to get too close to mortals…but do you? Let them go…but…there's no rule to say you can't use a tad of magic to help them.'

'I'll man this fire day and night if I must.' Brodd's eyes gleamed.

Mari's voice quavered. 'And for your peace of mind, I'll call on everyone in the forest with the least bit of magic in their blood to cast a goodwill spell. But Brodd, dear, how can a mere boy and girl – mortals at that – possibly break through the darkest layers of Caligo Castle alone.'

Startled, Brodd's head shot up. 'Surely there'll be a guide.'

'With Wairimu pulling the strings, can we be sure of anything? He's like a spoiled child yet so cunning. He'll use the ghost of his forefather…he'll use anything to scare them until he has them in his power and the Mage in his blundering hands.'

Remembering Lori's words just a moment before, Brodd bowed his head. *I wish I had more time to know you.* He didn't know the warmth of his eyes and gentleness of his handshake would stay with her, even in the tomblike chill of Caligo. The others gave Lori and Cade their special Forest Folk salute, murmuring farewells and wishing them luck, though some with dread in their hearts for what might be unleashed by this intrusion into the dark domain. Nobody noticed poor Briony trying to push through the wall of bodies. 'Ah…excuse…excuse…if I could just squeeze through,' she stammered. 'There's just one thing more, and that's me…the boy and girl will need me as a guide or they'll fall…fall into the pit.'

50 Zagan's Transformation
Caligo Castle

Why does Wairimu leave wine half a finger deep in his tankard before topping up? Surely not to hide something? It was a question that had always puzzled Mandel until this moment – the few seconds between his tankard being empty and then hastily filled. That was all it took for Mandel to see a shining object that told her everything. Her head spun. Her legs were jelly. It took all her will to go on pretending. *Breathe…breathe…don't give yourself away…not yet…not here, not now.*

A knock on the servants' door and she responded. Even to her own ears, her voice seemed strangely distant. 'Oh…Captain Ironbar…do…do come in.' The chief Axehead nodded with a faint look of curiosity, but he walked past her to bow deeply before the Scorpion.

'Bad news, Sir,' he said, uneasily. 'Dame Grey has taken to her bed and the boy and girl got away.'

Wairimu's face suffused with colour. He fully expected to have the Mage around his shoulders before night fall – the girl and boy paraded before him with due pomp and ceremony.

'The pair have taken refuge in Rhizanthella Forest,' said Captain Ironbar.

'Starvation and bat poo rain on their heads,' Wairimu howled. 'So, you're telling me Gatekeeper Mari let them in?' Grimly, he signalled Mandel for food and was soon digging into the plate of sausages dripping with tomato sauce. Waving towards the captain, he spoke with a full mouth. 'Dang it, those brats will be full of half-baked magic by now. I want every Axehead we have, to guard the bridge…they have to come out of the forest sooner or later.' In one noisy gulp, he swallowed a mouthful with a gulp of wine to help it down. 'Don't be fooled by any of their tricks.'

'Sir…there are rumours about.' Captain Ironbar cleared his throat. 'The gossips reckon the forest folk dug a great fat hole into the side of Orchid Hill last night. The door to Caligo Castle is uncovered, and…they reckon…the Rhizanthella is blooming. They say it's on the move…Sir.'

'Asch, don't believe it. Who is this person called They?' Wairimu spat out words like a snake spits venom. 'I put a curse on that orchid when I threw it away and when they locked me out of that old rubbish site, I put a curse on the lot of 'em. No mortal has seen the Rhizanthella bloom, I tell you. Those weirdos might have a place but they're locked in it forever. As for Orchid Hill, it's a grave…a grave that belongs to a dead Rhizanthella.'

Captain Ironbar shifted uncomfortably. 'But what about the old story?'

'I know the old story so there's no need to spell it out…pig's mud to that. It's rubbish.' But the words played in his head and would haunt his dreams. *When the Rhizanthella show its blooms to brave mortal hearts, the Chiefdom of Caligo will fall.*

'They say when it happens,' said Captain Ironbar, 'the lawfully elected Chief Wizard of Aberash will cast a nature spell and the orchid gets back its land. That land, Sir, is in the middle of your chiefdom.'

'And who is the lawfully elected wizard of Aberash?' he sneered. 'The very same Samuel who is strung up in my basement.' Pretending calmness, he took out his mirror and examined his tongue. Pin pricks of pain shot through his tongue tip with its new diamond stud. He wondered irritably if Judd had put a curse on it.

'Will we hold Mo?' the chief axehead cut in. 'He's the mawk with speech who came with news of Dame Grey.'

'Never mind Dame Grey. Go get the mortals…as for Mo, throw him off the bridge and let him sink or swim.'

'Yes, Sir!' Grimly, the giant turned on his heel and hurried to the big noisy hall where the other guards waited for their orders.

'Forget the bridge. We're going downstairs.' He glared at his team. 'A small working party should be enough to catch 'em. The rest of you stand-by.'

Downstairs in Deep? There came a grim silence and then mutterings about Zagan. What could you do with the ghost of a pirate who simply dissolves if you touch him? One who can make you see double or make up look like down? A ghost with eyes that might freeze you? Or send you into a trance that makes you forget who you are.

'You won't be anywhere near *Zagan,*' said Captain Ironbar, impatiently. 'You'll find the mortals in our own timber yard and storage area on the eastern border of Deep. That's as far as any mortal child could surely go.'

Meanwhile on the low-lying western border of Deep, Zagan emerged from the captain's cabin of the *Blade.* Though his ship – a stolen brigantine, was forever in dry dock, the old pirate was dressed in his favourite buccaneer garb. As if for action, with broad hat, frilled shirt, breeches, buckled shoes, a flared cape and a cutlass at his waist. He climbed out onto the deck and breathed deeply.

'Ah for a whiff of the sea,' he wheezed. It came from a blowhole that filtered through minions of fissures in the corals and rocks below ground. Zagan was tempted to cast a spell over the underlying sea to make it stretch and grow. On occasions when he summoned it, the huge swell would rise through the blowhole to break over the bow of the *Blade.*

Strangely, instead of salt and sea today, Zagan breathed in the green smell of forest and more worryingly, the pungent odour of burning gum leaves with a heady tang of eucalyptus. He listened for the hush and sigh of the sea, but heard something else. It was a low wizardly chant. *Hearth and home, fire over ice…fire over ice.* It was the voice of Brodd, the smoke reader. Zagan replied with a snarl.

Ice over fire…a mortal boy…a mortal girl…ice over fire

Invisible ropes, to bind them, shrouds of my ship to tie them

I've a bargain to make…my freedom to take…ice over fire.

Zagan scanned the huge under-cover space called Deep. Divided in two, one for castle business with storage bins and the Axeheads' timberyard, the other, his own domain. Once his playground and the site of his collections, now it was his prison.

Soon…very soon I'll be out of here. Zagan was heartily sick of the sulky blowhole and worried by thick earthen walls that kept him prisoner. *Give me the open air and icy waves of the South Seas. Give me freezing winds.* He longed to see great cliffs of ice sliding into wild white waters. It wouldn't take much to cross over the line into the land of mortals. He could be at the South Pole…in a blink. What a laugh it would be to send snow and sleet to mortal folk in summer when all they wanted was to lie about in the sun or ride the odd wave on a surf board.

Zagan, blustered and blew. His lungs wheezed and his ancient bones creaked as he prepared a place for the mortals. He would soon have them on the *Blade,* spread out across the rat-lines for Wairimu to see. No amount of harping from his heir would release them until the bargain was struck. His freedom in exchange for the boy and the girl.

'Ice over fire….' he chanted loudly to block out the sound of Brodd's seriously intense – 'Hearth and home, fire over ice.' It weakened his own spell to prevent Wairimu or any Axehead who dared, put a foot on the *Blade.*

As captain to the blood thirsty crew of more than one pirate ship, he had learned to be clever, cold hearted and cunning. 'There was a time when I'd have frozen Brodd's blood if I had a mind to,' he muttered.

51 Stolen Waters
Caligo Castle

In the castle kitchen, Wairimu removed the Sunny Isle Crystal from the bottom of his wine cup and replaced it with his tiny mirror. Then he slipped the crystal into the pouch he wore round his neck.

Catching sight of the shining object for the second time in a day, Mandel stopped herself from screaming at Wairimu, *Liar, thief. You transformed my people's fresh water pool into that crystal.*

Fearing a nasty payback, she held onto her rage and forced herself to act as if it were any other day. She picked up a tray of bread rolls and placed it in the oven, then asked about the resident ghost in Deep.

'I trust you'll find Zagan in good spirits…you're heading that way?'

'Aye,' he grunted. 'But don't ask me to take him bread, and don't feed the wretched mice while I'm away.' Lately Mandel's guesses were far too close to the truth and there was a glow about her…almost like happiness. It set his teeth on edge.

Indeed, Wairimu was on his way to see Zagan. He hoped to make the old git look into the Sunny Isle crystal. The thought of doing it himself was too frightening. He was so close to owning the Mage – so close to having power over Samuel and the mortals that surely the crystal would show him to be the most powerful ruler and magician of all time.

'Their story I will take, their story I will make.' With closed eyes, he chanted.

On his way down to Deep, Wairimu passed through the wine cellar. It was too cold after the warm kitchen, but cleaner and brighter since he handed over the keys to Mandel. She had scrubbed every surface and somehow made it lighter. How could that be? There was an earthy smell that might be a Grum. Sneaking back for kitchen scraps?

'Nope…the wretched Grums and Ms Alayah will be trapped and suffering in the pit.' He moved on, with a final sniff, never guessing that Ms Alayah was hidden behind barrels of his precious Vintage Black.

Thanks to Mandel, Judd, and the clever Grums, the wounds Ms Alayah had suffered were slowly healing. Though her aching heart longed for the sky and freedom, she had a cramped but clean space to stay in and kind friends with whom to share her light and to hear and tell stories.

'If the Alayah woman is dead,' Wairimu snarled, 'it's her own fault and the Grums? They're only Grums.…' The Chief Wizard of Caligo dismissed any last thought of them as he stepped down stairs into the basement. He was pleased to see Samuel awake in the holding cage and the shackled Judd, hard at work. In the haze of heat from the forge, the re-captured Judd worked on a new wizardly hat for him, decorating it with precious stones and gold leaf – booty from Zagan's treasure chest.

'What good is a treasure to a ghost, eh, Samuel?' A spark of greed flared in Wairimu's eyes. 'It'll be grand to have a new hat along with the Mage don't you think?' He glared at Samuel who seemed not to hear. With parched lips, the young wizard murmured some gibberish of his own.

'Don't pretend you have magic I don't know about.' Wairimu stepped towards the cage, but a stab of fear in his soul stopped him from moving closer. Vengefully, he muttered, 'You'll soon see what a real magician can do.'

Slipping between the curtains to his dressing room, he regarded his full reflection in the mirror before him. His mind drifted. *I can turn myself into anything…and I'll be, not a monster but something cool.* After deep concentration, chants and spells, Wairimu opened his eyes and whispered, 'Oh yes. Yes. Yes. Yes, to this nose, mouth and chin. Yes, to these shining eyes and glowing skin.'

He threw off his baggy gown and donned the clothes of a prince. Standing before the mirror he observed a golden-haired youth dressed in creamy satin. He touched the little leather pouch hanging from his neck…the Sunny Isle crystal was safely inside it. *Soon…soon you'll show me what I want to see…*

Wairimu flicked out his tongue. Today it was pleasingly pink with a row of sparkling studs. Unsure of his word power he chose a sword from his collection of weapons on the wall.

'S plus WORD equals SWORD.' Wairimu warbled his evil magic, willing his word power into the sword. Ignoring Samuel and Judd, he headed for the passage where the trapped wind waited to push him into the Arena. The Arena was his playground below the basement and above Deep. Gladly, he leaped into a circular gladiator's ring. Sometimes the Axehead guards held a wrestling match there to entertain him. Or he might show off his word power.

'Sa…Sa.' Wairimu tried a few lunges and a counter parry with an imaginary enemy. Sprawled over the tiered seats above the ring, a bevy of ghouls, ghosts and a big lazy giant slept on.

'I'll summon you when I have my sport with the mortals,' he crowed. But right now, he needed to see his ancient forefather downstairs.

At ground level, Zagan's domain in Deep was a decaying celebration of his pirating days. Apart from the *Blade*, the ground was littered with old mast heads and the hulks of rusted ships. Some harked right back to the Golden Age of piracy and slavery. In his ghostly form, Zagan regarded Wairimu from the bridge of the *Blade*.

'Lower the drawbridge and let me on board,' Wairimu demanded. His new glowing skin goose-bumped with cold and his teeth began to chatter.

'I'm rather busy right now,' said Zagan in a slow drawl. 'Perhaps tomorrow?'

'What?' came the terse reply. 'This is the only ship you run. The rest is mine, so hop to it.'

'Tell me,' said Zagan. 'Why has the dutiful heir decided to visit at this inconvenient hour?' Taking his time, the old pirate moved from aft to forward, and with ease, climbed the shroud and then balanced on a forward spar by holding on to the mast. 'I must say your visit is most inconvenient.'

'As if I can't see that!' Wairimu shivered as he felt the touch of Zagan's long icy fingers resting on his shoulder. It moved to his neck. Only a ghost would do such a thing from a distance. They stared at one another across the ice laden mist.

'So, what is it you want Scorpion, all dressed up in your finery? A favour I suppose.'

'I'm not asking, I'm telling you to do a reversal of the spell that stops me getting on your ship and then you will look into the Sunny Isle crystal and tell me what you see.'

'You never like what I see.' Zagan looked up at the mast head. 'And you never take heed of what I say.' He looked down and then across to his heir with his piercing green eyes.

'But you're the only one who will tell me the truth and I need to know.' Wairimu hesitated. He could smell something and he heard a sound he didn't like. It wasn't the usual mixed up boat smell of tar, rope, stale bilge water and so on, it was smoke from burned gum leaves.

'Hearth fire over Ice…hearth fire over Ice.' As the pitch of Brodd's chant increased, Wairimu stiffened. It could mean only one thing. That half-baked wizard was batting for the boy and the girl, attempting to protect them from Zagan. So, the rumours about the Orchid Hill door might be true. Captain Ironbar should have made it clear.

'I'll sack him as chief, come morning,' he muttered and then shouted at Zagan. 'If you capture the mortals, they're mine.' Perhaps it wasn't the right time to see his own image in the crystal. Better to believe what the mirror in his dressing room showed him.

'Sa…Sa…' Wairimu pushed the jewelled sword all the way back to his playground. Soon…soon he would have the Mage and the young prisoners, paraded before him, bound and shamed.

52 The Long Drop: Cade and Lori
Caligo Castle

Through the jewelled door to a rickety old lift – down, down, down. A powerful wizard had eyed them and no chant or spell would soften the dizzying drop into Deep. A bone jarring thump shot them out, head over heels.

'Bro, you're in my face,' Lori groaned and sat up, gaping at her brother. 'Where on earth did you learn to do that?'

'It'd take me too long to explain. Let's go.' Somehow Cade had landed on his feet with a neat somersault and a grin. He was already checking out the surroundings.

'Creepy…eh?' Lori's, voice echoed eerily in the tomb like space. At ground level, huge stone pillars supported the storeys above. Dim light from wall lanterns revealed a slick of slippery black ice on the ground. Cade slid for a metre and almost fell.

'Danger,' he warned.

Too late, Lori had already tripped. 'A bloody great stone hit me.'

'No, you hit the stone,' he teased, but his skin prickled when Lori read the words on its face.

'Here lie the bones of those who dare.'

'The Axeheads are coming,' he gasped. At first – giant shadows flickering- helmeted heads, jutting jaws, hefty shoulders, huge arms swinging. Giant feet tramping. Cade had studied maps of this same space. Made a model of it in clay. He pointed to the timber mill further along – its long bench and giant circular saws. A place where, in a working mill, the logs were sliced into boards. But this was an unused mill and the sawdust shoot and pit beneath the bench would be hollow. A small space. True. But a good place for kids to hide.

'Come quickly.' He grabbed Lori's hand, thankful for the magical footwear from the Now wizard. 'In skating mode, or we'll fall on our bums.'

'Can we blend?' Lori asked.

'No, it's too dark.'

'Yeah…dark and creepy.' Lori breathed sharply through her teeth.

'Be quiet,' Cade said in an urgent whisper. 'There are scouts around.' He cursed himself for not guessing. The loud tramping was a ruse. Something to distract them…two dumb kids…easy pickings…

Oh yes. He got a whiff of body heat and a strong garlic breath. Cade grabbed Lori's hand. They took off just as the lurking Axehead lunged. More agile than the clumsy giant, they slipped past him and raced on, past the sawdust pit and up a clear passage between timber stacks.

'Veer left,' Lori gasped. 'Now veer right.'

'Get them, Faradale!' A female giant yelled. 'Tighten up your turns.'

Lori prompted softly to tighten their own turns as they hurried on. 'Turn…turn…turn…'

'We're leaving him behind,' Cade gasped. 'But look!' A young Axehead came out of the blue, waiting for them in the middle of the path with open arms and a ghastly grin. The name 'Hooksie' blazed across her armour. Big drops of perspiration dripped from her brow. Quickly, they turned, but she was on their heels – so close they could smell her sweaty armpits.

Unlike Faradale, Hooksie was sharp-eyed and quick on her feet. The twins in turn were spurred into action. Their adrenalin kicked in. At a rattling pace, they shot up a pathway between timber stacks. Round and round the timber yard, they flew. Faster and faster – with Hooksie's large hands snatching at their backs and her steamy breath blowing hot on their necks. For a split second, Lori was held by her waist but she twisted sideways, away from the giant hands.

Enraged, Hooksie leapt at Cade and flung him down. Lori gulped, horrified, but sighed with relief when he summersaulted backwards and slipped out of her reach. She grabbed her brother's hand and again, they hurried on, doubling back on their tracks and running for their lives. They ran until their gasping lungs and thundering hearts screamed for a break. It came with the sound of Hooksie falling flat on her face.

'Rotten tomb stone,' she yelped. 'Eat rat fleas and bat worms why don'tcha? Faradale! The little titches have got away. Gong your fat head and call the rest of the gang to order.'

Cade and Lori had left Hooksie behind. Using a clear pathway, they shot around the boundary of the timber yard, hoping to find a clear way in to the sawdust pit before more Axeheads arrived. But it was too late. Faradale had alerted the others and more giants streamed out of the dark.

'Yikes,' Cade breathed in so sharply, it hurt his chest. 'We're surrounded.' *Assess the situation* the guide book had advised. *Look for a way out.*

'There's a gap between the Axeheads,' Lori hissed.

'Be quick,' Cade snapped. 'We gotta outrun them…and climb into the sawdust pit.' *Then what?* He secretly wondered. *Be holed up forever? Oh, shut up*, he scolded himself. *You need to trust.* Suddenly – a crackle like thunder and a flash of light. It lit the darkest corners of Deep from east to west. A light so bright it hurt Cade's eyes.

'Now we'll blend,' he said, with wonder.

Their hoods were already over their head.

'Blend Now,' they cried. With hands tightly linked, they hurtled towards the giants. Blinded by the burst of light, the puzzled Axeheads rubbed their eyes. Captain Ironbar tried to work it out. 'It's the kind of spell only an experienced wizard can do. What's going on here?'

'I can hear the titches,' screamed Hooksie. 'Grab them, you great clods. They're using an old trick from a cloth wizard. They're blending.' Clumsily a circle of big hairy hands clutched the air, but Cade and Lori were through the gap…and away.

Led by the clever Hooksie, the Axeheads thundered towards them, drawing closer…and closer…

'Stop,' Lori hissed at Cade. It was a surprise move – one they often used on each other on their way to school. They stopped so suddenly the Axeheads who were on a roll, dashed past.

'Turn you dunderheads,' Hooksie screamed. 'They're still blending but I saw the girl's eyes. The titches are behind us.' Weighed down with their cumbersome armour, by the time the Axeheads turned, Cade and Lori were gone. Breathing hard, they slipped into the old logging mill, past a giant circular saw and then crawled on their bellies along an old sawdust trail under the work-bench. Panting, they squeezed through the narrow hatch into the pit. In the gloom of the timber lined space, they were met by a pair of bright eyes.

'Briony…how did you get here?' they cried as one.

'Upon my word,' said the Grum. "Why did you rush away? I made up my mind to be your guide but with all the ballyhoo and farewelling I was left behind. I had to chew my way through a weak spot under the door. Broke a tooth doing it. The drop into the pit nearly killed me, but I must say I had to laugh just then, when you outsmarted the Axeheads.'

Above them the giants shouted at one another, arguing about tactics. Hooksie was by far the most vocal.

'Dumb clods, don't you know how wickedly clever your average mortal kid can be? They can't be too far away.' The giantess was silent for a moment as if drawing breath, then howled. 'Where have you got to you bite sized ninnies?'

'We're over here.' Lori popped her head out of their hiding place. She threw her voice so that it bounced back at them in the opposite direction. The giants immediately took off with a lot of yelling from Hooksie and Captain Ironbar, along with a few giant's swear words thrown in for good measure.

'Now we're over here,' Lori called. The giants ran back and forth like a herd of mad bulls chased by a pack of yellow eyed dingoes.

'Argh! We're all knocked up,' Hooksie roared, 'I'm taking a break.'

'Okay, it's your call,' said Captain Ironbar, with an exasperated sigh. 'If we leave a guard, it should be okay, but we need to come back after lunch. And I mean after lunch, on the dot.'

Noisily, the Axeheads signed off. Grumbling among themselves, squabbling about who should remain as lookout and guard until finally Faradale volunteered with the proviso that he would get to sleep-in come morning. The rest passed through a revolving door that took them to a long flight of steps and passageway to their living quarters on the western side of the Castle.

'The blundering fools,' the ghostly pirate muttered with nobody to hear but a scrawny albatross hovering around the *Blade*. 'They were supposed to wear the mortals out…not let them hide out.'

When all was quiet again in Deep, Zagan climbed to the lookout on the main mast of his dry-docked ship. With his peculiar telescopic eyes, he spotted three figures. They emerged from the logging mill to sneak past the sleeping form of Axehead Faradale. When at last they stepped across the invisible barrier from the eastern side of Deep into his domain, he smiled.

The boy and the girl had found a guide. Zagan had no idea how, but he recognised the castle Grum. She looked around with curiosity, wondering aloud about the origin and age of the stone pillars that held up the Castle.

'Hmm…pre-ice-age,' Briony mused with a studious air. 'And I'd say their uniform size is a fluke of nature…but my word, it's pretty chilly in these parts.'

'Hardly pretty…it's bloody freezing,' Cade muttered. Lori shivered and within a short time just as Zagan had planned, the twins were desperately blowing warm air from their lungs to their fingers and stomping their feet. Lori held up her hands. Her fingertips were white.

Briony pushed her own hands deep into her pockets. 'Y…y…you n…need to get your blood flow…flowing.'

Lori tucked her hands under the sleeves of her hooded top, while Cade burrowed his into his armpits. They couldn't think of anything else but warming themselves. All three travellers shivered uncontrollably. Their teeth rattled.

Within a short time, Cade saw that Briony's small body had rapidly passed from the shivering stage. Her eyes were already dull and unfocused.

'We need to find a shelter before her blood freezes.' Cade remembered what to do from first aid lessons at Scouts. 'Look there's something there.' With Lori's help, he guided the little Grum towards the burnt-out hull of an old ship. It was packed with coiled ropes and rigging, offering the shelter she so desperately needed. The Grum was soon tucked up in layers of sailcloth and bagging, but when Cade gestured for Lori to do the same, she backed off.

'I can't go in there…it is…never mind…I'll keep going.'

'Then I should come with you. But what? Why?' he looked at her with questioning eyes.

'That's the remains of a Guineamen– a slaver,' Lori said. 'You know the kind o' thing…galley slaves worked to death…cargo holds crammed with people torn from their homes.' Sensing her distress, Cade steered her away. Yet he felt it too, as if the weight of past cruelties and death were heavy on his shoulders. They staggered on until the shivering stopped but the cold had crept into their bones.

'It's freezing our blood,' Cade gasped.

'I think we're gonna die,' Lori was too surprised to be frightened. She stopped then, and stared. A sleek fully rigged two masted brigantine filled the world. In that moment nothing else existed but the *Blade* exuding warmth and light. Though unfurled, the snow-white sails beckoned.

Cade took in the soft sheen of old wood – the glow of brass. The mystery of old instruments that once guided sailors to the edge of the known world. Before either of the twins knew it, they were clambering up a rope ladder to the deck. Already their blood began to thaw.

'Come in, come in…be my guests.' A kindly old gentleman helped them onto the ship. He gave them each a bowl of hot porridge with cream and a swirl of honey on top. It was laced with something strong that made their bellies warm. They ate hungrily while their host stood back observing them quietly. Under his broad hat they glimpsed a thin-lipped smile.

'Thank you, thank you so much,' Lori murmured uncertainly and Cade echoed her words, adding, 'You saved our lives.'

What happened next was like a dream. A bad dream. The kindly old man had turned into something else again. A ghost like figure with burning blue-white eyes and steely hands. Grasping hands – too strong for them to fight. Binding them with twine they felt but could not see. Tight and tighter around their wrists and bodies.

'Ah.' A sigh of satisfaction, a long slow breath and the pirate sang:

Come dear children…your loss will be my gain
Come to Deep, the ice-king's domain
Come be the prize that will open the way
To the pirate Zagan's freedom today.

Dizzily, Cade struggled to see the ghost like figure more clearly. It shifted and changed. One A pirate with eyes that could burn you.

'Ah…I feel like I'm drowning under his spell.' Cade's legs, his arms, his body didn't belong to him anymore. 'We…gotta…get away from him.' So why was Lori being mean? Shouting angrily into his face. If her hands had been free, she might have slapped him.

'He's weaving an enchantment spell,' she scolded. 'Don't be taken in by him.'

Lori tried to work it out. *I need to think and I need to think fast. He's a mean one. A sly one and he's powerful. I can't hide or fool him by throwing my voice. I can only fight off his mind game by making a voice spell stronger than his, but I'm not a wizard and I don't understand what I do.* Lori avoided his dreadful eyes while calling on her sisters, the Lorelei to make her strong.

'*A song to repel, his binding spell,*' she chanted.

Cade shuddered at the touch of the pirate's icy breath on the back of his neck. Surely if you cut off Zagan's head, he'd grow another one and still capture you with his searing gaze. As if to tease them, the pirate moved away, only to hover again.

This time he focussed on Lori who was chanting some song about her sisters, the Lorelei. *But that's not right.* Cade was puzzled. Lori had no sisters. But he felt something – an undercurrent. There were no clear words, to Lori's chant, just a sound that might have been the sea or the wind. Or the earth turning from night to day. It was a sound that soothed him in a strange way, but the dreadful contest went on. And on. It was life or death. A contest between his sister and this weird other. Neither an invention of bad magic nor a true wizard. Neither ghost nor man.

Cade shivered with apprehension. How much longer could Lori go on? For now, she took the full force of the pirate's blazing eyes. Balanced precariously on the rigging, the pirate stretched and swayed back and forth. Again, and again he slipped, half falling, grabbing at the rigging, dropping onto the timber deck and then, with a faint wheeze, returning. Slowly, slowly with long icy fingers clutching at the air he stared eye to eye with Lori.

Lori probed the desperate pupils with her own eyes. *How much longer will he go on?* To see human fear in the eyes of such a demon startled her – but it made her understand.

'You come back for as long as I choose to keep you here, even if it kills you.' Lori was startled by her own voice and it scared her. 'Is that what being a Lorelei is about? Does that make me evil?'

Though weak, Zagan wheezed out a cunning reply. 'It isn't your power that is evil, it's what you choose do with it. Spare me. The weight of innocent death has become too much for me to hold. I'm done with causing grief.' The pirate knew all about changing sides in mid-steam. You did what you had to do.

Once released from Lori's spell, Zagan spoke in frail quavers. 'I should have remembered about the Lorelei…oh poor old *Zagan*…poor me. It has been a close call…why didn't I think about the Lorelei? And me a sailor too.' He was quick to haul the twins down from the mast, telling them he wanted nothing more than to escape to the south pole, to the land of ice and snow. 'Oh…oh, I just want to see the Aurora Australis…did you know you don't have to wait for a midnight sun Downunder? You can see it all year round. Oh, dear children, do I see pity in your eyes? Oh, thank you, thank you.' He was skilled at softening up a new ally.

'You won't leave me to rot in this awful place, will you?' he pleaded 'I'm going to need a little help up the stairs.'

The ice began to thaw. The ground underfoot squelched and the air soured. Zagan looked back at the *Blade*, seeing it in its true light. A discarded ship with tattered sails and peeling paint. It reeked of tar, of oak, of rope and canvas, of grease and filthy bilge water. The albatross perched on the main mast appeared as a black outline against the murky light. It let out a mournful croak.

Taking up her duty as a guide, Briony appeared, round eyed and watchful while Cade and Lori moved forward to face whatever it was they must face. Was it to meet the wizard who eyed them? In a wizard zone you have to wait and see. *You have to trust.* As they climbed the stairs towards the floor above Deep, the raggedy old pirate limped along behind them.

53 Mandel's Moment
Caligo Castle

Child of the moon beware, the beast is awakening, stay clear of his lair.'

Mandel chanted her warning then tapped the floor with her message stick. A faint scratching on the other side of the wooden floor boards, and a little hand waved. It was a signal from Da Grum.

'All well, down here,' said Da. 'The others are sleeping, but I fear our poor Briony has met foul play.'

'She is so clever, I'm sure she'll stay out of trouble.' Mandel's hand closed over the handle of her message stick. She felt the marks on its surface with her fingertips. Since Alayah's reading lessons, the message stick spoke to her often.

'If your greatest wish is above you,' it whispered, 'then look below.'

'My greatest wish is to see the sky every day,' she replied. 'Below is the wine cellar and the basement where Wairimu does his darkest magic. Below is the prison of Zagan, a ghost who keeps alive old chants and spells that create misery.'

'You must go below,' the message stick insisted, 'to finish unfinished business.'

Mandel pictured the underworld beneath the floor she scrubbed every day. Unwanted memories heaped up around her.

'Yes,' she whispered. The usual crackling fire in the big kitchen stove was out – the oven cold. Mandel found Wairimu's wine tankard and fished out his little mirror along with a bonus of two tiny keys. She took these, and a basket loaded with her last batch of bread to the wine cellar where Alayah and the Grums were sleeping. She left them some bread and tiptoed on to the basement with a nice savoury bun for both Judd and Samuel.

Samuel slept, while Judd looked up from his work, alarmed.

'Mistress Mandel,' he whispered, 'it is not safe for you here. Wairimu is armed and dangerous. Don't you want to live to see the sky again?'

Mandel watched the terrible heat of a Wairimu's forge and then said softly: 'Please call me Mother. You're like a son to me. And yes, I do want us both to see the sky…whenever we feel like it. That's why I'm here.'

She whispered more words and Judd nodded. With fear and excitement dancing together in his eyes, he lay down his tools and took her arm, showing her the way into Wairimu's Arena.

'I'll come with you,' he offered, but she shook her head. 'I must do this myself.' She pressed two tiny keys into his hand. 'Neither key will take us to the sky, but one will undo your shackles, and the other will free Samuel from the holding cage.'

She entered a long passage, buffeted by the tortured wind. As if knowing she wanted to be rid of it, the invisible rope that tied her to Wairimu cut viciously into her ankle.

'*Devil – devil rope*, get away from me,' she hissed. To comfort herself she put her right hand on the message stick that was tucked into her belt. 'I need you to speak to me,' she pleaded.

'I'll tell you a story,' said the message stick. 'It is about a young girl who lived with her people on Sunny Isle. Each day she drew water when her people were thirsty. Can you tell me what she saw when she bent over the pool?'

'She saw her own face,' said Mandel. 'It was round and smiling with a glow that made her beautiful.'

'You are that same person,' said the message stick.

'I am that same person,' Mandel said in a small voice.

'Say it louder.'

'*I am that same person.*' The rope slackened at once. Invisible until now, it took on a solid form. Sticky as a spider's web – intricately knotted, but because she was able to see it, Mandel unravelled it easily. Unleashed from her ankle, the rope sprung away. It leapt ahead of her, all the way into the Arena. Snake-like and silent, it slithered towards Wairimu and hid in the dust at his feet. Slowly, Mandel followed.

In the guise of a youth, Wairimu sat on a throne lined with red velvet and decorated with skulls, demons and a gaping mouth that spewed puffs of acrid smoke. When he saw Mandel standing before him, he threw her a look of contempt and spat out the words he was sure would sting her.

'Mandel…oh Mandel…you are hopeless. Why are you here? This is not your domain. Go to the castle kitchen and bake me bread…'

'The fire is out,' said Mandel, 'I can't light it because the rope that ties me to you pulls too tightly.'

'Then I will loosen my end,' said Wairimu.

'Very well.' Mandel came close, and moved her head beneath his chin where the Sunny Isle crystal shone up at her from inside the open pouch that hung around his neck. With a sleight of hand that surprised her, she took out the crystal and replaced it with Wairimu's own little mirror.

'Thank you for loosening the rope,' she said. 'I'll go and light the fire.

The painful tips of Wairimu's tongue eased. 'You know I might have burned you with my words for letting the fire go out,' he said, 'if I were not such a good husband.'

Mandel held the crystal up to his face. 'See for yourself and tell me you're a good husband.'

'Get it away from me.' Affronted, Wairimu stood up, his face contorted into something so evil, Mandel had to look away but she heard his words. 'Of course, I'm not a good husband and you're not my wife. I am *Wairimu* – Scorpion.' He shot waves of tongue fire at Mandel but the flames blew back. Those that did touch her left her unmarked.

'Why are my words not burning her?' he screamed.

With the lightness and ease of a dancer, Mandel ran from Wairimu's terrible curses. She flew up the passage, leaping the stairs to Ms Alayah's hide-away in the wine cellar. Only then, with Ms Alayah watching, did she look into the shining crystal. Her own kind face looked back at her. It was no longer young, but it reflected back an inner glow and a beauty that time had not taken away.

Behind the reflection of her own face, she glimpsed the sky. What did it mean? Within the cellar itself, no sky could be seen, no light but the magical moonshine that came with Ms Alayah. Gradually it grew brighter revealing a flight of stairs.

'Until now it was hidden by Wairimu's curse,' Mandel said, 'but where is the door to the sky?' The space where the door should have been, was blank and dense as a sun spot.

'There's an old story'. Mandel remembered it clearly and it made her heart heavy. 'It's about a mortal boy and a mortal girl. Until they break Wairimu's wicked spell we are all prisoners of Caligo.'

54 Face to Face
Wairimu's Domain

It's weird,' said Cade. 'I can feel the weight of Zagan's heavy clothes on my back. Lori's own shoulder's sagged. Just moments before, an agile ghost, Zagan now trudged along beside them – a weary old man with a gammy leg, stirring pity in their hearts.

'Dearie me,' he whimpered. 'Do help me up the steps…ah yes, the girl on my right and the boy on the left, if you please.'

With Briony leading, they struggled up the steps out of Deep.

'Today was a close call,' Zagan muttered to himself. Lori's spell might have been the end of him. But he was doing quite well as things stood, with both kids lending a hand. The pirate hid a smile. Ah yes, they were still his passport to freedom. It just meant a switch in sides…just like in his pirating days. You back a winner, no matter the rights and wrongs of it.

He hummed a little chant: 'A mortal boy, a mortal girl, eyed by a wizard must fall to his spell…or pass the test, and yet, with a coin and a key may prove the best…the prisoners of his bind to free. You've heard that before? Yes?' A flicker pride crossed his face. 'It was I who added that clause to Wairimu's curse on the castle door. The best anyone could do, as it turned out, and the Supreme Council passed it.' At the top of the stairs, Zagan let go their arms. 'Ah yes, a mighty good clause it was. Now all you need do is outsmart *Wairimu*.' He shook his head. 'A scorpion from way back. I really don't know where he got that bad streak from…oh do wait for a poor old git.'

He staggered along, wheezing out his advice. 'Only you two young mortals will be able to *see* that door, you see. It is in the wine cellar at the top of a secret staircase.' Again, the old pirate clutched at them with long icy fingers that sent chills down their spines.

'What can we expect?' Cade asked. 'A vile monster, or what?'

'Vile he might be.' Zagan shrugged. 'But you can be sure he won't look it. He's too vain for that. He'll look a picture. But remember, he's armed and dangerous. He wants the Mage and will stop at nothing to get it.'

The thought made them jumpy. As they approached the Arena, Zagan lagged behind chanting in a low croon until he turned wispy and thin as smoke. His pirate clothes now a discarded soggy pile.

'It's better than having him cringing at our side,' Lori whispered.

Ghost like and strange, Zagan floated above them as they scurried after Briony. Their Grum friend led them to a cave like hall filled with portraits of Wairimu's ancestors. Beady eyed and cruel faced, their mouths whispered hideous warnings of what might happen to two dumb kids. The words stung their skin. It messed with their heads. Their fears came at them like fists in their faces. *The Mage is just a pretty rag. It's all been for nothing. Samuel is finished. Renana is dying. Ms Alayah is trapped. You're just a couple of dumb kids and you don't know anything.*

Pain shot through their ears and their legs seemed to melt. Gasping for want of clean air, the twins sagged against each other. Their eyes met. With shaking hands, Cade reached out to steady Lori. *Oh brother*, she thought. There was a heart wrenching hurt in his eyes.

'We gotta get out a' here.' Cade dropped his shoulders and straightened his spine. A trick learned from their Mum. Lori, too, straightened her spine.

Cade knew what came next from the map in his head but felt less alone with Briony leading the way. He was shocked by the size of the Arena and the unexpected stink of farts and belches from the ghosts and ghouls. Sleepily, they looked on with yawns and stretches. One raised a large head in slow motion, as if waking from a dream and then began a lugubrious chant. One by one, the others joined in.

'They're so creepy.' Lori moved closer to Cade. 'What are they?'

'Ghouls and ghosts.' Zagan hovered near, a ghostly wraith himself. 'They're held in thrall by Wairimu.' An eerie silence followed.

'Show yourself *Scorpion*,' Zagan bellowed.

A laughing youth leapt from behind a screen, his corn coloured hair like a splash of sunlight in the dreariness. He was dressed in cream satin and his tiger eyes gleamed like jewels.

'Wairimu?' Even Zagan was dazzled and confused.

'I am *he*,' said the youth in a crisp clear voice. 'What is your wish, dear forefather?'

A prick of his shining sword on their bare ankles woke the twins from a trance. Cade whipped out Mia's tchield and the fight began. A slow and dangerous dance. Eye to eye, Cade and his adversary. They circled each other. Wairimu lunged. The point of the sword hit the tchield with a ping and he reeled back.

'*Djoo…djoo*…shame…shame,' the ghouls muttered.

With fresh energy Wairimu hit back and Cade had to fend off the wild blows. Hot sparks flew while the strange audience hooted and cooed. There followed a grinding test of strength – tip of sword pushed against tchield.

With barely a sound in between the clashes, the contest went on. Lori followed every move – the silvery gleam of the tchield and the glow of Wairimu's jewel encrusted sword. Instantly, she tuned in to every nuance of Cade's laboured breath or a soft 'Sa. Sa. Sa.' from Wairimu as they locked together, sword against tchield.

Cade slewed the sword off once again.

'Go Cade,' Lori whispered.

Infuriated, Wairimu swiped at her, herding the twins away from the arena while the ghouls roared their pleasure and their disappointment.

'Stay with us…Scorpion…our own hero…Wairimu.'

The fight continued along the long passage leading to Wairimu's basement where the trapped wind whipped at their clothes and hair. Unprepared for the force of it, they found themselves pushed upwards into the Wairimu's workspace, the basement. He arrived before them, deep chested and powerful, with raised weapon ready to strike. Mesmerised, they froze. Their eyes glued to the sword in his hand. A powerful gleam of copper and bronze elegantly scrolled along the blade to a lethal tip.

'Wake up from your trance, Samuel.' Wairimu cried. 'See me take the Mage and tell me you're still the wonder Wizard of Aberash.'

Vicious and reckless, he thrust the sword at Cade forcing him close to the forge. The heat was terrible. Wairimu thrust the sword low and flipped the tchield out of Cade's hands. For a moment it was suspended in the air and then fell past outstretched hands into the flames.

55 The Contest

The Basement

It happened in slow motion. There was nothing Cade could do. Small pictures in his mind. People and places. Brave Mia and her brothers. Bb the horse. Serval the swamp boy. And the wonderful wizards of Rhizanthella Forrest. But the most striking picture of all – his own name curling in the smoke of a fire – *Cade, Keeper of the Mage.*

'No! I was meant to keep it safe and now it's gone.' A tight band of sorrow squeezed his heart – the Mage and Mia's tchield that protected him, gone. Cade struggled to breathe. *Please somebody tell me it has not been for nothing.*

'It's not over, mortal.' Blinded by his own fury, Wairimu lashed out. He wanted to punish Cade – for what he had done himself.

Dodging one blow after another, Cade yelled at his sister, 'Look for the door.' At this, Wairimu swiped at her. Sharp eyed, Lori spotted a trolley laden with test tubes and other paraphernalia. Using both hands, she thrust it forward to block him. Wairimu smashed it against the wall and went on with his rampage, destroying priceless treasures collected by Zagan in his pirating days. It was Cade he wanted and Cade he would get, regardless of whatever stood in his way.

Cade began to believe it. It was only the thought of sparing Lori now that kept him going, for his heart was heavy with a sense of failure. *It's all been for nothing.* He felt like curling into a ball but the twang of Wairimu's sword was close. Looking on, Lori guessed from its angle, it was about to land squarely on the back her brother's skull. She opened her mouth and screamed, a rasping sound that froze the deadly weapon for a precious second of two. It gave her time to push another object towards the rampaging wizard.

Using two hands, Warimu lashed out with the sword. One more treasure smashed. A beautiful wooden cabinet carved by one of the Axehead guards who, before being ensnared into the Scorpion's corrupt domain, was a gifted wood wizard. The maker of this piece would have cried to see it.

The chase went on, up and down, and across the basement floor. Home to Wairimu's darkest transformations and magic. Cade's heart was in his throat when Wairimu, having missed him, lunged at Lori. She twisted sideways, ducked beneath a table and slipped through to a space on the other side.

'Leave me with him,' Cade begged. 'Go find the door and take my coin.' He threw it to her and though it passed through the fingers of her outstretched hand, she caught it with the other and slipped it into her pocket.

'I'll find the door.' Tears streamed down her face. 'But I won't go without you.'

Led by Briony, she leapt up a flight of stairs, past barrels of wine and a small audience. They watched, open-mouthed as she leapt up another flight of stairs. There, standing at the top was a shining door lit by a window above with a tantalizing glimpse of a bright blue sky beyond.

We're nearly there. Lori willed her brother to keep going. But with Wairimu snarling at him, ready to strike, he struggled to breath. Cade's heart raced more wildly and faster than any boy's heart could surely stand. There were black spots before his eyes and his brain felt woozy. He hardly knew up from down. Surely that was a voice coming from the rafters. For an instant, the face of a fair-haired boy appeared over the edge of a platform between the rafters. A face he had seen in a dream.

'Grab hold of this rope,' the boy yelled, and the rope swung by him. As his hands closed over it, doubts clouded his mind. *Is this a trick? Can I trust what I see? Is the boy a servant to Wairimu and under his spell?* Something clicked in Cade's brain. *I have to take a chance. Because I want to live. And I want to live, just because life is precious.* With his fingers clenched tightly around the rope, he pushed off with his feet towards Wairimu, missing the raised sword by a fraction of a centimetre. On the upward swing, he landed on top of a display cabinet, sharing space with a row of highly polished trophies. Human skulls – each and every one.

As Cade's heartbeat returned to something like normal, he pictured his own name written in smoke. Cade, one-time Keeper of the Mage, now Skull-Trophy of Wairimu – Scorpion.

Cade shivered as the wizard threw his sword down to arm himself with a sledge hammer. With powerful strokes he aimed at the structure that held the cabinet together. Skulls crash to the floor. Cade floundered until he realised the rope was still in his hands.

'Cade!' A familiar voice called to him from some place over his head. 'It has not been for nothing.'

'Hah?' His cousin's voice steadied him more than he could say. Maybe it hadn't been for nothing. He swung himself back towards Wairimu, landed with a two metre start and ran. Each time the thrusting sword came at him, all Cade could do, was to leap out of the way.

'The Mage is gone, and you're going to pay, boy.' The Scorpion took a moment to recover his balance after another failed attempt to cut him down. It gave Cade time to call out to Lori. 'Get out while you can.'

She yelled back, 'You're coming with me, brother. You must.

With split second timing, as Cade appeared, Lori scanned for a key symbol on the door and she heard a click. Now for Cade's coin, she placed it in the slot ready for him to push through. No way was she going to desert him now or risk messing up Zagan's spell.

'Quite right…quite right,' muttered the pirate ghost from his vantage point above. 'It takes a girl *and* a boy to open a door to the sky.'

'The coin is ready to go, Lori yelled. 'Get yourself up here and push it in the slot. You're doing well, bro.'

In truth, it wasn't looking good. Cade sprinted towards the steps that led to the door, only to feel the bruising thud of something hard against his shin. It was the blunt end of the wizard's sword thrust. Cade yelped with pain and stumbled, rolling over to avoid lashes from the razor edge. Angry swipes whipped the air. Closer and closer. Once, twice the teasing prick of the sword caught and then ripped the shirt that covered Cade's back. He was hurting all over and gasping for breath. Stubbornly, a voice in his head tried to make sense of something that made no sense.

'First the Mage and now this,' he sucked in a ragged breath. He's just destroyed my shirt. A shirt that was hand stitched by Nyan, a loyal friend. What is it with Wairimu?

Cade reached for Lori's outstretched hand, knowing they had lost the fight. She sighed and together they observed Wairimu in all his finery, like some kind of devil archangel. Resplendent, he towered over them with the gleam of his sword poised to strike.

'We're done.' Lori said, believing it to be true. It was all over, surely. But being Wairimu, he needed to gloat – he wanted every ounce of pleasure from his triumph.

'Be my slaves or die,' he hollered, and then Lori's heartfelt cry rang out with all the power and force of a true Lorelei.

'Never…er…never…er…never…' The word echoed and re-echoed like nothing ever heard in that land out west across the waters. For twenty long seconds Wairimu 's weapon froze. In a flash Cade reached forward and pushed his lucky coin through the slot. At once the door swung open.

Recovering from the shock of Lori's cry, Wairimu followed the twins onto the rooftop and the inmates of the castle poured out after them. The fight went on: the thrusting sword, the leaping and dodging, the cries and gasps of fear and wonder.

'Wairimu – coward,' Mandel cried, 'how is it you attack defenceless children with such a weapon?' She threw her message stick to Cade. For a sickening moment it looked as if the stick would fly out into the wilderness. Taking a chance on his left hand, Cade caught it just in time.

With the stick solid and warm in his palm, his reflexes sharpened. He tossed it into his right hand, using the flat middle of the stick to ward off the blows with a woody thud…thud…thud. Wairimu came at him, again, but then, in a surprise move, turned on Lori. Quick as a flash Cade threw the message stick.

'Magic,' Lori shouted. She was quick to catch it but not fast enough to use it like a shield first time round. Instead, she leapt out of harm's way. On the second strike, she used the message stick to slew the sword to one side. With a curse, Wairimu lunged towards Cade and Lori threw the stick back to him.

For a very long time (measured by Hooksie), the contest went on, waxing and waning. The giantess had no great love for the mortals. They'd given her grief. Wairimu had threatened fines and even a long stretch in the Caligo Dungeon for failing to catch them. But no doubt about it, the tykes had courage. After mastering Mandel's stick, their actions became sharper and quicker. But what hope did they have? Wairimu was so powerful. He had ruled over so many for so long and with such a heavy hand. It looked to Hooksie that he'd have those kids for breakfast. Red faced with effort. Shirts hanging off their backs in shreds. Gasping for breath. At the end of their tether. But what was this?

Wairimu gritted his teeth as Lori and Cade used the blunt end of Mandel's magical stick to ward off his blows. It jarred him. In a weird moment his gaze met Mandel's accusing eyes. It was as if she and her whole tribe were punishing him for taking away their water and turning it to a crystal. The thought weakened him. With the next swipe and blow he faltered. He felt wobbly in the knees.

'The brats are smart, I'll give 'em that,' he muttered. His gorgeous mask slipped. It burned a lot of energy to take on the form of a youth. He never meant it to go on for so long. *If only I hadn't lost the Mage…I'd be top magician now.*

'Guards,' he yelled, 'I've had my sport, now grab the pair of 'em. Ironbar? Hooksie…Faradale? Where are you?' He couldn't believe the guards were standing about gawping. Some were soft-eyed as they gazed at the twins. A boy and a girl, battered and bruised, their clothes torn to ribbons. A boy and a girl destined to free the prisoners of Caligo, a place of darkness, misery and lost dreams.

And weren't the Axehead Guards prisoners of a kind? Robbed of their right to work as professional wood carvers and tree planters? Those whose pay he had recently docked, clapped when either of the brats got the better of him.

'Hooksie?' He waited for the brightest of his slaves to jump to it, but she and the rest of the gang were busy taking side bets on the itty-bitty mortals and, by gosh, they were getting the better of him. How do each of the fleabites know what the other is thinking? Their timing was perfect. Dang it, why didn't he have a twin who could help out? But then again…maybe not.

'Mandel!' he shouted between swipes. 'Get that dang parrot here now!' Surely that bird could give the boy a nip to slow him down. 'Scorpions and death adders, redback and whitetail…get him off of me. *Djak,* where are you, smart bird?'

Wairimu turned towards a pink flash of wings. A bad blunder. The distraction caused him to fumble his thrust and the boy had him. Cade swiped the sword clean away into the blue air, while the sharp end of Mandel's message stick pointed at his heart. The stony silence of his slaves filled him with dread.

Cade might easily have thrust the message stick into the Wairimu's heart. But his boy heart said, no. 'I can't do it. I'm like Bb and Brodd. We don't attack. We defend.' He offered the stick to Lori and she shook her head.

'It would make us like him.' Her face hardened 'I might be a Lorelei, but I would never use my powers or a stick to take a person's life.'

56 Time of Reckoning
The Roof of Caligo Castle

Wairimu came to himself with his tongue furry as mouldy bread. *Why haven't they killed me?* He opened heavy lidded eyes, only to see himself in his true form for the second time in a day...*not* a pretty sight. He looked away from the Sunny Isle crystal in Mandel's hand.

'What will become of me?' He saw pity in Mandel's eyes, but she turned her face away and called for a carrier and four guards. 'Take him across the bridge. Dame Grey will take good care of him.' Ironbar and Hooksie helped the four strong giants. The hand-held carrier was lowered to the ground and the pair rolled him into it, and then drew the silk curtains around him.

'Up now,' said Hooksie, and the giants stood. The young giantess strode jauntily ahead of the little procession while Captain Ironbar marched behind, descending along a graduated ramp which led to the guarded bridge.

'Wait...wait...' a feeble call from behind the curtains. 'Djak...if you don't mind...I have something for Mandel.' Wairimu fumbled under the cushions for a wine tankard he recently planted for emergencies. Dipping his fingers in, he drew out an object. 'That's for Mistress Mandel,' he told the waiting bird.

With dull eyes, Wairimu stared ahead at the shadowy scene through the silk curtains. Not once did he shout at the guards or utter a single curse. He slumped into the cushions without moving. Only when Djak came with a whispered message from Mandel, did he put his head out between the curtains. He nodded his head at her and waved a last goodbye. The message she sent him was something about a garden…about him making a garden. For the old folk in the Dame's nursing home. A garden…of all things? As if it were something he might possibly do….

The little group on the rooftop watched the slow passage of the carrier. It bobbed up and down in time to the jarring thump of the giants' feet as they tramped along the winding slope. They watched until it was a tiny spot making its way to Dame Grey's domain. At the same time, they sensed the fleeting presence of the ghost – *Zagan* the pirate.

Zagan had his eye on the South Pole. Ah, it was wicked how he'd been locked up all those years with only the Justice Ants for company. How fortunate he'd been to get a free ride with the mortals. 'I owe them a favour,' said *Zagan* and then hearing his own words a terrible thought struck him. *Does this mean the Justice Ants have got to me?*

Cade watched the passage of Wairimu 's carrier until his eyes stung. The blue sky was all around him, but the darkness of Caligo still weighed on him. He waited for something – anything – to make him feel better. The Mage was burnt up. Samuel was nowhere to be seen and it looked like Ms Alayah was still lost in the murk of the Scorpion's poison. So, what good had come out of any of it? *My name is Courage…I'll always be with you in spirit…* The words of a long-eared brumby played in his head.

'Courage?' Cade murmured. 'When you *fail,* that's when you need courage. So where are you now, Bb?

Lori had to know. 'Tell me, you're alive, Renana,' she whispered. How did you shake off the power of bad magic? Words came to her and softly she sang:

These castle walls must crumble, the chiefdom of Caligo must fall
To the realm of precious things, where the honey myrtle sings
Of its own secret love, ruby red and glowing in its earthen cave.

Lori thought about the miracle of seeing the Rhizanthella blooming, but she was waiting for a sign. She looked at the stranger who stood beside her. A boy with fair curly hair and calm blue eyes.

Judd blushed shyly under the girl's gaze. He was feeling weird and wobbly without shackles on his ankles, but it was magic to walk about freely. He couldn't believe the sky was so wide and high. So forever and blue. For the first time in living memory he saw a bird flying there. Its dark wings were glazed with colours of a forest. A soft goldish green with a tinge of sunrise red. Without knowing why, Judd ached with love for it.

'What is that bird?' he gawped

'You have the gift,' said the girl. 'That bird you see is Renana. She is the Night Protector and she feeds on magic.' When the girl spoke, her eyes were like stars…not that Judd remembered seeing stars, but he'd heard about them.

'I'll never really understand what my gift is,' the girl murmured. 'How can you? I am so lucky to have known Renana.' Together they watched the bird circle around them until it drifted away on the thermal winds above.

'If she is the Night Protector, she will see the stars tonight,' Judd said, wishing with all his heart that in his new life he might be so lucky.

Ms Alayah saw Lori with Judd gazing at the empty blue sky with rapt eyes as if they beheld something magical and beautiful. Beside them Cade stood forlornly, yet she knew he would be alright.

'The Mason twins have come through, and so have I,' she whispered to the blue air. She remembered feeling her way in the dark with the Grums, climbing through narrow runnels, stretching and reaching, hurrying and scurrying. Driven by hunger and deprivation, she had stretched her body to the limit, reaching the unreachable, crawling through impossible spaces, holding at bay, the fear. She would miss the magical moonlight that lit the way and also the Grum's and Mandel for a special set of friendships that warmed her when she was cold. But it wasn't in Ms Alayah's nature to be downhearted for long. By the time Lori and Cade noticed her presence, she gave them her most dazzling smile.

'Is it really you?' Lori gasped. 'You look different. Younger. But you're still you.'

'Yes, and I'm free, thanks to you and Cade.' Their favourite teacher smiled warmly.

'But…we didn't do anything,' Lori stammered.

'We were supposed to free you.' Cade stifled a sob. 'I'm so sorry…we…you see I was….'

'You were magnificent. And you did free me.' Ms Alayah hushed him. 'We were all in total lockdown and because of some curse, we couldn't even see a way out. I'm so proud of you both.'

'And so am I,' said a voice behind them. It was Samuel, finger combing his now longer than shoulder length hair. But it was the Mage that made them gape. It was a little rumpled, but the same cloak with its lovely mix of darkness, its light and those leaping colours like the Aurora Australis.

'Thanks to Mia's tchield, the forge is cold and the Mage is fine.'

Sammy passed the tchield to Cade and he yelped, 'I should have known any magic from Mia would have been super-tough. But I was supposed to give the Mage to you.'

'You did, even though it came to me in a roundabout way. Thanks to you, Cade, Lori and everyone who helped out, the magic of the Mage is stronger than ever.'

Samuel took in a great gulp of cool sweet air. He had told a little white lie, but for the good of Aberash, he was sure the Supreme Council of Wizards would forgive him. In fact, there was far less magic in the Mage than he or anyone else had ever imagined. With the help of his mortal cousins, Samuel had discovered, the true source of his wizardly magic resided in his own heart.

He gulped in another huge breath of air. How beautiful it was – just right for a good old-fashioned nature spell. There was quite a lot to be done. To begin with, those orchids needed honey myrtle if they were on the move. If he couldn't summon a fly or a wasp crew to pollinate the orchids, he was sure the Justice Ants would oblige.

Samuel's fingers itched to begin a spell with no bad vibes from Wairimu to spoil it, but what was this? Oh no, not the extra-long green taxi…now what could have called Ruby and Roger already? Was it the Lorelei cry that drew them from Inn Between?

Before Samuel could blink twice, the extra-long green taxi had landed on the helipad next to the Hellican.

'Are there a couple of kids here who could use a lift?' Looking quite flustered, Roger ran across the rooftop with Ruby close behind. The Pronto team had broken quite a few Zone rules by coming here, Samuel noted. It would take a tinge of luck and fast talking to fix it with the Supreme Council.

Stylish as ever, Ruby kicked up her shiny red boots before rushing over to hug the children with tears in her eyes while calling them her 'darling chicks.' Lori and Cade were surprised by the show of affection from somebody they hardly knew. It was embarrassing, but somehow it seemed alright. Pretending to be quite unaware of the rules, Ruby handed Samuel the keys of the taxi.

'I see you have already switched over to flying mode,' he remarked.

'Yes,' replied Ruby, nonchalantly. 'The rotor blades work like a dream.'

'Good, then I'll fly us all home.' Samuel looked about. 'Who's for a lift then?'

At once, Ms Alayah, Lori and Cade, along with Roger and Ruby all put up their hands for a lift. Before they took off in the taxi, Samuel cast a wonderfully impressive nature spell. He stood in a place on the castle roof that looked like the top of the world with a see-through daytime moon in the blue sky behind and the Mage billowing around him.

'How lovely is the Mage,' the Grum family whispered. 'Full of magic if we're not mistaken…oh how lucky we are here to see it.'

Samuel's fingers thrummed. He touched the smooth seams of the Mage. The silkiness of it helped draw out his store of good magic for a huge transformation. Yes, indeed, with a little time, Caligo Castle would crumble away. The Axeheads would go back to their wood carving and tree planting, he supposed. There would be another Wairimu in some unknown part of the zone, making trouble no doubt. But for now, all was well.

Mandel smiled at Samuel. The Chief Wizard could do with a little filling out, she thought. It gave her an idea.

'Thank you for the offer of a lift,' she said, 'but I have my own way of getting about now.' When Wairimu whispered to Djak from behind the silk curtains of the carrier, he sent Mandel the one and only key to the Hellican. She held it up for Samuel to see.

'Now it's up to me, to use it for good, to break the pattern of bad deeds. I owe it to the clever inventor of the Hellican whoever he was…and to the good folk who were hurt by Wairimu.' Until this moment, anger, and then pity, for him stirred Mandel's heart, making her silent and sorrowful for the loss of dreams. But now with the vast blue sky above her, the clear day beckoned, just like the Sunny Isle pool and she was ready to dive right into it.

'First, I'll give the Hellican a good scrub,' she said softly to Djak and Judd. 'I'll fix the lower deck as a mobile bakery, the middle for a comfy place on rainy days and if you want it, you can have the upper deck for a jewellery workshop, Judd. You can open the roof and see the stars on clear nights.'

'The stars…oh Mistress…I mean Mother.' At this, Mandel's eyes brimmed and her heart swelled with happiness.

The Grum family blinked from the odd tear and too much light in their eyes. Ma broke the silence to thank Samuel for his kind offer of a lift. 'We'll be heading off on foot for the Grum runnels,' she explained. 'Our dear Briony knows where we can find nicely cured scraps from the forest folk.'

'Oh, how delicious,' the young Grums chorused.

'Mushrooms and truffles? How ab…so…lute…ly delectable. Da licked, his lips…what do you think my sweet? Can we go now?'

'Manners…manners….' Ma spoke sharply and at once Da stammered out a hasty apology. 'Oh please, forgive our rudeness and thanks so much to all, especially our dear Alayah. How wonderful it's been…we must meet again…do come to the runnels to see us…if you fancy.'

With final waves and well wishing, they scurried into a crack that had already formed between the rooftop and the walls of Caligo Castle where tiny green shoots sprouted from seeds of honey myrtle.

In the darkness, their whiskers twitched – how it thrilled them – to take in the pungent smell of the Grum runnels and freedom. What more could they wish for?

57 From Aberash to Brightday High
The Grounds of Aberash Castle

Dawn broke with a rosy spread of light and a clear throated call from Renana. It was a big day in Aberash. One look at Ms Cora brought a lump to Lori's throat. Today was a last goodbye to Castle Keeper Caius who had lost his life in Wairimu's raid. All the villagers and children of the treetops were there for the memorial service.

The twins fell into step, one on each side of Ms Alayah for the procession. From all around, came the solemn sound of feet padding on the soft moist earth. They were led along a pathway to a special place in the Castle garden where the ashes of Mr Caius would be scattered.

From the eulogy by family and friends, the twins learned that as well as being a loyal Castle Keeper, Mr Caius was a clever inventor and magician, well-loved and respected. When Samuel spoke to the mourners, he looked grand in the newly washed Mage and his words went right to the heart of the matter.

'Nobody will forget our beloved Castlekeeper, nor will they forget the harm inflicted by Wairimu both inside and outside of Aberash.' Sammy paused and it seemed that his warm gaze was directed at each person — for him or her alone. 'But the bad memories make the good times more precious.' At this, Cade and Lori exchanged a smile. They were proud of their cousin. 'Yes, yes,' they said together. There were nodding heads and murmurs of approval all about. Afterwards the villagers made music and there followed several days of feasting and celebrating a new era of prosperity and peace.

For Lori and Cade, the happy days with trusted friends ended in a dream. When they wakened, the extra-long green taxi was through the barrier and gliding gently into the Undercroft of Brightday High. Minnie was waiting with lemony lemonade, raspberry muffins and a special welcome-home cake for Ms Alayah. The usual fare was on offer too, with heaps of toast to go with the cheese. You could order ham plus cheese and best of all, great shakes to go with the milk. A relaxed and smiling Mr Trihardy led the whole school community in cheering for the safe return of Ms Alayah to the fold. Even Ms Rake mouthed a faint 'Hooray'.

There were more speeches, handclapping, whistles and cheers when each of the twins received their first ever Certificate of Excellence. But the story of Ms Alayah, along with that of her young rescuers, would soon become yesterday's news. The strange events would fade from people's memories. So would the unusual appearance of a gleaming extra-long green taxi in the pick-up bay. Only Lori and Cade were there to wave goodbye to Samuel as it drifted towards the shimmering wall at the far end of the Undercroft. The other kids, teachers and parents had already rushed away to toboggan in the snow.

It was in the newspapers and all over town: First Ever Snow for the City of Brightday – of the fairy-tale kind with a spectacular sky show from the South Pole – the famed Aurora Australis in full bloom.

Everyone was too busy dodging snowballs to ask awkward questions about the rescue…a great relief to Ms Alayah and the twins. For how could you properly explain everything that took place out west across the waters? That mysterious no-go zone where the sun goes down?

For Lori and Cade, there was a joyful reunion with their parents. Robert and Petronella Mason arrived late, as usual, puffing and panting after a run in the snow. Amidst bear hugs, kisses, laughter and tears, they talked over each other to say how proud they were to have such wonderful children.

'We should have known you were not quitters,' said Robert.

'So brave,' said Petronella.

'So marvellous…how lucky we are.'

'But how do you *know* we were so marvellous?' Cade asked. 'You can't believe everything you see on TV.' His gaze flashed from his dad to his mum and then to his sister.

'Or fake news on twitter….' Lori's words fell away as she glimpsed the hem of a shimmery green dress under her mum's coat…and those tough clunky red boots that you wouldn't want to mess with. Their mum's face was almost as red as her boots.

Their dad's clear water eyes twinkled with laughter, but his voice when he spoke, was serious. 'Before we say a word, you must each make a vow of silence. The utmost secrecy is imperative.'

'I'm in,' said Cade quickly. 'Dean told us a bit about…whatever you're about to tell us.'

'I'm in too,' said Lori. 'Am I right in guessing that our Mum and Dad are not only Roger and his dear Ruby, but a part of the pronto team?'

Cade opened his mouth, whether from astonishment or whether he had something important to say, nobody ever asked because his mother's hand was firmly clamped over his mouth.

'Not one word,' said Detective Ruby. 'You have earned your places as full partners in the firm, and you abide by the rule of silence. You work only in the holidays, of course.' There is to be no slacking off at school, no missed days, no excuses and all school assignments to be completed on the due date.

'Sorry we didn't brief you before we left you,' Robert said. 'But to make the most of the magic, we had to let you find it for yourselves.' He went on. 'As members of the team you'll be on call. It will mean a spell in the country now and then. You'll keep the coin and the key under lock and key…if you get my drift?' Cade and Lori nodded vehemently without speaking – serious, thoughtful investigators, but their lips twitched with runaway smiles.

The family were on Bus 303 when Cade turned towards Lori to whisper, 'We didn't get to eat at the party, are you hungry?'

Lori's eyes danced. 'Want some chocolate?'

'Oh yes…yes please.'

'No trouble…besides, I do owe you one,' Lori said. 'I hope your chocolate from Minnie keeps going for Serval, but I have a feeling this will be the last of mine.' It was a delicious morsel after their long journey from a land across the waters.

'Remember when Bb said to look for his shape in the clouds?' Cade asked. 'I think that will be the sign that tells us we must go back.'

'Sure,' Lori murmured. She remembered their last golden days and magical nights at Aberash Castle: feasts and rooftop concerts, boating with Mia, rock climbing and abseiling with the River boys and every morning greeted by the sound of Renana. One moonlit night the big bird sang for Lori, telling her, *Look for my shape in the clouds for a sign.*

'Yes,' she told her brother, 'For you, Bb. And for me, Renana.'

Author Notes

The land of Aberash was inspired by the many carefree hours I spent as a child with my siblings exploring the swamps and bushlands of Southwest, Western Australia. With due humility, I have used some Noongar words as a mark of respect for the people who knew its beauty and understood its subtle riches eons before my family migrated to the land Downunder in the early nineteenth century.

As Wilf Douglas (1996), reminds us: "…languages not only have their own set of speech sounds, but they also have their own way of making words and sentences and each has its own beauty of expression."

I am hopeful that my limited use of Noongar words for the names of familiar landmarks, birds and animals will inspire young readers to learn more about the Noongar people and the music of their spoken language.

References

Noongar Dictionary (1997) composed by Rose Whitehead for the Noongar Language and Cultural Centre (2nd edition 1997).

Illustrated Dictionary of the South West Aboriginal Language by Wilf Douglas (1996), Edith Cowan University Press.

Chapter 9 – "Nyungar" compiled by Alan Dench in *Aboriginal Words* (multiple contributors), Macquarie, 1994.

Noongar words:

Features of the land: *moyootj* – swampland, *bilya* – river, *manang* – pool, *kardil* – tree with hard wood used for shields, *mangatj* – banksia tree, *bidi* – path, *gnamar* (rock hole – source of water), *karl* – camp fire, *muller* – large flat cooking stone.

Animals: *marloo* – red kangaroo, *djooditj* – native cat, *noorn* – black snake.

Birds: *dirl-dirl* – plover, *dwarnart* – twenty-eight parrot, *kooraa* – smoker or regent parrot, *kaawar* – small purple parrot, *nyoolam* – night hawk, *werloo* – curlew, *yoondoordo* – osprey, *yaatj* – night owl.

Fish: nyola – cobbler, yolka – snapper.

Other foods: *djoorla* – honey drink, *koolah* – edible part of emu plum flower, *koorak* – bush tucker in general, *mangk* – leaf tea, *marda* – oily nut, *mol* – sweet berry, *yoork* – potato (referred to as spud).

Objects: *mirlkoorn* – wooden carrying dish, *wadi* – club

Language: *kaya* – yes (a form of greeting in the story), *kwoba* – good.

Note: *Red Jack* (Ch 36: Bb and the Stranger) reference: poem *Red Jack* by Dame Mary Durack (1913-1995), Australian writer and historian.

Acknowledgements

Thanks to artist Amy Trevaskis for her artistic skill and especially for the delightful subtext in her illustrations.

For their critiques of earlier drafts: Victorian writer, Alyson Reynolds; English graduate and discerning reader of children's books, Caroline Mayes; WA poet and successful writer of children's fiction, Sally Murphy.

In preparing the work for publication: Deidre Savage for her fine editing skills and audience awareness. Her suggestions have been invaluable; Carolyn Switzer, English graduate and editor for her meticulous reading and final edit; Sari Smith who readily shared her writerly wisdom with me.

For those friends and family who listened patiently to my ramblings: You are too many to name, but for my sister artist, Dolores Lamb, thank you for your encouragement that never wavered.

To the marvellous Paige Gardiner for voicing the audio version of the book, and last but by no means least, Ian Hooper of Leschenault Press for your patience and promptness in dealing with the detail.

About the Author

For me, writing this story has been a joy. I have loved the characters and the writing process so much it has taken a long time to send it on its way.

Aberash: A Mysterious Land Downunder has undergone many transformations. Yet, in spite of constant rewriting, the essential story remains true to the original which came to me in its entirety from somewhere in a dream space.

I was raised with told stories and books resounding in my head, mostly set in other lands or from the point of view of new migrants but my personal sky was Downunder and my landscape, bushland and swamp. It was the whip bird with a song that filled my nightscapes.

And so I set this story down that it might allow others to love this, my homeland, as much as I do…and in doing so I pay the greatest of respects to its original custodians, the Noongar People who came before all of us and nurtured this land with their care and love.

Other publications by Helene Smith for young and old readers:
Operation Clancy 2nd edition 2019
Leaping the Tingles 2nd edition 2019
Children of Morwena 2nd edition 2019
Dreamstone 2nd edition 2019
(Leschenault Press)
The Potter's Son, Macmillan Ed., 2009
"Flood Zone" in Reading Safari – Xtreme Weather, Macmillan Ed. 2001.

Family History
To be a Man of Independent Means, Aleda Books, 2015

Short fiction and poetry for adults:
A Tiny Light (SF), Bookmark Dreaming (poem), The Little Gardener
(poem) in Glimpses, Milli-Milli Writers, 2017.

These are some of several titles shared in community collections by
Helene. Her books for children appear in school and public libraries.

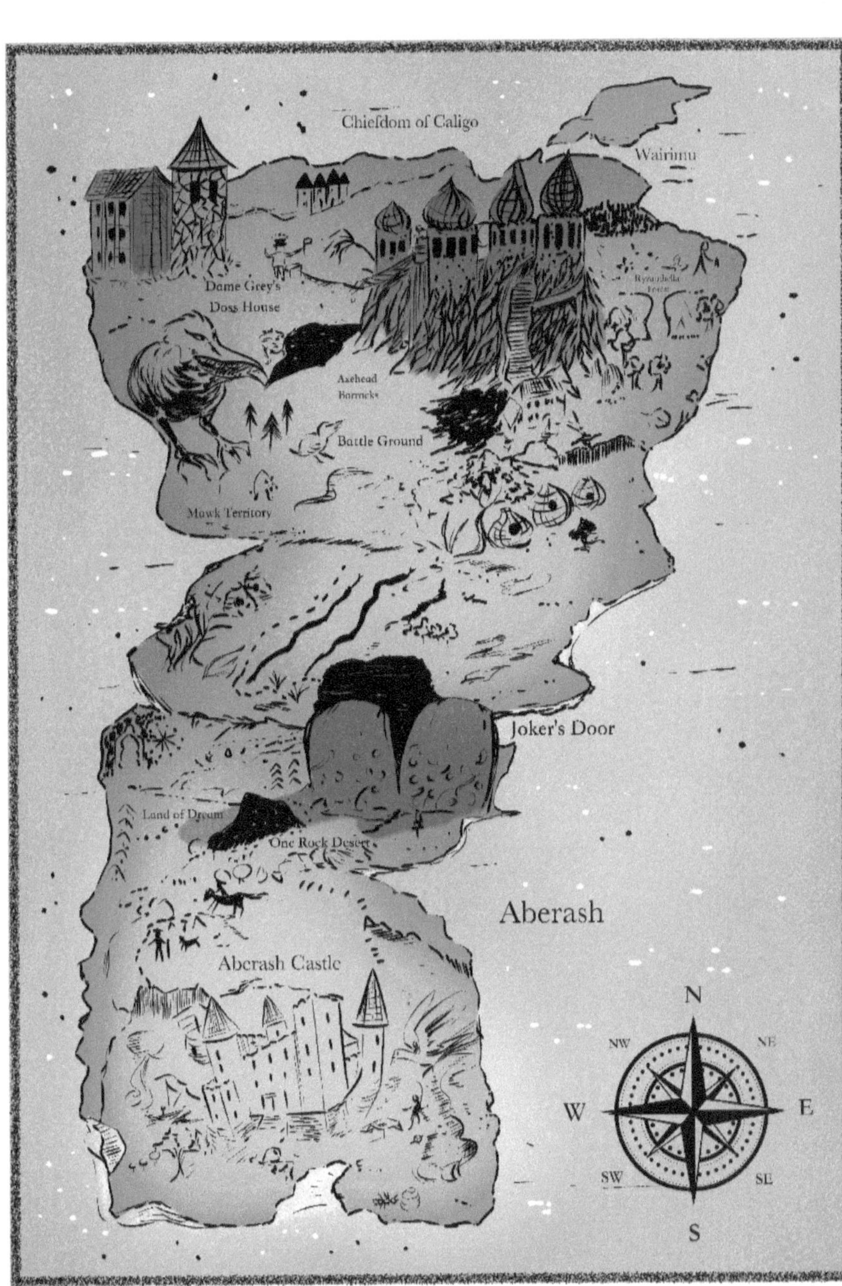

Chiefdom of Caligo
Wairimu
Dame Grey's
Doss House
Axehead
Barracks
Battle Ground
Mawk Territory
Joker's Door
Land of Dream
One Rock Desert
Aberash
Aberash Castle
N
NW
NE
W
E
SW
SE
S